CATALYST

THE ALLIANCE SERIES: BOOK FIVE

EMMA L. ADAMS

1

———————

KAY

"You're absolutely sure they aren't going to eat us?" asked Raj, one of the Inter-World Alliance's Ambassadors for Earth. We stood on the threshold of Cethrax, the most notorious world in the Multiverse, and for once in a lifetime, it wasn't because of some atrocity committed by one of their runaway monsters.

Didn't mean I'd trust them not to dismember us if we got too close. "Can't say for sure," I said, "but even they wouldn't be stupid enough to attack Ambassadors. Especially given the situation."

'The situation' being the reason we were there in the first place: a potential cross-world war. To be honest, if I'd ever imagined a war with any other worlds in the Multiverse, I'd have expected Cethrax to be on the opposing team. Firstly, because they hated the Alliance. Secondly, because they hated everyone else, too.

When I joined the Alliance last summer, if anyone had told me I'd ever be making a trip into Cethrax's territory, I'd have told them they were talking crap. Or just laughed. It went against common sense, not to mention survival instinct. Cethrax's monsters were predators. And humans were their prey.

But, for once in a lifetime, we had a common enemy. I finished sketching Cethrax's symbol—a wyvern's handprint —on the wall of the Passage with the end of a thin black-glass-looking stick, a world-key, and pulled back. The wall glowed in the patch around the symbols I'd drawn, an arrow-head pointing to the right, and two others I wasn't sure of the meaning, and a rectangular door opened in the wall. I nodded to the others—Raj and Iriel, fellow Earth Ambassadors, along with representatives from six other allied worlds and two council members—and we entered the monsters' lair.

Cethrax as I'd experienced it was an uninspiring place of swamp and mud and the occasional beaten-up-looking stone building, so it was somewhat jarring to open a doorway right into the heart of a city... of a sort. The central point was what looked like a pile of garbage—bits of rock and wood and god-knew-what-else heaped on each other to form a fifty-foot stack. Had to be the palace. Rather than putting in windows, the Cethraxians simply kicked a piece of the wall away whenever they wanted to take a look outside, evidenced by the number of holes in the construction. Apparently it hadn't occurred to them that at some point, the entire structure would collapse on them.

Hopefully we'd be lucky enough to avoid it happening while we were here.

The palace was the home of the Vox, who, for the first time in a hundred years, had agreed to meet with Alliance representatives on his own territory. Considering Cethrax usually responded to any incidents involving escaped monsters wreaking havoc in the Passages with blank indifference or outright threats, I supposed to most people, this plan was a long shot. But I'd seen the Vox, leader of this area of Cethrax, subdued by a monster even more powerful, and by freeing him with Ada's help, earned a favour from the king of the swamp. Granted, he'd already allowed us access to his territory in exchange, but only to stop the same monsters enslaving him from destroying the Multiverse. Generally, the only way to get through to the monsters was to threaten them with bodily harm. It was the one language they understood.

Unfortunately, knowing that wouldn't make negotiations any easier.

Raj shook his head at the palace. "Place is going to come down around our ears," he said. "That is, if they don't lock us in a dungeon."

"Ever the optimist," said Iriel, the other Ambassador.

"You did memorise the guidebook, didn't you?" I spoke in an undertone. "Talk legal speak at them and it'll put them to sleep. Besides, we've common ground."

"Because you almost blew the place up."

"Hmm." That was one way of putting it. Our common enemy, the Stoneskins, were monsters with skin made of unbreakable adamantine. They'd enslaved the Vox and used Cethrax's doorways indiscriminately, trying to find a way to break into a world that had been locked off because of a worlds-spanning magical war. They'd almost wiped out the Multiverse in the process, and Cethrax could no longer deny they were in way over their heads. The monster-ridden lower levels of the Passages had been a nuisance as long as the Alliance had been around, but no one guessed the monsters hadn't been acting alone. Something had been influencing them. Either we ignored the problem and hoped it didn't happen again, or took the initiative and made a deal with the devil. Or rather, the Vox.

Shadowy shapes moved through the mess of discarded metal and tree and rock surrounding the central palace.

Ramshackle stone houses belonged to the goblin-like foot-soldiers, while the smaller variations of the vox-kind had been kicked out of the city before we were due to arrive because of their unpredictable habit of attacking people. We were armed, of course, with adamantine daggers and Valeria's new stun-guns designed to pierce even the stony hide of a chalder vox, but the whole point of our visit was to *avoid* hostility.

The higher council members took the lead, as they'd apparently been here before. Zan Izen was Klathican, a war survivor with cybernetic replacements for both arms and an enhanced-sight upgrade to one eye, giving it an unnatural pale blue glow. Then there was Alexis Greene, Valeria's leading council member, who insisted on wearing shoes with hover-tech built in so she didn't have to walk through the swamp. The representatives of the other allied worlds followed. Earth's council had been forced to remain at Central, locked in videocall meetings with the Republic of Thairon, as they had been for the past week.

Right now, I'd rather think about the monsters than anything to do with Thairon.

"Also," Raj said, his voice dropping as we got closer to the palace, "we've killed quite a lot of them. Just saying."

"True." When Cethrax's monsters trespassed into the Passages, they'd attack any human unlucky enough to stumble into them. Alliance guard patrols were trained to show no mercy to any opponent from Cethrax unless they planned on taking up a new existence as a human-shaped mural on the Passage wall. Besides, Cethrax didn't show much more kindness towards its residents than people from Earth. This became evident when the leading council members finally tracked down the palace's door—or rather, a hole in the wall where one of the vox-kind had clearly barrelled through it, leaving a gap the size of a large boulder.

The entryway—if it could really be called that—was filled with skulls that looked like they belonged to dreyvern or ravegens, the smaller goblin-like creatures which roamed through Cethrax.

Oh, crap. Those rocks lying around definitely weren't rocks, but sleeping vox-kind. I made a mental note to assume anything unmoving was alive unless proven otherwise.

Alexis Greene looked back at the group as though hoping someone else would go into the palace first. When no volunteers were forthcoming, she went in, hand twitching in the direction of the magic-gun at her waist. Valeria's residents were allowed to carry weapons offworld, though use of most was forbidden in the Passages, on the quite reasonable grounds that weaponry was liable to explode in the user's face.

Personally, I thought daggers were a safer bet.

The inside of the palace was all one floor, and looked no different to outside apart from the mud on the floor being trodden down. It was dim to the point of near-darkness, and I had to take out my communicator and switch on the torch-light app to keep from tripping over anything in the dark. Like sleeping chalder voxes, for instance. Cethrax's inhabitants apparently had night vision. That, or no common bloody sense.

The dark made the ceiling feel lower and the walls closer than they actually were. We walked through to the centre of the room where a dark wooden table was set up surrounded by lumps of rock. No one sat down in case their seat grew teeth and ate them.

At the head of the table was a being the size of a small bungalow. The Vox was the largest and ugliest of its kind, though also the most intelligent—not that 'intelligent' was generally a word used to refer to Cethrax. The monster blinked eyes the size of plates, looking down at us as though closed, I wanted to put as much distance between us and the swamp as possible.

"It makes no sense, I admit," I said. "Total change of heart… I reckon someone might have bribed him. Or coerced."

"Impossible. The Stoneskins are dead." Iriel walked alongside us, her cyber-eye rotating in its socket. "Who else can threaten the *Vox?*"

"Technically, they fell into the abyss," I said. "They didn't die. If they found a way back to Cethrax…" *It'd be our fault. My fault.* I'd been the one to open the abyss, while Ada and the other Alliance guards fighting the Stoneskins had pushed as many of them as possible over the edge. Those who'd fled had been arrested on Valeria and locked up.

The other Ambassadors and council members split up as we reached the main corridor of the Passages. Zan Izen and Klathica's other delegates headed to the mecha-guarded door to the Klathican Embassy, while Greene went through one of many doorways to Valeria. Meanwhile, Raj, Iriel and I headed for the smaller corridor to the side, which led to the Passage door behind Central.

I'd expected my boss, Ms Weston, to meet us in the Passages for debriefing, but instead an irate-looking Carl, head of Central's guards, accosted us.

"Are the council…?" I started.

"Still occupied," he answered. "I take it the mission didn't go as planned?"

"The Vox said he had a change of heart and ran us out of the swamp," I said.

"As expected," said Carl, shaking his head. "At least some of the guards who made bets will be happy."

"Wait, they bet we'd get eaten?" asked Raj indignantly.

Carl shrugged. "I couldn't stop them. It *was* the first

mission into Cethrax in years, and you all came back in one piece. You're free to go now."

"It wasn't a total bust," said Raj, as we walked back to the main Passage corridor. "At least we get to go offworld now. Or get horribly drunk and forget all about it."

"Hmm. I think I'd rather ride a hover bike." My words received a predictable incredulous reaction. "Come on, you can't deny the risk factor's lower than Cethrax's swamp."

"No, you're right, I can't," said Raj. "That was too close. You're going to Valeria now?"

I nodded. "Might as well. I arranged to meet Ada there." I didn't mention I intended to spend as little time on Earth as possible. Like most people, Raj hadn't made the connection between the recent announcement of negotiations re-opening with Thairon and a certain council member who'd been off-grid for the past five years, but it was only a matter of time.

People stared as I headed through the crowded main Passage to Valeria's door. I shook off the paranoia. They had good reason to stare at me, and it didn't mean they'd found out about Thairon. I'd opened the Alliance's eyes to the threat of the Stoneskins—not to mention crashed an invisible car into a wall outside Cethrax.

If not for the more present threat of a potential upcoming war, I was pretty sure most of the Alliance members who'd witnessed what happened would want to avoid me, the unhinged magic-wielder who'd trodden a very fine line between necessary risk and breaking every law in the Multiverse into pieces. As it was, Dr Helm, creator of the invisible car in question, had pressured Valeria's Alliance into issuing a cross-world statement detailing the recent events in a way that made sense to the public. Usually the word "magic" was enough for people on Earth.

whatever experiment had turned them into adamantine-coated monsters, and Dr Helm and the others had seemed genuine when they'd denied it. I'd learned to tell when someone was lying. They really hadn't known. The question was... *who* did they mean?

After checking no one was close enough to overhear, Dr Helm said, "They mentioned they were part of a project, but there was never such a project at our lab. We took the name from our sister company in Klathica."

"That's where they were from," Ada cut in. "I forgot—I totally forgot. With everything that happened..."

"It's okay," I said. "I know you told the Alliance everything important." Our supervisor, Ms Weston, insisted on detailed reports, but it was impossible for Ada to remember every tiny detail of her time with the Stoneskins. Amanda, Ms Weston's sister, had put her foot down and said Ada shouldn't *have* to relive it. Even though we needed as much information as possible if we wanted to prevent a similar attack from ever happening again.

Ada shifted her feet, subtly, but I noticed. A sudden unease prickled the back of my neck. *Had* she told the Alliance everything important? Ada wouldn't hide the truth on purpose. But I had good reason to avoid the company's sister branch on Klathica, especially now.

"Yeah," she said, "of course. But they did mention Klathica. That wasn't the world they said the experiment was on, though. They said they were created on Thairon."

My heart missed a beat, then sank, hard, like someone had punched me in the chest. Thairon was the world my father would be returning from. The world the Alliance was in negotiations with. And the world my mother had died on.

2

ADA

"Dammit." I looked up at Kay from where I'd sprawled on the floor of the training area. "You got me again."

"You okay?" he asked, shifting back into position. I'd lasted all of five seconds in this round of one-to-one combat before he'd knocked me down. The guy was freaking *fast*.

"Sure." I sat up slowly, waiting for my opening. Then I lunged forward in an attempt to knock his legs out from underneath him.

I might as well have telegraphed my attack before even *I* was aware of what I was going to do. Next thing I knew, he had my arm in a lock. Gentle, but firm. If I moved, it'd hurt like hell.

"Damn you," I muttered. "You did this to me when I tried to escape prison, remember?"

"Oh, yeah," he said softly in my ear. "I also did this."

He flipped me over his shoulder. I yelped, kicking. "I told you, I—hate—being—carried!"

He stopped moving. The pressure on my arm loosened. "Ada, are you—?"

"Gotcha." I pulled my arm free and shoved him in the

"Kay, you aren't banned from my house, you know," I'd said. "What's the problem? Nell didn't say anything to you, did she?" That seemed unlikely. Kay tended to have the same reaction to being told what to do as I did—that is, he'd probably do the opposite.

"No." I couldn't put my finger on it, but something in his tone was different. Hesitant. Which really wasn't Kay's style.

I exhaled. "If you don't want to see me, Kay, just say so."

"What? No. I just wanted to make sure you're okay with this. After what happened, you don't need to feel you have to—"

"Are you kidding me?" I started to laugh, but stopped. "Kay, you ran across half the Multiverse to find me—which is *very* flattering, by the way. But I'm capable of making my own decisions, you know. I'm an adult."

He laughed quietly. "I'm very much aware of that."

"So we're good?"

"Yeah." His tone softened. "We're good."

Okay. "I'm not used to this either, you know, but we need to actually talk to one another. By that, I mean *tell* me next time you plan to go gallivanting offworld or break the law. And for the love of Cethrax, don't go up against any more gods."

"Got it," he said. "Is that your only condition?"

"Hell, no. I'm just getting started."

"Ada…"

"Huh?"

He paused. "I'll try my best, but being accountable to someone else isn't something I'm used to. I'm not trying to make excuses, but I can't promise to tell you everything about before I joined the Alliance. Before the Academy. It's not a time I like to remember."

"I… you don't have to tell me anything until you're ready, Kay." Sure, a big part of me was curious as hell, but the other half suspected the experiment that turned him into a magic-wielder wasn't the worst part of Kay's childhood.

"Okay," he said. "When we first met, I said I didn't lie. That… wasn't always true. I lived in the same house as two council members, before my mother died, so I was always under the Alliance's confidentiality agreement. Old habits die hard."

"It's all right, Kay," I said, sort of surprised. He'd never brought up his parents in front of me. Then again, we hadn't had the chance to discuss the future of our relationship before I'd been taken by the Stoneskins. "Want to come over now?"

"Sounds good to me."

And that was that. I had to hand it to Kay for putting up with Nell's questioning, too. She'd interrogated him about every world he'd been too—I guess in case anyone tried to kidnap me again.

"Nell, I've been with him almost every single time," I'd interjected. "I'm the one who—" I cut myself off before I said *went to Enzar.* I'd been close enough to breathe in the burning air and feel the magic of my homeworld against my skin. I still woke in the night convinced I'd open my eyes and see through that doorway again. Every detail was burned into my brain.

The line of shielded soldiers, split apart by a deadly third level magic attack. The world lit up in white, as my contact lenses were reduced to nothing, revealing the mark of an Enzarian magic-wielder. The thrilling call of magic as my homeworld beckoned to me.

The Alliance now knew, including the council. But I was under their protection. And I was glad of it now. Even when I'd thought I was safe, my homeworld had never really left me.

I didn't tell my family, or even Kay. I figured he knew I

people making stupid comments, I said, "Because I don't want to dazzle everyone at Central."

Vic laughed. "Yeah, you messed up the camera images on Valeria."

"Good," I said, not finding it half as funny as he did. "The fewer people who know what happened the better."

"Didn't you see the news?" said Vic, eyebrows raised. "Half the Multiverse knows what happened."

No, they only knew what they'd seen on the TV. I'd watched part of the video online and then switched it off, unable to stand it a moment longer. Someone had sold footage of the battle that had almost taken out Neo Greyle to Valeria's media. Thank the gods the videos hadn't shown what had happened on the other side of the doorway, on Enzar. Because for all their excitement, Valeria's media would start a mass panic if they realised *that* was where the doorway had opened. They could pass Cethrax off as a joke, but Enzar... I was amazed the magic flying around there hadn't done more damage to Valeria's capital.

"Your boss isn't happy about it," said Jeth. "She wants the footage taken down, but the council's wound up in this mission to Thairon."

"Thairon?" I echoed, and my blood went cold.

"We're not supposed to know about it," said Vic. "But Iriel couldn't keep her mouth shut when she came in here earlier."

"Not supposed to know what?" I asked. *No. The Stoneskins are dead. It can't be about them.*

"There's not much to know," said Vic, glancing over his shoulder as though worried someone might be listening in. "Something about a meeting. That world's been out of contact with Earth—with anyone, really, for years now. Then out of nowhere, they called our council over there for negotiations."

Andy looked up. "You'd think they'd have more important

problems. Instead, half the offworld council's gone, including all three members from Central."

"Maybe they're looking for allies," said Jeth. "Seeing as Cethrax didn't work out."

"Yeah, it sounds like it was a train wreck," I said. "Kay's still writing the reports."

"Speaking of reports," said Andy, "your boss bit my head off when I asked where the records of Thairon were. You'd think I'd torched her office or something. I was just curious about what made the council up and leave right after a cross-world threat."

Thairon's records aren't here? Given how the Stoneskins were linked to Thairon, it seemed too big a coincidence that they'd suddenly contacted the Alliance. Maybe Nell's paranoia was rubbing off on me. Except the Stoneskins claimed to have nothing to do with the Alliance. *Enzar* had created them. But I knew the StoneKing was dead for sure, unless he'd survived me stabbing him in the eyes, the only vulnerable part of his unbreakable body. Still…

"Why'd Thairon cut themselves off from the Alliance?" I asked. "Was it like Karthos?"

Jeth's former homeworld had been exiled from the Alliance after a civil war in the one free nation on that world had resulted in a bloodbath. But the doors hadn't been permanently closed, like my homeworld. Or Thairon, apparently.

"I think there was some kind of natural disaster," said Vic. "Some reason they had to shut all the Passage doors there. To be honest, I think everyone forgot about them."

"It's confidential, isn't it?" said Jeth. "The council took the world-keys, anyway, so we know they mean business."

"They did?" *What?* "All of them?"

"Central only has three. Why?" said Jeth.

They were our backup. Kay had used a world-key to find

me when the Stoneskins had taken me across the Multiverse. Aside from the Passages, world-keys were the only way off Earth, and the Passages weren't as safe as they used to be. It'd been one of Valeria's world-keys that Kay had used to go to Cethrax yesterday.

"Do any of you know anything else about Thairon?" I asked.

"They provided the simulator tech," said Vic, and everyone looked at him. He shrugged. "That's all I know. They used to be pretty close to Klathica ages ago, before they cut themselves off."

Klathica. The Stoneskins had come from there originally, before being taken to Thairon to be turned into monsters for the war. I didn't know any more than that. But suspicion crept up my spine all the same.

"Yeah, the Klathican reps have been nosing about Central," said Andy. "I don't trust them. I think they're after our tech."

"They've been here?" I looked at Jeth.

"Yeah." He shrugged. "They always want in on the latest tech."

"Probably wanted to take credit for the 'badass booster'," said Vic.

"We're *not* calling it that," said Jeth.

"The sciras boosters, right?" I asked. "I think it's a cool name."

Jeth rolled his eyes. "You would. I hope you'll take the gloves for a spin," he added, indicating a pair of lightweight black gloves amongst the tangle of computer wires on the desk. "They're safe, I swear. I made sure these two didn't tamper with them."

"Tech head would murder us," said Andy. "You know, I didn't sign up to make fancy gloves or build weapons."

"Yeah, none of us did," said Jeth. "Valeria's people keep

trying to recruit me. Makes me wish *I* could turn invisible sometimes," he added, with a smile at me.

"You have the Chameleons, you evil genius. Anyway, I'll see what I can do with these." I picked up the gloves, which did match the guard gear we normally wore on patrol or on missions. The leather-like fabric was protected against damage even from magic. Gloves sure would be useful if my magic kept acting up.

"The protection's built in," said Jeth.

"Hmm." I tentatively tried to use magic, but the level was too low on Earth at the moment to do more than conjure a spark. "I'll keep them handy when I'm on patrol." Though I hadn't been assigned to guard duty since I'd got back. I had the impression Ms Weston didn't want to tempt fate by sending me into the Passages.

I headed back to the first floor, thinking. Sure, the Alliance seemed to be on high guard against any threats, but guilt nagged at me for being less than thorough in my explanation of the StoneKing's plan, and for not going direct to the council before they'd disappeared to Thairon and telling them that the Stoneskins had been created there.

But it was probably for the best that they didn't know the StoneKing had decided to trick the magebloods into thinking the Royals had implanted me with the core of all the magic in the Enzarian Empire. It was impossible, of course. I hadn't even *been* on Enzar since Nell had smuggled me out as a baby. The magebloods only knew I was missing, and that was far from uncommon on a world which had been at war for over twenty years. If they'd believed the StoneKing, that I had the nexus inside me, they wouldn't have been able to kill me without risking destroying themselves. The StoneKing had said everyone would believe the story. I doubted so, but just in case, I hadn't told the Alliance. Or even Kay. No reason to worry everyone when it wasn't even true. Nell would want to encase me in a bubble, and I might even be forced into hiding again.

No. I wouldn't hide in the shadows any longer. I wanted to know who the Stoneskins really were, and what they had to do with Enzar. And if, as Kay had said, the answers weren't here, then...

I stopped outside Ms Weston's office. As our supervisor, she was the only person who might give me authorisation to go to Klathica, a world that didn't normally let tourists in. I couldn't begin to think how I'd explain my quest for information, but maybe I'd be able to get a permit. It was more likely that I'd be allowed there than Thairon.

"Ada? What are you doing?"

Busted. Ms Weston frowned at me through a crack in the door. My boss hadn't left her office much over the last week, and right now, she looked as close to dishevelled as I'd ever seen her. I tried not to stare. She always looked impeccable, not a single hair out of place, her smart suit without one wrinkle. Now, her chin-length dark hair was in disarray, and the papers in her arms stuck out at angles like they'd been gathered together in a hurry.

"Er, nothing," I said. "Just came back from the tech office."

"Can I have a word?"

Her appearance wasn't the only thing that was unusually slapdash. Papers were scattered all over her desk, some weighted down with communicators. I counted five of them.

"What're you doing with those?" I couldn't help asking.

Her eyes narrowed, as they always did when she was displeased about something. "Not our concern right now."

"Okay..."

For someone who had two emotions—stern and angry— seeing my boss this jumpy was odd, to say the least.

"Your reports are very well written," she said. "I think they'll satisfy the council."

Ms Weston had told me to keep the details of the Stoneskins' origin between the three of us—Kay, her and me—until the council came back. I'd nearly brought a war right here, and I'd bet the Stoneskins weren't the only ones who were looking for me.

"However, there's one part I'd like more detail on—the path through the worlds you travelled down with the Stoneskins. Every detail you remember."

"I wrote down everything." I hadn't recognised any of the worlds they'd taken me through, aside from Cethrax. They were worlds abandoned and desolate, bare of human life. "You had the files on the world with that plant, right?"

"Yes." Her mouth was a tight line. "But there needs to be an enquiry into the deaths there."

My insides twisted. The bomb the StoneKing had planted had nearly killed Kay.

"It's not your fault, Ada," she said, as though she'd guessed what I was thinking. "But still—our image matters, especially given recent events and what's ahead."

"What's ahead?" She didn't really think there was going to be a war, did she? Nobody had made an outright attack since the Stoneskins. We didn't even know who the enemy was. Someone was manipulating Cethrax, yes, but the worlds which were a threat were closed off. Literally—the doors in the Passages leading to those places were impossible to open from both sides. I'd asked. As for the Stoneskins, they were dead, and the few who'd been arrested on Valeria claimed not to know their boss's true goal *or* to remember the exact circumstances of their creation.

"Just a precaution," said Ms Weston. "You can't be too prepared. And I wanted to talk to you for another reason, Ada. I think the time has come for you to be promoted to Ambassador."

What? I stared at her, my mouth hanging open. Of all the

things I'd expected from the past week, a promotion was the least of them. I'd violated most of the Alliance's laws. Not to mention, as Kay had said, we'd probably blown the laws of *nature* sky-high when we'd opened the doorway to the void.

"Um," I said. "That's… unexpected." Great, now I'd lost the ability to put words together coherently. "I'd love to."

It wasn't a lie. Or at least, it hadn't been. I'd helped people from my homeworld over half my life, and the idea of being able to legally visit other worlds as an Ambassador was literally a dream come true. Better, I'd have an ironclad excuse to go offworld and look into other Alliance branches' files. If they let me.

"Excellent," said Ms Weston. "Here is the necessary paperwork."

She piled a heap of papers into my arms, on top of the gloves.

"Oh, they're from the tech team," I hastened to explain. "They want me to test-drive—not drive, you know what I mean—their magicproof gloves."

"I see," said Ms Weston. "If there's a fire risk, I would ask you not to do so near my office."

"Uh…" I never could tell if she was being serious or not when she said things like that. I'd seen a handful of moments where she acted like a human being, but still.

"And there's one more question I had, actually," she said. "I wanted to ask… what you know about Thairon."

Again? "What's happening there? The tech team were talking about… something about it being closed off, and now it's opening again."

"Yes. I want to know what *you* know about it."

"Nothing," I repeated. "The Stoneskins were created there, I think, but I don't know anything about the world itself. It's been locked down, Vic said. Is that true?"

She gave a tight nod. "Thairon is in an unusual situation.

It has, for the past twenty years, remained in a permanent state of stasis, of a sort. After a wave of natural disasters, their entire population relocated to a satellite orbiting their homeworld. But the population, including the government, spend the majority of their time in a virtual environment, in a simulated state. This mimics the world they once knew, so in essence, their lives haven't changed since they were forced to leave their planet's surface."

"I... what? Simulation?" I didn't know what I'd expected her to say—maybe I'd been hoping for a clue about Enzar's connection with the place. "Like virtual reality, only permanent?"

I'd known some worlds had the technology. The Alliance themselves used it, of course. The training complex contained chambers designed to recreate imaginary scenarios in a simulated environment. Earth's technology was heading in that direction. Amanda had told me about a version of the tech on Klathica in which you actually controlled the experience. But you couldn't live in one permanently, right?

"Unfortunately, the government is, to use the Alliance's terminology, unstable. The magic level on Thairon was unpredictable—it still is, but the population don't know it. It's difficult to describe to someone who's never been there."

"*You've* been there?" I blurted.

Her hands tightened, her expression closing like a door slammed. "No."

"Oh," I said. "Uh. It's just the way you said it. Never mind. The government—they're like, controlling the population. Is that it?"

"You cannot even imagine." Something in her voice chilled me. She'd been involved with that world. *How?*

"I can." Well, I had to say something. "My world's torn to pieces in a magical war. My parents are most likely dead."

Guilt shot through me, unexpectedly—I'd spoken without any emotion. *I didn't know them,* I reminded myself. *Nell, Jeth and Alber are my family. Not them.*

"Yes," said Ms Weston. "You're right, of course."

"So that's why no one's heard from the council members who were on Thairon," I said, in a clumsy attempt to change the subject. "When they were in the simulation, I guess there was no outside contact."

"Correct. There was also no safe way to use any of the doorways, as they were located on the planet's unstable surface. Instead, they had to use a world-key to enter, which, again, is inaccessible in virtual simulation."

I shook my head. "Wow."

"You said the Stoneskins were created there. That doesn't add up with what we know of that world. The planet's surface has been uninhabited for twenty years. There certainly couldn't have been anything of that nature there."

"But it might have been hidden... How did the council get back in touch with Earth?"

"The council has yet to update me on the precise nature of their arrangement, but I don't believe in coincidence, Ada."

No. I didn't either, not anymore. Something was happening on my homeworld. The Stoneskins... Thairon... even Cethrax. We might as well be walking under a thunder-cloud, taking bets on when the storm would break. Worse was not knowing where they'd strike first.

"So... Thairon had contact with Enzar?" I asked. "Do the council know that?"

"If they do, there's no proof," said Ms Weston. "Did the Stoneskins happen to say the name of their creator?"

I shook my head. They hadn't. "Just it was on the mage-bloods' orders. But... they might have been lying." Like when the StoneKing had told the group it was just a revenge mission. There was more going on. He didn't just want revenge, he wanted to rule. To be king of the empire, not destroy it.

What if he'd told more lies? It was beyond me to figure out how his mind had worked. Not to mention the others. He'd convinced them so thoroughly they'd been left without a purpose when he'd died. He'd said he wanted me to be his queen. My skin crawled at the thought. I'd never be at his mercy—or anyone else's—again. Not even if Enzar came knocking on the door.

"You think he lied?" asked Ms Weston.

"I don't know what to think." I was telling the truth this time. "I just wanted to get away."

"Of course you did," said Ms Weston, half to herself. "I'm sorry, Ada."

I blinked, startled. Why was everyone acting oddly lately? "It's fine."

Great. My boss was being weird, my boyfriend was hiding something, and the Alliance might be dragged into a war. Right now, I almost wanted to go back to filling out mind-numbing paperwork.

"Are any of the other Alliance branches likely to have information on the Stoneskins?" I asked.

She gave me a sharp look. "No. I've already asked at our most recent council meeting. As a newer Ambassador, it will take several days to get your offworld permit sorted so you can access certain worlds."

Dammit. I took in a breath. *Okay.* I could be patient for a day or two. We hadn't entirely cleaned out the archives here. It'd probably be best if I made a plan before wandering into the Klathican Embassy searching for information when their guards were notorious for arresting people on a whim.

"Anything else?" I asked Ms Weston.

"Go back to the office. You'll officially be on the list for ambassadorial missions as of tomorrow."

"Okay." I nodded. Act normal. That was all we could do, until we knew who the enemy was. I'd plan which questions to ask on Klathica, and figure out how to get more information on Thairon and the Stoneskins.

But I had the feeling, as I closed the door to Ms Weston's office, that my boss knew more than she was letting on.

3

———

KAY

Ada came out of Ms Weston's office, an expression of vague puzzlement on her face. I caught her eye and she smiled.

"I got promoted," she said. "To Ambassador."

"Really?" I probably sounded too surprised, though her smile looked strained. "That's... what you always wanted, right?"

"Of course."

"Fantastic," said Markos. "You can volunteer for the next excursion into the swamp."

"Yeah, no thanks." Ada deposited a ton of papers on her desk. The others had left the office, aside from Markos. "Anyway, I'll be filling these out for the next ten years. What are they, health and safety forms? What to do in face of imminent death?"

"Pretty much." I glanced down at my own written reports. "So the dragon's around?"

"Yeah..." She glanced behind her, and then said, "She's acting kinda weird."

So I wasn't the only person who'd noticed. "She said everything was okay with your report?"

"Surprisingly," she said. "She just wants more detail on the worlds the Stoneskins took me through."

"What, apart from the swamp?"

Ada shrugged. "It's what she asked for. They really ought to get a map of Cethrax in case anyone gets stuck there again. I have no idea whereabouts the Stoneskins took me."

"Onto the Vox's territory, apparently." I tapped my own pen on the desk. Files had a habit of multiplying, and I swore I'd written the same thing twenty times now, and typed a copy for the Alliance's digital files. They wanted written evidence to send to all the major Alliance branches, seeing as technology and magic went together about as well as fireworks and a lit match. "The specifics don't matter. Cethrax looks the same all over. It has about the geographical variety of Antarctica, only with swampland instead of ice."

"Ha." She smiled. "I think we got the better deal. I don't get why Cethrax acted like that, though. You'd think they'd want to form an alliance with the winning team."

"Hmm," I said. "They aren't team workers. They kill and eat their own kind, if they can't get anything else."

"Ew, really?" She shuddered. "Okay, I get they're not the smartest bunch, but the Vox seemed…"

"Intelligent? Well, he's the least stupid, but that isn't saying a lot," I said. "I reckon they've survived through sheer bloody-mindedness. But yeah, it doesn't add up. The Vox knew we beat the Stoneskins. Logically, they should be on our side."

"I hope not," said Markos. "They'd be as likely to kill us on the battlefield as the enemy. I'm going to talk to the dragon." He left the office, tail swishing.

"Everyone's talking about it like it's inevitable," said Ada. "It's all because of my homeworld. If I hadn't…"

"It's not your fault." I gave her a look I hoped was reassuring. "If you weren't here, this would have happened no matter what. The council were short-sighted for thinking they could just shut the war out and it would go away."

I spoke with more venom than I'd intended, my mind still on one particular council member, who'd issued the statement in the first place. Lawrence Walker. I almost wanted to go and knock at the council's door and ask when he was coming back to Earth, just to get it over with.

Another part of me wanted to run to the other side of the Multiverse. But that was cowardly. It wasn't like before. I was a magic-wielder now, and just yesterday, I'd walked into Cethrax's capital and come out alive. Dealing with Lawrence Walker should be nothing in comparison.

A dozen questions lurked in Ada's eyes, but she only said, "They couldn't have interfered. It was a full-on magical war."

I'd used the same justification, once. Part of the reason I'd helped her in the first place was to strike back against my father's insistence that the Alliance stay out of the conflict.

"They see no problem engaging Cethrax. The vox-kind have hated us for a thousand years."

"Yeah." She fidgeted. "But what if Cethrax… what if they're answering to someone else?"

The StoneKing? No. He was dead. Ada had killed him herself. The few surviving Stoneskins were under watch on Valeria. "If they were enslaved to a magic-creature like last time, we'd have seen it," I said, more confidently than I really felt. "The link with Vey-Xanetha isn't open anymore."

"Yeah." Ada closed her eyes, taking in a calming breath. "I know."

I took her hand, which rested on the table, and traced circles on her palm with my fingertip. She looked up, eyebrows slightly lifted in surprise, and her mouth curled into a smile.

"It'll be okay," I said. "We'll be using the new weapons the tech team have been working on later in training."

"Jeth didn't say. You're reading minds again, aren't you?"

"Check your communicator," I said, amused. "They sent out a message."

"Crap," she said. "There I was, thinking I'd caught your psychic powers."

"You'll have to do better. Though," I added, leaning closer. "I bet I can guess what you're thinking right now."

"Really, now?" A flush spread across her cheeks. In moments like this, when she looked at me—really looked at me—I could almost forget the shadow hovering over my shoulder.

The sound of hooves interrupted us and we pulled apart enough to look vaguely like we'd been behaving professionally as the centaur came into the office.

"Honestly." Markos closed the door. "Nobody put those files away?"

"You're the one who knows were everything's supposed to go," I said.

"Guess I'd better go and submit this report." Ada stood up. "If she wants it now."

"The boss seems highly-strung," said Markos. "She has reason to be, with the staff overworked and Aric kicking up a fuss downstairs."

I looked up. "Wait, Aric's here?" I'd totally forgotten about Aric in the wake of everything else. "I thought he got hauled off by Valerian law enforcement."

"Technically, he's an Earth resident, so they handed him over to our guards instead." Markos snorted. "Now he's claiming he wants to help the Alliance. To fight on our side."

"They'd better not let him near a weapon," I said. "Seriously?"

"Unfortunately," said Markos, "our delightful former colleague is, once again, on Earth."

"Not in jail?" I raised an eyebrow.

"Apparently, the guards didn't know what to do with him so they stuck him in the holding cells. He knocked two of them out."

Ada winced. "Ouch. He's still there?"

"You're not thinking of paying him a visit, are you?" I asked.

"Of course not. I just wondered what they'd done with him. I mean, he betrayed everyone, but he wasn't really on his father's side, right?"

No, I'd thought at the time. His family had been trying to get their hands on Aglaia's source, and he'd wandered into the plan by accident and got himself stuck on Aglaia. I'd spared his life, having learned it had been his sister who'd set a wyvern to attack me two years ago, and his father who was behind the scheme on Aglaia. But he was still dangerous to the Alliance.

"They do know he's a magic-wielder, don't they?" I asked Markos.

"Of course, human," said the centaur. "He was telling everyone who would listen."

"Really?" I raised an eyebrow. "That's one sure-fire way to get yourself in trouble."

"Tell me about it," said Ada. "I have no idea how he survived the Stoneskins. He doesn't have a lot of sense."

No. Ada herself was lucky to have survived. It still amazed me that we'd both walked out alive, much less that even after all the near-close calls with death, Ada not only wanted to stay in the Alliance. She wanted to stay with *me*.

Once we'd submitted our reports—without Ms Weston biting anyone's head off—we headed to the training complex for the compulsory weapons training. The warehouse-sized building was two streets down from Central and surrounded by high fences to keep passersby out. It looked like a fancy gymnasium, but allowed only to Alliance members. I spent a lot of time there anyway, but not at the firing range—normal guns weren't much use against monsters.

Carl, the scarred senior guard, was in charge of weapons training. A group of fifty or so of us gathered in the main hall of the training complex for instruction, ranging from nervous-looking novices to Ambassadors and other higher-up Alliance members who might need to go offworld.

"The current situation merits training in battlefield weaponry," said Carl. "Attacks from monsters are more numerous, and stunners and daggers are ineffective on many opponents. We cannot leave safety up to chance and the expertise of a few. So the tech team have been working hard with other Alliance branches to develop new weapons."

He held up a gleaming black gun. Not an Earth weapon, for sure—it looked a little like the semi-automatic magic-powered guns Neo Greyle's Law Enforcement Squads had carried before they were banned across Valeria.

"These contain bullets made of the materials you're used to in your stunners—obsidiate with a thin covering of adamantine. Don't fire them inside Central, nor in any place which is or may be made of a magic-based substance—especially the Passages."

"So what's the point, then?" asked a novice. Evan, the guy who'd been giving everyone grief for the last month. "If we can't fire them in the Passages? I thought we were using them to take down monsters."

"The same rule doesn't apply to the lower levels," said Carl, "which is where many of you will be patrolling now. Cethrax's doorways overlap with the hidden Passage we recently discovered, and a large number of our patrols will be covering the area to ensure nothing escapes to Earth."

"So we risk getting clawed to death or eaten alive," said Evan.

"Evan, if you have a problem, the door's that way."

Evan glared, but wisely shut up. He might be a loud-mouthed aggressive dick, but he wasn't the only one who didn't look too pleased with the arrangement. Most Academy students took training seriously, but how many people really thought we'd be on the battlefield when we graduated? At least Aric wasn't here. Everyone in the room had been triple-checked by security, especially the handful of magic-wielders amongst us. The Alliance were more paranoid about attacks than ever.

Carl demonstrated how to use the weapon on various targets. Fire a bullet at a concrete wall and it burned a hole right through it. The only thing it didn't work on was adamantine, of course. If the Stoneskins came back, the sciras was all we had. But the Alliance didn't think we'd be facing off against the Stoneskins again. They thought we'd be up against magic-wielders.

Enzarians.

I caught Ada's eye. She looked a little nervous, but I recognised the determined set to her jaw.

"Right," said Carl. "That's about it for demonstrations. Form a line. No screwing around, and it goes without saying you're not to point your weapon at anyone unless you're prepared to shoot. Got that?"

When it came to my turn to hold the gun, I didn't hesitate. I took aim at the target and fired. The recoil was more of a static tingle than anything it. Easy. Too easy. I shook off the thought. What was the matter with me? We had to be prepared, in case Enzar really did play their hand.

But the face I saw behind my eyes when I fired the gun wasn't Enzarian but Lawrence Walker. The enemy even the Alliance didn't know they had. The one person capable of undoing everything the Alliance had worked for, and dragging Earth into a cross-world war.

~

"That might have gone better," Raj commented, as the group of us sat in the Blind Wyvern later that evening. "I'd have better luck if I threw the gun at the enemy's nose rather than firing it."

"It's still more reliable than a third level magic shot," Ada said.

As Raj went to get more drinks, I leaned in to ask, "You haven't used magic since, right?"

As she went tense, I regretted speaking. But she shook her head. "Not since there. I can't use magic without remembering. I almost couldn't… couldn't stop it." She looked down, and I shifted close enough to brush her hand under the table. "Anyway, my brother made these magicproof gloves, and they help."

"Magicproof?" That'd definitely help. The magic level in the Passages was higher than ever, and if I used high level magic, I risked burning the skin off my hands.

Ada nodded. "I'm keeping the gloves on when we're patrolling. I won't be any use as an Ambassador if I can't go offworld without an escort."

"It'll calm down soon," I said automatically, and wished I could take back the lie almost at once. I hadn't dropped so much as a hint about Walker potentially coming back, but as long as he was out there, it was damned difficult to pretend everything was normal.

My communicator buzzed. "Simon's stuck on Klathica. Cethrax has flooded."

"What? Seriously?"

"Well, the lower corridor. Which might not even have

been Cethrax, if someone opened a door into the ocean or something."

Ada's expression relaxed into a smile. "Surprised you haven't done that yet."

"Nah, it's usually Zanthar. If you ever wanted to go there, by the way, there's probably only a month left before the whole place is submerged."

"I'll add that to the priority list for our next day off. Did you say he was on Klathica?" asked Ada.

"Yeah. He had to shortcut through the Embassy." Ada had asked me more than once if I'd take her on a tour of that world. I'd responded that Klathica didn't *do* tours. If you couldn't give the security mechas a good excuse for you being there, they wouldn't let you in.

"I don't get that place," Ada said now. "What's their issue with offworlders? Half of them weren't even born there, right?"

She must have got curious and read the files. "No, they weren't. They don't hate all outsiders, just people from any world that's aligned with Valeria... which means half the Alliance, including Earth." And now we came to the part of history I really didn't want to talk about—that half of Klathica's population was originally from Thairon, before that world had sealed all access. And that Klathica's hatred of Earth had everything to do with the reason Thairon had been sealed off. "Believe me, you're not missing much. Valeria's on the same tech level, with added hover boots."

"Ms Weston said it'd take a couple of days before my permit comes through."

"You really wanted to go?" *Oh.* I got it. The Stoneskins. If they'd been taken from that world to Thairon, there was the tiniest chance Klathica might have information. "I can have a look," I said quietly. "I don't have to be in the office tomorrow, strictly speaking."

She smiled. "But you planned to keep me company?"

"I owe you a lunch date."

"You already paid for our meals and drinks tonight."

"It's not a big deal, really." Money wasn't the issue. Nothing I bought her could make up for the fact that being around me might put her in as much danger as she'd been in around the Stoneskins. But I'd made the mistake of pushing her away before. Selfish though it might be, I wanted to be with her, even if only for a short time.

Markos walked up to the table, almost knocking the drinks over with his tail.

"By the gods, don't look so scared. I don't bite," the centaur said to a cowering novice, causing him to trip over a stool. Nearby, Aric's moronic friend Evan glared at us.

"Nah, but he might trample you a little if you annoy him," I added, raising my voice so Evan could hear. He backed away, hiding behind another group of guards. *Ha.*

"When will he quit?" asked Ada. "I don't think he even wants to be here."

I shrugged. "He has black marks on his record already, even more than Aric did. He'll be out, or Cethrax'll eat him before the year's over."

"Heard you guys had a narrow escape from Cethrax yesterday," said one of the other Ambassadors, and a few of the guards moved in closer to listen. The first formal visit to monster territory in twenty-odd years was kind of a big deal. I didn't mind telling *that* story again, nor knocking back tequila shots with the other Ambassadors and demonstrating my knowledge of Cethraxian curse words to general amusement. Markos opened a crate of Aglaian wine, which everyone declined. I was pretty sure the bar staff would have had protested if they weren't afraid of being trampled under the centaur's hooves.

"Want some?" I asked Ada, prompting a memory of the

time she'd fallen under the influence of the same wine on Aglaia.

She gave me an embarrassed grin. "No, thanks."

Simon arrived in the middle of our recount of Cethrax's attack, dripping water everywhere, and demanded to know why I hadn't bought back one of the vox-kind skulls from the palace.

"Because we were running for our lives," I said.

"As usual," said Simon, rolling his eyes. "Come on, though. I'm surprised the council don't have one in their office."

"Nah, our own council haven't set foot in Cethrax's capital," I said.

"Just us lucky Ambassadors." Raj gave a mock-cheer. "Who even authorised it, the council? It might have been nice of them to check the Vox wasn't going to change his mind before they sent us in."

Good point. But it was impossible for the council to be in twenty places at once.

"I think it was a snap decision," said Iriel. "But I did pick up something while we were there. Not a vox skull," she added, and placed a flattened piece of metal on the table.

"What in the world is that?" Everyone stared at it, including Ada.

"I think you mean what in the *Multiverse.*" Iriel flipped the metal plate over. Close up, it resembled a flattened version of a communicator. Like someone, or most likely, some*thing,* had trodden on it. "It's Klathican. I'd have taken it to the council, but they're locked in their offices and Weston bit my head off when I tried to hand it over with my report."

"Yes, she's too busy hiding in her office or breathing fire all over the first floor," said Markos. "What in all the gods' names happened to that?"

"Where'd you find it?" I asked. The thing had been

squashed flat. Wires and buttons were mashed into the metal casing.

"Inside the Vox's lair. I picked it up when you were having a staring contest with His Ugly Highness," said Iriel. "I figured he wouldn't miss it."

"So what does it prove?" Raj returned his attention to pouring tequila shots. "They probably stole it from some poor guard."

"It's a communication device," said Iriel. "Klathican guards don't need them." Her wired eye rotated in its socket, causing Simon to almost fall out his seat. "Most of us have implants for communication. This is an old-fashioned one."

Simon stared at her eye in horrified fascination. "Can you see through walls?"

"I can see through your skull," said Iriel, and Simon looked even more alarmed. Until he saw Ada laughing. "You're having me on."

"It's the mechas who can see through walls," I added. "Some of them, anyway."

"I'm not going to believe a word any of you say," Simon muttered.

"That part's true," said Iriel. "Creepy bastards. As for *this...* I actually can't tell what it's for." She flipped the metal piece over. "I only know it's Klathican because of the logo."

KimaroTech. My blood chilled.

"Have you spoken to their Alliance recently?" I asked Iriel.

"No, Izen disappeared after the meeting," said Iriel.

"They might have picked it up in the Passages, I suppose," I said, more to drown out my own doubts than anything. Ada had said that during her time with the Stoneskins, the other human prisoners had mentioned stopping off at points on Cethrax where tech from Alliance worlds had ended up. Cethraxians were hoarders, even if they didn't understand how Alliance technology worked. Still, considering the abrupt end to the supposedly peaceful meeting and the fact that their communications with non-Cethraxians were usually less than friendly, something didn't feel right.

"So Cethrax are communicating with someone offworld?" Ada asked, voicing the same question which crossed my mind.

"Maybe," said Iriel. "I suppose even they can understand Classical Klathican… but it's beyond me to figure out why they'd *want* to."

"Yeah." I took the device in hand. "Can't have been all that important to them if they trampled it." But the vox-kind weren't exactly intelligent. And the last time they'd cooperated with humans had been with the Conners.

"Maybe take it to the Embassy?" Raj suggested, knocking back another tequila shot. "Come on, forget about the vox-kind. We survived with all our limbs intact. Lucky us."

"The Embassy would confiscate it." Iriel turned to Ada. "Could you hand it to your brother? Not that I don't think it's a matter for investigation, but the council have bigger problems at the moment."

Yeah. Thairon. I just wished I knew what they were *doing* there.

"Sure can," said Ada. "But it doesn't look like there's much left of it."

The question was, had there been any other suspicious non-Cethraxian devices there in the Vox's palace? I hadn't checked. I'd been more focused on the vox-kind themselves. But it wasn't the first time I'd wondered if someone else had been giving them orders.

Maybe someone linked to the Stoneskins.

Right. I'm going to Klathica first thing tomorrow. I owed it to Ada to help her find out the truth, even if it meant revisiting my own demons.

A cliff. The opposite ledge is cloaked in mist, so it's impossible to see if the shadow on the other side is a person or not.

It doesn't matter, because I'm going to die.

My feet are too close to the edge. But the two fully-grown men behind me are armed, and there's nowhere to run.

I have a gun. One gun, which I hold in shaking hands.

If I don't kill them, I'll fall.

I raise the gun. Pull the trigger. Blood sprays from the man's chest.

The second keeps coming.

I'm sorry, I mouth, and the blast resonates in my ear. Head-shot. I don't miss. I never miss.

The ground shakes. Crumbles. Gives way beneath my feet. I can't even scream as I fall into the abyss. Somehow, even as I'm falling, I can see the outline of the figure on the opposite cliff, slant-wise, indistinct. This time, it comes into focus. This time, it looks like Ada. Her expression, like condemnation.

But I'm still falling, and I can't reach her.

A hand touched my shoulder. I jerked out the way and was on my feet before it registered I'd moved. I stared at Ada, lying dishevelled on the bed, like she was part of a different world.

"Kay…" She sat up. Her chalk-white face and wide eyes might have been a mirror of my own expression. "Are you all right?"

Not again. "Yeah."

"Are you sure?"

I just nodded. Cold sweat prickled my skin. I didn't even want to know if I'd been talking in my sleep.

I walked to the bathroom, turned on the shower, stuck my head under the icy water and concentrated on breathing.

You have to tell her.

Could I? Was it worth inflicting the truth on someone who'd already seen more than her fair share of grief? Ada deserved better than what I could give her, but she'd chosen to stay here with me. Every day I spent in her company made the notion of intentionally screwing up what we had even more inconceivable.

I came out of the bathroom to find her fully-dressed and going through my desk drawers. "What are you doing?"

I winced inwardly at the unintended sharpness in my voice. Ada turned and frowned at me. "Just looking for your communicator charger. I left mine at home."

"It's in my bag." I grabbed my guard gear and closed the drawer she'd left half open. *Stop being paranoid, Kay. It's not like there's anything incriminating in there.*

No, that wasn't the problem, but I didn't think I could explain to Ada.

"Hear from Ms Weston yet?" I asked her. "Guess we don't have to show at work early." Probably for the best, because I was feeling increasingly like I'd head-butted a wall. "If not, I'll check in on Klathica."

"I haven't heard from her, but I made coffee." She walked over to the kitchen area. "What was the deal last night? I had no idea you knew so many Cethraxian curse words."

"It's one of my many talents." I dry-swallowed two painkillers and joined her.

"I reckon I'm acquainted with some of the others."

I smirked, leaning in to kiss her. She tasted of coffee, which seemed a really good idea. I took the mug from the counter with one hand and grabbed a protein bar from the cupboard with the other. "What did you do with that device from Cethrax Iriel gave you last night, anyway?"

"I forgot about that. Guess I'd better hand it over to my brother today." She loaded a plate with toast and took her own coffee to the table. "Hope we're not violating any rules by keeping it here. Seeing as it's illegal offworld tech."

"Worried about breaking the rules? You?"

She lightly hit me in the arm. "Very funny. Seriously, though."

"We're not allowed to take offworld tech from Central or other Alliance branches or transport any magi-tech between worlds without permission… within limits. That thing's busted to shit, so it barely counts as technology. Besides, it's Klathican, and so is Iriel. Technically."

Ada rolled her eyes at me. "Nice subversion of the rules there. Anyone would think *you* were the one who sneaked magi-tech between worlds."

"Ha." She hadn't meant it in that way, but I couldn't help feeling angry with the part of myself used to conjuring up a lie at a second's notice. Even when I made a concerted effort to avoid doing so. "You can screw with the regulations more now you're at Ambassador level."

"What, bring luminous snails into the office like Iriel did that one time?"

"If you want. I was thinking…" I leaned over the table and placed my hand over hers. "You and I could take a few days out to Valeria."

She glanced down at our interlinked hands, biting her lip. "Maybe. I'll check with Nell. She's convinced the sky's going to fall on my head any moment."

"If you're sent on the next mission to Cethrax, that's a pretty valid worry." I paused. "There won't be one, don't worry. They just blew all chances of ever allying with Earth."

"Good," said Ada, taking a mouthful of toast. "Because I really don't like the idea of fighting on the same side as a wyvern."

"Riding one?"

"No!"

I grinned at her, the last threads of last night's dream slipping away. How just hearing her laugh made me feel like a ten-ton rock had lifted from my shoulders, I'd never know.

When no messages from Central showed on my communicator, an irrational surge of relief went through me—for one more day, I was spared.

"You go on ahead," I said to Ada, checking the time. "I'll go to Klathica and meet you there later, okay?"

"Are you sure?" she asked. "I could walk to the Passages with you."

"I need to take care of something first. You don't want the dragon to snap at you for being late."

"Doubt she'd notice." I knew she hadn't quite bought my excuse, but I didn't want to get out the papers with Ada still here. It would drag up questions I wasn't sure how to answer. She'd been patient with me so far, but it'd only been weeks since our return to Earth. If the truth came out, even if we had a shot at normality, I couldn't convince myself she'd stand with me in the end.

Once she'd left my flat, I retrieved the mini-safe, in which I'd locked my mother's will.

The letter she'd left still made no sense. Half of it was written in a code I'd never been able to read—and considering I'd at least *seen* hundreds of worlds' scripts, that was saying something. The other part read: *"Earth is safe. Central will hold, I will make sure of it. If he goes to Thairon, he's not coming back."*

"Guess you were wrong," I muttered to the now crumpled paper as I set it down, wiping the fine silver dust it had gathered off my hands. There were no clues in the writing. But there might be, somewhere else. Offworld.

4

KAY

My offworld permit easily got me past security at the Passage entrance, a concealed metal door on a deserted street around the back of Central. The buzz of static signalling the presence of magic came from behind the door, in the blue-lit corridors between worlds. Central's entrance was out of the way, down a corridor with only two, little-used doors.

Klathica, on the other hand, was wedged in the middle of the main Passage, and I'd inadvertently decided to go there in rush hour. Offworlders and Alliance guards alike jammed the way down the path, which was as wide as London's busiest roads only without the crossings. I had to elbow my way through with my ID in hand, searching for the right door. Hoping I didn't run into anyone I knew, so I wouldn't have to explain why, if my family owned the biggest company in Klathica's major city, I'd avoided setting foot on that world until I'd been promoted to Ambassador.

For one thing, as far as I was aware, my father hadn't gone to Klathica in years, either. He'd shown no interest in KimaroTech, even though he technically owned half their properties. He preferred to work for Earth's council. Officially, because he "wanted to spend time with his family'" I couldn't help but smirk at the thought. He'd spent less than half my life on the same *planet* as me.

I left the last of six rounds of security behind and followed a short metal-plated corridor into a large room like the waiting area at an airport, except staffed by mechas—Klathica's most basic model of robot. The information desk was on my left, so I headed that way, trying not to look to my right, where a row of monitors hooked up to a series of wires. Every major entrance to Klathica had a free testing area for their sim-tech. Two spaced-out guys slumped in chairs before the computer screens, visors over their faces. I had no idea which model they were testing this time, nor did I particularly want to know. The standard one projected you into a detailed hallucination, a 4D movie of your own making.

"Can I help you?" said the mecha, in the overly-chirpy tones of one programmed for customer service. She spoke Classical Klathican, as I'd expected. Klathica had tried to install a 'universal language' about a hundred years ago, supposedly because it made it easier to communicate over the virtual network. It hadn't quite succeeded because there were still a thousand dialects and variations, but everyone learned Classical, including most new Alliance members. Even on Earth.

I checked no one was close enough to listen before I said, "I'm here to access some information as an Ambassador for the Alliance. My name's Kay Walker."

"Walker." Her tone had no curiosity. Of course not. They hadn't created mechas with actual human emotions yet—that would defeat the purpose. "May I ask which information you wish to access?"

"All available information on the activities of Kimaro-

Tech, including interactions with other worlds, for the last twenty years."

That ought to cover the Stoneskins, if they had any information at all. If there was any history of Klathica's connection with Thairon, Ada and I needed to know.

"I cannot allow that."

"What?"

"I cannot allow access without prior permission."

"I have permission." I lowered my voice and flashed my ID again. "My family owns the company."

"Officially, ownership passed on to Lilian Greyson five years ago, when Lawrence Walker formally announced his resignation."

I swore under my breath, in English, though they probably understood me, given how they were equipped to understand a thousand languages. Klathican was the least expressive language in the Multiverse.

"That may be," I said, "but certain information is public knowledge. I want to access everything you have."

"Very well."

I followed a series of instructions to get my communicator hooked up to a box-shaped mechanism, one of their terminals. Unlike Earth's Alliance branches, Klathica stored all their files digitally. I had no doubt passcodes and firewalls would keep me out of the deeper layers, but all the basic information would be mine to access.

A beep told me the information had downloaded. I unplugged the communicator, checking the contents of the files. As I'd expected, half of it was blacked out, though at least they had all KimaroTech's staff's names, seeing as they were officially employed by the Alliance. This Lilian Greyson had been President for five years, since a week before my father had left Earth. So he'd replaced half the staff and probably terrorised the others into confidentiality. Figured. It wasn't worth my while to pay an actual visit, because I didn't even know where to start.

The history information was standard, with no mention of Thairon. Not surprising. Even Earth's records were bare minimum. Nobody, not even me, knew why my father had gone there, five years ago, taking a team of his own. Nor why he'd come back now.

The timing was too suspicious. And that didn't even drag up the connection with *Enzar*. I scanned through the files, looking at the earliest records. Enzar… that would have been before I was born, in all likelihood. But I found no mention of the name.

My hand clenched around the communicator. What was I thinking? That all the answers would land in front of me as soon as I walked in here? It was like expecting an answer as to why someone had pinned me to a chair when I was eight years old and shot an illegal offworld substance into my arm.

Illegal offworld substance. *That came from here.*

A prickling feeling crawled up my spine. I looked up, scanning the room. A vacant-eyed man staggered past the desk, high on something. I stiffened, every muscle locking in place, as a familiar smell washed over me, one I'd tried to forget. Klathica's stimulants had a potent aroma, one not comparable to anything on Earth. Like oil, maybe.

Hands clenched, I turned back to the communicator. *It's not him.*

But it reminded me. Which company was in charge of offworld magic-based substances? KimaroTech, of course. And lustre had been *discovered* here on Klathica.

I ran a search on lustre. *Access denied.*

I swore again, not bothering to lower my voice this time. As much as I needed the information, I wasn't about to start shouting about magic sources in the middle of the Embassy.

Wait. I loaded up the information on the magic boosters.

They had to disclose what they actually contained, for legal reasons. The list flashed up on-screen. *There it is.* Lustre appeared on the middle of the list. I clicked on it, and this time, got what I was looking for.

Lustre... discovered fourteen years ago in what appeared to be an ordinary sciras deposit in the northern territories. All known samples are in the hands of Klathica's Alliance.

No. It wasn't true. *He'd* got hold of some... but Kimaro-Tech was deep in the Alliance here. He had contacts.

This substance is rare, but demand is not high. Only works in conjunction with other magic sources and in large quantities.

It only worked with other sources. Had my father know-ingly turned me into an amplifier? He might just have asked the scientists to inject me with every available source. I was no more than a pawn, and expendable. But whose idea was it to use lustre? The same people who'd made the Stoneskins?

KimaroTech.

I glared at the screen, and a bunch of sim-addicts scurried away from me, looking frightened.

Despite myself, I ran a search on Walker's name.

Access denied.

Great. If I stayed here much longer, someone would get suspicious. Even turning invisible wouldn't get me past secu-rity. It was designed to pick up on magic-based enhance-ments, after all. Klathica's Alliance would never let an outsider into their files, maybe not even Walker's son.

My communicator buzzed with a new message. From Ms Weston: "The council has issued a statement on the events surrounding the group known as the Stoneskins. All missions to that effect have been disbanded as there is not sufficient evidence that they are a threat to the Alliance."

What?

I stared at the message. The council had denied our

reports? *Not sufficient evidence?* They'd damn nearly killed Ada and me.

My heart stopped. Only one person had the clout to deny every word I said, no matter how much proof we had. Only one person would *want* to.

He's back.

ADA

Something's wrong. The thought followed me all the way to Central. I stopped at the tech office first to hand over the device Iriel had picked up on Cethrax to Jeth, before heading back to the first floor.

I knocked on Ms Weston's door, but got no answer, so I joined Markos in the office.

"No sign of the dragon?" he asked me from behind yet another mile-high stack of files.

"Apparently not," I said. "What's all this, anyway?"

"Admin," said Markos. "A bottomless quagmire. You're supposed to join me." He passed me a stack of papers.

To Markos's exasperation, I kept putting the files in the wrong cabinets until the centaur took over, leaving me in charge of passing him the right documents. Worry about Kay gnawed at me, keeping me from focusing on anything. What did admin matter, if there might be a war at any moment? Did Ms Weston seriously think alphabetising old files was more important than looking for information on the Stone-skins, or figuring out what Cethrax might be up to? Even Jeth couldn't glean anything from the device Iriel had found in the Vox's lair.

I jumped when my communicator buzzed with a message. I read it, then reread it, twice. I looked up at Markos. "What… what the hell?"

"What?" The centaur tapped a hoof. "This had better be important. I've almost made an alphabetical puzzle out of these file titles."

"They're deprioritising everything I told them. About the Stoneskins… and my homeworld. The council say there's… not sufficient evidence?"

It looked like a *joke*. But the message went out to the whole of Central. *What the hell?*

"They said what?" The centaur looked genuinely shocked. "I've worked here for ten years, and they've never dismissed anything without looking into it properly."

"First time for everything." The *something's wrong* feeling grew even stronger. Even if there turned out to be no threat to Earth, there was no way they'd be confident enough to outright dismiss a threat on the Stoneskins' level.

I walked to Ms Weston's office, but it remained locked, an 'out of office' sign on the door. The message had been sent from inside Central, but it sure didn't sound like the council. My thoughts ran in circles. I paced around the office, skimming through my communicator as though answers lurked inside it.

Kay appeared behind me, causing me to drop all the files I was holding.

"Really, human?" said Markos.

"Sorry," said Kay and I at the same time.

"Did you get that message?" asked Kay.

"Yes!" I dropped to my knees to recover the files. "Dammit, Kay."

"Sorry. I came back as quickly as I could."

I took in a breath, clambering to my feet with my arms full of papers. "Tell me I'm not losing my mind here. There were witnesses on more than one world. The council can't expect everyone to accept that there's no evidence the Stoneskins are a threat to us."

"I know," said Kay. "If it was in the interests of preventing a nationwide panic, I'd understand. But that's not what it is. It's a cover-up."

"I don't get it." Understatement of the century. "I thought the priority was keeping Earth safe. Seriously, they can't just de-prioritise the Stoneskins." I didn't even care if it meant people would stop staring at me like I was about to detonate. "Did you find anything?"

"No," he said irritably. "Klathica's security's airtight. We'd need authorisation to access the higher levels."

Damn. "Ms Weston? We need to find her."

Both our communicators buzzed again. Markos snort-laughed as we scrambled to turn them on. "This office was so abominably dull before you two arrived."

"Looks like you're on your own," said Kay. "We've been called to Covent Garden. How'd she even know I was here?"

"Witchcraft," said Markos, taking the files I passed to him.

"Crap." I read the message, which did appear to have been sent from Ms Weston's communicator. "Magic-wielders causing trouble in a public place. There are witnesses."

"I'm betting it's those bloody Klathican implants," Kay said.

Unease stirred inside me—*Klathica, again.* "Whatever it is, I'm wearing the gloves." Luckily, I'd had the presence of mind to shove them into my bag.

The offworld districts in London were scattered around the capital, but Covent Garden was a major one. It was also the site of the black market where Nell had run part of her business, and Jeth had bought illegal pieces of offworld technology. Now, he could get everything legally through the Alliance, but there were still people who depended on those markets for news of their homeworlds. Not Enzar, though. I doubted anyone would have recent news, especially not now.

Kay and I had to take the tube across London, which didn't improve Kay's mood, even if our Alliance IDs let us skip by the ticket barriers. Everyone stayed away from us, though that was probably more because of our guard gear and visible weapons. Pushing through the flood of commuters, we made our way to the exit.

Once outside the station, we turned right and ran down James Street towards the already-audible sounds of a commotion.

"Crap," I said. "They're not *inside* the market, are they?" Fear shot down my spine as we crossed the piazza to the covered market, pushing through the crowd that had gathered outside. Screams rang out from below the glass roof, and I saw the clear reflection of purple-red sparks. *Oh, hell.*

"What's going on?" Kay demanded. "We're from the Alliance—let us through."

The glass-roofed market was definitely the source of the screaming. Sparks of magic ricocheted around, creating a panicked rush. A winged man had climbed onto the underside of the glass ceiling and hung from one of the lights, a manic glint in his eyes. A teenage girl flew overhead, shrieking with laughter, a pair of mechanical wings attached to her shoulders.

"Stop that!" yelled a voice. We weren't the only Alliance members here. Two guys in Alliance guard gear were trying to coax the man down from the ceiling, the rest were crowded around one area of the floor—the source of all the sparks.

Kay swore and pushed through the crowd. I followed. Magic buzzed under my skin, and the crowd parted enough to see where someone had dug their way down through the middle of the floor, leaving a gigantic hole. The sparking magic stopped the Alliance members going near it.

"What is that?" I asked the guards.

"We're calling magic-wielder backup," said the guard, a blond woman. "It's some kind of magic-based bomb. They buried it under the marketplace—none of us can touch it."

Crap. "We *are* the backup," I said. "Let me at it."

"Who did that?" Kay asked, as I edged closer to the hole in the floor.

"They dug it up," said one of the guards. "With their bare hands. Must have some kind of strength enhancer."

"No kidding," muttered Kay, as I tentatively moved closer to the hole.

Nervousness fluttered under the surface as my skin tingled from the closeness of magic's presence. *I'm in control,* I told myself. I'd been in trickier situations, and I could pull the magic right out of a source without even touching it. I'd done it before. But never with a live bomb.

The ceiling exploded. For a heart-stopping second, I thought *I'd* done that, then I tilted my head to see the guy on the light had managed to yank it out of the ceiling further along, sending glass raining down on the crowd below. I cursed under my breath as the crowd fled, screaming. I reached for the magic again, and this time, the static buzzing rose, higher than before.

Higher than it should be able to on Earth.

"Shit," said Kay. "There's another source."

He must be amplifying the tracker in his pocket, which let him zero in on a single magic signal and find where it was coming from. All I sensed was the one nearby, but now I dragged the magic towards me again, and nothing happened.

"It's blocking me," I said.

And only one thing had managed to do that before: a *living* source.

A purplish glow surrounded the magic-wielders—the girl flitting across the ceiling, the man pulling the roof down, and others running amok through the crowd. I jumped back, drawing my stunner. A living magic source controlled them. Had to be. Veyak, the magic source on Vey-Xanetha had done the same to the summoners—but if there really was a kimaros, how the hell did it get over here?

I waved my stunner, a warning to everyone to back off before anyone got hurt. We needed to find the source, if there was one. Kay seemed to have a plan of his own. He'd moved into the crowd, his own stunner out. Then he turned invisible.

Going to sneak up on it? I had no idea. My gloves muted the charge, but they also stopped me using magic. I slid my left glove off, keeping my right one on my stunner hand. I let sparks jump from my left palm, hoping to lure out the kimaros.

"I'd stay back," I warned the crowd. "As for *you*," I said to the magic-wielder who'd dropped from the ceiling, "if you don't want to blow to pieces, I'd suggest getting away from here."

My words had no effect. The man's face was utterly blank, his eyes glassy. No, he definitely wasn't in his right mind. Cursing, I blocked his clumsy punch and zapped his arm with the stunner. He fell, convulsing, and I grabbed for the magic again.

A force slammed into me, throwing me back. I rolled over on the hard ground, the thick sleeves of my guard jacket blocking the impact, and heard Kay swear from somewhere alongside me.

He appeared, eyes wide, magic sparking from his hands. "Bloody kimaros is too strong. I can't see it. It's here—really close, but it must be hiding itself."

Hell. Last time he'd gone up against a magic-creature,

Veyak had almost killed him. I was the only person strong enough to resist, most likely due to the adamantine in my blood.

"Together." My hand brushed against his. He could transfer power to me through skin contact, while my adamantine protection kept magic from harming him. We hadn't used our magic like this for a while, and I'd forgotten the moment of intense contact, the absolute trust we needed between the two of us to combine our magic. The light of my own power was reflected back at me as our gazes connected and we raised our hands to the sky.

A shape appeared above us like a malevolent red cloud. It might have been Veyak's twin, though smaller and less apocalyptic. Sparks danced off the shattered glass roof, and a fresh trickle of alarm slid down my spine—everyone in the crowd was vulnerable to magic burn.

"Let them go," I said. "Now."

Anger brushed against me, anger that wasn't mine, but it wasn't like the overwhelming sense I'd had with Veyak. Not a voice in my head. More like a mildly pissed-off thundercloud.

"Fight me," I said. "Not with your puppets. Fight me yourself, unless you're too cowardly."

This time, sparks flew—literally. Purple and red spiralled from the creature and bounced off the ground. Screams rang out from the scattering crowd, but I couldn't protect everyone at once.

I pulled on the magic again, like yanking a rope, and the creature finally took form, leaving the humans behind. It swirled like smoke into a yowling clawed bundle of sparking magic. A kimaros.

I raised my stunner-hand, sending a second level wave through the air with the palm of my hand. The kimaros collapsed into smoke and re-formed, snarling. I raised my arms to protect my face from another volley of sparks, and drew my stunner, swinging it in an arc to send a bolt of magic at the creature. It collapsed, writhing, more smoke than anything solid. The magic level dropped, the jolt fading to a trickle.

The creature spun around, hissing like a cat.

Kay appeared beside the hole in the ground. The creature lashed out, but Kay had already jumped out the way, drawing his own stunner. As its back was turned, it was too late to stop my attack sending it writhing to the ground. Kay flicked his own stunner on to join mine. Sparks flew, and a torrent of red-purple magic combined from both our stunners. In one zap, the beast was reduced to smoke. Though the kimaros might be gone, the other source remained. The flying sparks had died down, but I didn't dare let myself move too close to the hole in the ground.

I used my free hand to yank the magic from the source again, letting it flow into me. My skin tingled, but not as intensely as around the kimaros. I gritted my teeth and pulled harder, feeling the small hairs on the back of my neck lift in response.

"Shit," I said. "I can't channel it all."

But Kay had already jumped over the edge.

"Kay!" I shouted. What was he doing?

"Got it," he said, one-handedly climbing back out. He held the source in the other hand. It wasn't a pure source, but looked like a remote-shaped device not unlike our own Chameleons. The adamantine-coated glove stopped it burning him, and also stopped the flow of magic pulsing into me. Then he snapped it in two. "This toy is useless now," he added.

The magic disappeared, like a candle snuffed out, and my hands dropped to my sides.

I gaped at him. "Please tell me you knew I'd taken most of the charge out of that thing before you picked it up."

"I was pretty certain you had." He flashed me a quick smile. "Now…"

Silence had fallen over what was left of the crowd. The avian man staggered to his feet, staring at us. "Who are you?"

"You were being controlled," said Kay. "We're from the Alliance. Can any of you tell me what happened?"

Luckily, more guards from West Office had arrived by now, and Carl sent a message saying he and some others were on the way. From the fragments of stories we picked up from the witnesses, it sounded like the kimaros had appeared from the other Passage entrance, near Leicester Square, and all magic-wielders nearby had been caught in the spell. They'd lost all sense of self. None of them even knew what the magical device was.

And they had one thing in common: they'd all recently acquired an enhancement, originally from Klathica, which boosted strength, speed and agility—and wasn't supposed to work on Earth.

"The seller said it would," insisted the claw-footed man. "Said it worked just fine, magic or no magic."

"We'll have to look into that." Kay tapped his communicator. "Right. Some others will be here soon, including representatives from the department of offworld affairs—you'll have to give them your story."

He still held the broken pieces of the source. Gleaming black metal. It might have been any source, because they looked so similar. But they never showed up out of nowhere. Least of all on Earth. I definitely hadn't seen anything like it at the market before—I'd have remembered.

"That *is* safe to handle, isn't it?" I asked dubiously.

"Probably best if you wear both gloves," said Kay. "You all

have magic-based implants, right?" he asked the avian man, who shifted, uncomfortable.

"It was just a bit of fun," he said.

"If it turns out any of you were complicit in creating an explosive, there will be consequences."

Silence fell as the words sank in—not so much the words, as Kay's cold Alliance guard expression. Though I suppose the fact that we'd both killed a magic-creature between us helped. Judging by the number of people with their phones out, we'd be the next YouTube sensation by the end of the week.

"Did they know?" I said. "The Alliance? They should have evacuated if they thought there was a bomb. They never even told us."

"Yeah." He frowned. "You're right. I should have thought of that, too. We need to get back to Central."

5

———

ADA

An hour later found us in the tech office. As the council were still gone and Ms Weston's office bore a sign telling us she was in a meeting upstairs, we took the pieces of the bomb to Jeth, who acted as though we'd discovered a windfall. At least, until I'd explained the device had almost blown us up.

"What do you think?" I asked Kay, as Jeth painstakingly took the device to pieces while the other tech guys sheltered behind their computers in case it exploded again. "Did the magic-creature order those people at Covent Garden to make the device, or did someone else give it to them?"

"Someone else," said Kay. "It was a weak creature, for a kimaros. Someone was controlling it for sure. Besides, I'm pretty sure those creatures don't have their own will, not in the way humans do."

"Like Veyak." And it had been the Vox who'd controlled *that* magic source. On the orders of the Stoneskins.

Kay nodded. I'd bet he was thinking the same.

"So we have out-of-control magic sources, strange messages apparently coming from Ms Weston's office, and the Alliance won't believe the Stoneskins are a threat," I said. "Jesus. You'd think someone was out to get us."

"Imagine that," muttered Kay. "Seriously. If Ms Weston doesn't believe the situation needs looking into, I'm going right to the offworld council. Valeria, for starters. Whatever they think's so important, it can wait."

"Yeah," I said. "Question is, where did the kimaros come from? I mean, they're usually on high-magic worlds. I thought they were originally from Vey-Xanetha." Except one did get into London before.

"I'd be careful, sis," said Jeth. He'd poked open the battery, revealing its gleaming innards, and was in the process of extracting the various wires.

"Always am. I'm pretty sure someone was filming us fighting that magic-creature." I almost laughed at the look on Kay's face. "Jeth, run a search on the Internet. It'll probably be up by now."

"Oh, man." Jeth returned to his computer. "This, I gotta see."

"Bloody hope not," said Kay, and my heart sank. He was right—the way videos went viral, our battle with the kimaros might be around half the allied worlds by the end of the day. The last thing I needed when I was supposed to be keeping a low profile. Alliance employees in general were advised to avoid being caught on camera. I'd always assumed that was the reason Kay didn't have any photos at his apartment.

"Here it is." Jeth grinned at us.

I leaned in to see the monitor. There wasn't a lot visible on the grainy image except for a lot of purple-red flashes. You couldn't even see us. I breathed out.

"Magic and cameras don't really go together," said Kay.

"Yeah," said Jeth. "Your secret identity is safe, sis. By the way, Nell was asking about you."

"Okay." I cast a guilty glance at Kay. I'd been pretty much

living in his apartment lately. "I'll go home later. She won't be happy to know the council's gone walkabout, though."

"They have?" asked Jeth. "The whole council?"

"Don't tell everyone," Kay warned. "It'd start a mass panic. Besides, it's not like Central's incapable of taking care of itself in their absence—all our best fighters are here."

"Damn," said Jeth. "Well, our team's busy mass-producing those magic-based guns, and we're seeing what we can do with sciras, too, now we have permission from Klathica's Embassy."

Kay looked at him sharply. "You do?"

"Yeah. Why?"

"Those magic-wielders all had implants from Klathica which aren't supposed to work on Earth."

"They did?" Jeth frowned. "Klathica's on the level, even if they're a bit obsessed with human enhancement. You should see their tech team—they're more machine than human."

"I can imagine," said Kay. "But there were issues with those magic-boosts before."

"Yeah," I said. "Is it the KimaroTech Institute you're working with?"

"They provide the technology, yeah," said Jeth. "We're due to meet with the team in a few days, we'll talk to them then. See if they know anything."

"Be careful," I warned. "I wanted to go there, but my Ambassador's permit's still in the works. They don't give away information easily."

Jeth's brow creased. "I can promise we haven't seen anything dodgy."

I doubt it. If Klathica *did* know about the Stoneskins, it'd be classified several times over.

"All right. We should probably head back to the office." And find out why someone had sent Kay and me to dismantle a bomb that could easily have killed one of us.

"Let me guess," said Kay, as we climbed down the stairs to the first floor. "You want to go along with the tech team?"

"Jeth and the others have no idea what they might be getting into," I said.

"They'll probably be fine," he said. "It's the people who bought those devices who might be in trouble."

"Shit. Loads of people did," I said. "Like Aric."

"I forgot about him," said Kay. "Maybe we should talk to him first. See if he knows anything. He's clueless enough to overlook vital information even if it's staring him in the face."

"Who's clueless?" Markos called over from his desk as we walked towards the open booths of the main office.

"You." Kay and I both glanced at Ms Weston's office, and the post-it note on the door.

"If the council's gone, who's she even meeting with?" I asked nobody in particular.

"Maybe videoconferencing with the offworld council." Kay took out his communicator. "Question is, was she really the one who sent us to Covent Garden?"

"What have you done this time?"

I explained to Markos, growing more impatient by the minute. I almost wished we'd stayed to help clean up the mess at the market, just to do something useful. Ms Weston might not be acting like herself, but of all people, you'd think she'd have looked into the situation before sending us in.

"Magic," Markos muttered. "Good for nothing but trouble. Klathican implants, you say?"

"They're supposed to be programmed to switch off if you leave Klathica," Kay said. "There are strict laws about bringing *anything* magic-related to Earth, everyone knows that."

"Except the black market." I worried my lower lip. Jeth

and Nell had used to buy things from sellers all the time, when we'd been living under the Alliance's radar.

Kay looked at me. "Black market?"

I shifted my feet, though his gaze wasn't accusing, more curious. "It's usually at Covent Garden, but I didn't see anyone I recognised there. I don't think anyone would bring in magic implants. The markets are run by people who don't want to draw attention to themselves. Especially now. Generally they sell stuff people need for survival here, not fancy gadgets or anything. Not the people we traded with, anyway. But most of them closed up shop, Nell said."

"And the Alliance has shut some of them down," added Kay. "Like the one the unicorn came from. It's not easy to set up a secret market now, not with offworld activity being watched so carefully. As for that source, god knows. Every single piece of technology belonging to the Alliance is tagged. *And* the instructions on how to make them."

"Yeah." I shivered. "I didn't know. I mean, imagine if someone outside found out how to make Chameleons. They have sources in them. I didn't realise there were so many on Earth."

"Sources burn out quickly here," Kay said. "That magic-creature wouldn't have lasted long. They thrive in high-magic atmospheres.

"Yeah," I said. "But they also don't have the mental capacity to give people complicated instructions. Veyak didn't, and he, it, was a living god. More or less. I reckon there must have been an intelligent being behind the attack. Those creatures aren't really self-driving."

"Good point." Kay frowned. "It just seemed to want us to unleash magic energy—which came from that device. Someone must have built it and left it there. I don't know any non-human species who have that kind of knowledge of how to manipulate Alliance technology. Even Cethrax."

"It can't have been *them*, could it?"

Kay looked down at his communicator. "I have no idea. I wouldn't have thought they'd have the patience to put something like that together. Let alone give orders to someone else. Besides, Cethraxians can't get here without the Passages, and all access is monitored. Including the hidden tunnels, now."

The image of the flattened communication device flashed into my head. No matter how many defences the Alliance had, the enemy always seemed to be one step ahead. Whoever was plotting against us hadn't died along with the StoneKing.

It was a relief to escape the confining office at the end of the work day and go to the training complex. I had more than enough frustrated energy to burn. I was starting to get the hang of the gun. I'd developed killer hand-eye coordination thanks to years of knife-throwing lessons, and I could hit a target from any distance.

Every time, I imagined it was the StoneKing.

As I fired the gun a final time, I accidentally sent a bolt of magic along with it and burned a hole right through the centre of the target.

"Oh, crap." I shot a guilty look at Carl. The other guards, behind a wall of protected glass, gaped at me. "Sorry."

"Lucky you've got an excuse." Carl shook his head as I handed the gun back over. "Really, the Alliance ought to offer classes specifically designed for magic-wielders."

"Kay said something like that once." I wiped my sweaty hand on my top. "I think it would help, for sure."

Whatever the others said, I was glad of the extra training. Yes, they were weapons designed to kill. I knew the guilt and horror of taking another life, even by accident or if I'd had no choice. I had a nice montage of nightmares as testimony.

But I needed every defence possible, if war really was

coming to the Alliance. Would I fight? I couldn't yet answer that question. I'd killed in defence of the Multiverse before, but my own magic was unstable enough I didn't feel safe setting foot in a high-magic world—not for myself, but for anyone who might get caught in the crossfire. I saw the suspicion in the other trainees' eyes, the ones who'd heard the rumours. I couldn't help what I was any more than I could help being related to the Royals who'd started the war on Enzar.

But it didn't mean I couldn't control it. I *would* control it.

If only our progress on finding out more about the Stone-skins had gone as smoothly. I'd all but given up looking in the archives now, but with Ms Weston gone, nobody could give me permission to go searching for information on Klathica. No one at Central even knew who'd really sent the message ordering Kay and I to go after the magic-creature at Covent Garden—according to Carl, all the guards had received the same order. Which begged the question: was Ms Weston really the one to send it?

I paused outside the doors to the simulation rooms, where Kay had disappeared after the lesson. Wait a minute. There *was* someone who might know more about what was going on.

I was in luck. In the reception area, I found my friend Amanda, one of the novices' training instructors, stacking papers on the desk.

"Hi, Ada." She gave me a rather forced smile. "Are you doing okay?"

"Yeah. I've been in weapons training. I think Kay's in the simulator." I paused. Ms Weston was her sister. Maybe she knew what was up with the boss and why she'd been so cavalier lately.

"Have you heard what's been happening at Central?" I asked her. "The council are gone. Did you know?"

Amanda tucked a strand of blond hair behind her ear. "Yes. Danica told me the situation required all the council to be present. I can't imagine they'll stay away from Earth for longer than a day, but Central has reliable defences."

"Of course," I said. "It just surprised me. The council's gone and… and they issued a statement saying they don't believe the Stoneskins are a threat."

Amanda was one of the few people I'd told the whole story of my capture to. She wasn't a magic-wielder, but she was a good confidant and she'd helped me a lot in training.

"The Stoneskins? They were the ones who…?"

"Kidnapped me. Yeah. I don't understand why the council wouldn't take it seriously. Whoever created them, it happened right under the Alliance's nose."

"No," said Amanda. "That certainly doesn't sound like a decision the council would make."

"They're on Thairon." I threw caution to the winds. Though for so-called confidential information, it had certainly spread quickly.

Amanda gave a tight nod that, for a moment, made her look like her sister. "Yes. Danica told me. Thairon is a priority."

"Yeah, I get that," I said, "but a doorway to *Enzar* opened. The Stoneskins could have wiped out all the worlds. It felt like part of something bigger, too. They were from Klathica. An Alliance world. I don't understand why the council would just dismiss that."

"The council have their reasons," said Amanda. "Thairon is a particularly precarious zone because thirteen years ago, seven Alliance members were murdered when they attempted to free the population from a slave-like simulation-state their government had put them into. One of the dead was my brother."

I clapped my hands to my mouth. "I'm sorry."

"It's not well-known," said Amanda softly. Tears trembled at the ends of her eyelashes, though her voice hadn't wavered. "Not to new Alliance members. There were no eyewitness accounts, because there were no survivors. It was a terrible tragedy for all involved, and worse for the council because the mission wasn't approved. They went behind the Alliance's back."

I bit my lip, sorry for bringing it up. "They did?"

Amanda nodded. "The council ruled against interfering. Thairon had advanced weaponry, and refused to listen to reason. Nobody could get close enough to save the people trapped in the simulation."

"Your sister said they'd been trapped there for years. That kind of technology… how's it possible to keep it running that long?"

"I wish I knew," said Amanda. "Initially, they intended to recreate the world they lost when their planet was ravaged by natural disasters. More than forty percent of the world was evacuated, and integrated into Klathica's population. But those who remained swiftly fell under a totalitarian government. They were imprisoned on a satellite with no way out—no doorways. Nothing. The only way to free them was for someone to close the simulation from the outside, but when the team arrived, they immediately ran into a trap. My brother…"

"God. I'm so sorry." I never could have guessed. Now it made so much more sense that Ms Weston wanted to keep Central safe. Maybe that was why she'd argued against getting involved in Thairon. She wanted to protect us.

Amanda shook her head. "This just brought it all back to the surface. The guards I train—I know some of them will die. It's the risk of the job. Like everything. We can fight, but as individuals, nothing we do can stand up to a force like that. In any case, Thairon refused any more contact with the

Alliance, and the doorways were closed. No one's been there in years."

I couldn't say anything. Just imagining what it would feel like to lose Jeth or Alber tore me in two. Made me want to run home. I'd never have guessed Ms Weston was hiding something so… tragic.

"I'm sorry, Ada. I didn't mean to offload on you. Danica won't talk about it, and I…"

"It's okay," I said. "I get it. Really. I never tell anyone people's secrets. I won't tell her you told me."

"The way things are going, she might have to tell you herself. She won't risk anything on Thairon. If there's the slightest chance of any of you going near that place, my sister will shoot it down with everything she has."

I had no doubt that was true. The question was, what did it mean for the Alliance's council meeting over there?

"The council are already there," I said. "Do you know if she planned to send a delegate to Klathica? Because they might have information on Thairon—on the Stoneskins."

She wiped her eyes. "I can ask. You're newly qualified as an Ambassador, right?"

I nodded. "Yeah. It's pretty important that I go there. Kay, too."

"I can do that, but not—not Thairon."

"But you do know what their situation's like," I said quietly. "The council—are they safe?" I felt awful for asking, but it seemed as though events conspired to pull us closer to Thairon by the day. I couldn't lie down and let Enzar take the Alliance while the council were gone. Even the thought that Nell would never let me leave the house again did nothing to quell my urge to see what the hell was happening over there. For the first time, I wondered… someone seemed dead set on nobody investigating the Stoneskins. If not Ms Weston or even the rest of the council, who might have sent that message?

"I only know the little information they left behind." Amanda pulled something out of her bag—a photo—and unfolded it. "I shouldn't have kept this, but I can't get rid of it. Even Danica doesn't know…"

She held it up. The photo showed a row of seven people, wearing what looked like Alliance guard gear. At the forefront of the group was a striking woman with sweeping dark hair, maybe thirty or so. The way she stood, slightly forward, made it clear she was the leader of the group.

"This was taken thirteen years ago," said Amanda. "Alliance members don't usually go for photographic records, for obvious reasons, I can't remember why they made an exception—maybe for the press, in case they succeeded. I was only twelve at the time. The seven of them were from different Alliance branches across the Earth— except Caris, he was from Valeria. That's Sam," she added, pointing at a guy on the far right who was clearly the youngest of the group. Like the others, he was smiling.

"He—he'd just joined the Alliance." Amanda dabbed at her eyes. "He was twenty-two. Danica was two years younger, she was an intern at the time. She was here at Central when she found out."

I swallowed. I didn't know what to say.

"They all died only a couple of months after the photograph was taken. If they'd succeeded, they'd have been heroes. Liz already was, really, she did so much already, but they removed all evidence after—after they died."

"Liz?" I echoed.

"Liz was the one who organised the whole thing." She pointed to the raven-haired woman. I could hardly believe, looking at her confident smile, she'd died only a few months later.

"She died, too?"

Amanda nodded. "She planned to be the first one into Thairon, from what my brother told me before he left. The next the Alliance heard—they were dead. But—I couldn't have stopped him going, even though saving everyone was a long shot."

You can't save everyone, Nell always told me. Thairon wasn't their world, but in another life, I could see myself doing the same. The image of my homeworld flashed before my eyes. If there was the slightest chance they could be saved…

Amanda dabbed her eyes. "I'm not about to condemn Sam or the others for what they did. Yes, it was essentially a suicide mission—even Liz knew. She risked everything. She was married, too." She paused and looked at me. "Had a son, left at home."

"That's… awful," I said. "For them, I mean."

"He's just like her."

"Huh? Who?"

In answer, she flipped the photograph over. A list of names was scrawled on the back, underneath the date. Thirteen years ago. The first name on the list was… Elizabeth Walker.

I stared. *No way.*

"Kay's *mother?*" I turned the photo over again. Damn. How had I missed the resemblance? I'd seen when I'd researched the Walker family she'd died in Thairon, too. Thirteen years ago. I just hadn't put the pieces together.

Elizabeth Walker smiled at nothing. Like she was immortal. Holy hell, the resemblance was uncanny. Kay wore the exact same expression whenever he faced down a Cethraxian monster.

"She died on Thairon," I said. "But the Alliance is still in negotiations there right now. Your sister told me."

Amanda nodded. "Several council members from different worlds have been there over the course of the past twenty years, and some remained there after the world was locked in stasis five years ago. One of them was from Earth. They're still there, as far as I know, but it's a mystery what they've been doing all this time."

The ground tilted under my feet. Somehow, I knew the answer before she spoke the words.

"Who was the person from Earth?" I asked, sealing the inevitable.

"Lawrence Walker."

6

KAY

I slid the visor over my eyes and prepared to fight for my life. Again.

A cliff's edge, shrouded in mist, the faintest outline of another cliff on the other side. Standard backdrop. If you fell over the ledge, you were dead—at least, until the simulator restarted itself. Nothing like living dangerously.

So that's how you want to play, universe. I moved right up to the cliff's edge, feet treading a path I'd walked too many times to count. I waited until my feet were right up against the end, over the abyss, then hit the 'ambush' button. Quickly, I spun around to intercept the attacker with a strike to the throat. He crumpled and fell, and I caught myself at the cliff's ledge, heart beating fast, adrenaline flooding me at the near-miss.

I hit the reset button and the cliff disappeared. *Okay. Maybe I don't have a death wish.* But I had to be sure.

I'd lost track of time. The real world looked distorted, the walls of the room shifting like they were closing in on me. I removed the sleek, future-tech helmet and threw it down.

The floor was padded to prevent injury, so it bounced, undamaged.

Get it together, Kay.

I found Ada in the reception area after I left the locker room. The guilt on her face was readable even before she opened her mouth.

"Why didn't you tell me you knew about Thairon before I did?"

And just like that, I felt for all the world like I was still standing on that cliff, waiting for someone to shove me into the abyss.

"I didn't realise they were linked to the Stoneskins," I told her as we walked out of the double glass doors to the car park.

I looked sideways at her. She didn't meet my eyes. "Kay… was your father involved with them?"

A pause, like we stood on the edge of a blade, poised to fall. *This is it.* I'd been lucky to have a precious few weeks with her. Now my father was going to return to Earth—if he hadn't already—and everything I'd worked for the past five years was set to unravel.

Anger rose, hot and unexpected. *Is that how it's going to be? You're going to give up before he even gets here?* Five years was a long time. I didn't live in the Walker house any longer, I was a goddamned adult with a life I didn't care to lose. And Ada had killed the StoneKing, for god's sake.

But if she got near Lawrence Walker, she'd lose her trust in me. No question. She might well lose all faith in the Alliance—I would, if I were in her position. If I didn't know the truth.

"I don't know what my father was doing on Thairon. There hasn't been a word from the place since he left five years ago. It's closed off."

"In simulation," said Ada, with a glance back at the training complex. "How can a world function like that?"

"It can't." An uncomfortable measure of relief rose as the conversation moved away from dangerous ground. "They killed all the dissidents who dared to challenge the system, got the remainder of the population hooked on drugs, and locked them up. It's been that way for thirteen years."

Thirteen years ago. The same time I'd been experimented on, turned into a magic-wielder.

The same year my mother's team had gone there, and been killed.

Thairon. It really was Thairon. It was the Multiverse's idea of a joke, for sure, that Thairon would land at the centre of everything again. The Stoneskins had the Walker name written all over them. But I didn't know for certain my father had been the one to come up with the project. Even though it sounded remarkably close to the experiments he'd pulled on Earth.

"Thirteen years." My heart dropped at her tone. She knew. Somehow…

"Yeah," I said. "There was an attack on Alliance members there, when they went to try and shut down the simulators."

"I know," she said quickly, interrupting me. "Amanda told me."

I blinked, momentarily stunned. *Idiot.* Amanda was Ms Weston's sister. Of course.

"Her brother was involved," said Ada. "I—I understand if you don't want to talk about it, but…"

"It's fine," I said, ignoring the sinking feeling in my chest. *You have to tell her.* It was all tangled together with what was happening now—Thairon, the experiments, the Stoneskins. All was tied to the Walker family. "I guessed Ms Weston knew something." I didn't add, *when she was telling me not to go after you.* Ada didn't need to know the boss had opposed me trying to save her. She hadn't wanted me to sacrifice my life for a lost cause, like she thought my mother had. "That was the last time anyone tried to liberate Thairon, but did the StoneKing say *when* they were created? It must have been more than five years ago for them to have access to the Passages. Maybe longer. The doors were more or less closed thirteen years ago."

"No," said Ada. "I have no idea how long they were around. They might have been looking for a long time. Their methods for navigating weren't exactly reliable."

True. They'd used the StoneKing's built-in tracker to follow the nearest magic signal, wherever it happened to be, while using pieces of auros—the substance world-keys were made from—to open doors to whichever world the signal came from. They'd caught Ada completely by accident through following her magic signal, because we weren't supposed to be in that part of the Passages in the first place.

"Yeah…" *For god's sake. Just say it already.* "I'd tell you if I knew the truth. You know that, right?"

She looked at me, her eyes concerned. "Yeah, I do, Kay."

Her words didn't make the guilt go away. "For all I know, my father did take the experiments offworld. I wouldn't have known."

"You were a kid," she said. "Of course you wouldn't. It wouldn't change anything."

They all say that, whispered a voice. *Always. Then they get a hint of the truth and they shrink away. You see it in their eyes. They're scared of you like they're scared of him. You saw it from Ada already.*

Shut the hell up, I told the voice. I wouldn't be at my father's mercy again, especially when he wasn't even bloody here.

"Okay," I said, softly. "You should go and see your family. I have some things I want to deal with tonight."

Most of which involved messaging members of various councils. I might even take a trip into offworld district, though that was a precarious risk at the best of times, especially after today. But I needed to look at those implants again.

Damn it all to hell. Quickest way to get answers was to visit my mortal enemy, Aric.

Someone up there really was laughing his arse off at me. After saying goodbye to Ada, I about-turned and headed for Central, and the holding cells—or, the rooms where Ada had been imprisoned back when the Alliance had arrested her.

I went to the guard office first, half-expecting to find it deserted. Instead, Carl appeared behind the door to the small room.

"Hey," I said. "I never asked—did you find out who sent the message calling us to Covent Garden?"

"Ada asked me the same question," he said. "No. It was sent in Ms Weston's name."

"It doesn't seem like her to send us into a situation with a live magic-based bomb without at least forewarning us."

"I got the impression the caller's information was vague," said Carl. "We need more people keeping an eye on potential problem areas. They're bringing guards in from some of the other Alliance branches soon. Central doesn't have nearly enough backup if another incident happens, and London has one of the highest offworlder populations on Earth."

"Yeah, I'm surprised they haven't done it already. It's basic common sense."

"It took a message warning of a potential threat to Earth via Central to convince them." Carl's eyes narrowed in suspicion. "Someone messaged all the head Alliances at once."

"Someone had to do it," I said evenly. "If the council and Ms Weston aren't around."

"Kay, sometimes paranoia is justified. Sometimes not. If the council have made their statement, then that stands."

"That may be," I said. "But they're not on Earth."

And *that* didn't add up, either. It just seemed downright irresponsible to leave Central unattended after the Stone-skins' attack, whatever the crisis on Thairon.

"Is Aric in the holding cells here?" I asked.

"Who told you that?"

"Markos did. What's he held for, conspiring against the Alliance? The magic-based implant isn't illegal."

"It is on Earth," said Carl. "Klathican, is it? He wouldn't tell me."

"Yes," I said, "just like the people who attacked us today. I want to talk to him."

I'd expected him to argue, but he nodded. "Maybe you'll have more luck than me. He doesn't respond to reasonable arguments." He handed me a key.

"I'll keep that in mind." I took the key and turned it over in my hand. "It's not a magic-proofed room?"

"Doesn't need to be. He has only first level shots left in him. Burned himself out, I'd guess. If anything happens, I'll transfer him somewhere more secure."

"Okay," I said. "I can promise he won't be getting out on *my* watch." I had to emphasise that. Ada had escaped the cells twice when I was supposed to be responsible for her. So much had changed since then.

Aric's cell was the only locked room in the corridor. I turned the key and shouldered open the door slowly in case he was behind it, ready to make an escape.

Instead, he leaned against the back wall, and glared at me when I came in. He wasn't cuffed, and still wore guard uniform, now more than a little worse for wear.

"What do you want, Walker?"

Any brief thoughts of diplomacy went clean out the window.

"Don't," I said, closing the door with a *snap*, "call me that."

"What hit you, Walker? Your girlfriend get herself kidnapped again?"

Fury rose like a tidal wave. Even beating the shit out of countless monsters hadn't been enough. My fists itched to punch a real target. But it wouldn't get me answers.

"Leave Ada out of this," I said, through clenched teeth. "Did you sense any change in the magic level today?"

"No fucking clue."

"Glad we're keeping things polite and friendly."

"I've been locked away, haven't I?"

"My heart bleeds for you. There was a rise in the magic level earlier. Bunch of people with implants under the control of a magic-creature. You wouldn't happen to know anything about that, would you?"

"I've been locked in here," snarled Aric. "No idea what you're talking about. Magic-creature?"

He didn't know. At least it ruled out one possibility.

"Okay," I said. "Just checking. We caught some people trying to plant a bomb. They'd been brainwashed by a magic-creature—a kimaros. You heard of those? Your father set one loose on Aglaia."

"I didn't know what my father was going to do, did I?" Aric's jaw clenched. "Sounds like you don't know what yours is doing, either."

I froze. "What do you know?"

"The guards were muttering about Walker being back. Figured they weren't talking about you, seeing as everyone worships the ground you tread on. They *hate* your dad, though."

Hell. "He was here?"

"I'm not a fucking psychic, Walker, I can't walk through walls."

I was torn between rolling my eyes and leaving him to his own stupidity, or just clocking him in the face. At least, unlike with the Klathican Embassy's mechas, I was less likely to end up decapitated. "Yeah, I was asking if you'd overheard anything. Apparently, you're too stupid to make that logical leap."

"Piss off, Walker," he muttered.

"What, so you can carry on staring at the wall? Do you not *want* to get out of here?"

He half-shrugged. "Not too fussed. My family's all dead, aren't they?" His eyes narrowed to slits. Guess he probably didn't know the centaurs had killed them, though I'd been on the brink of stabbing his sister when they did.

"Thought you hated the Alliance."

"It's them or no one. Guess the fucking Stoneskins are dead, too."

"You saw the fight in Valeria's capital."

"I'd have killed them if they hadn't been invincible," he snapped. "I don't know what you and the Valeria guards drugged yourselves with."

"Temporary magic boost," I said dismissively. "It worked. We knocked them into the abyss. That's not the point. Did they happen to say where they came from?"

"You've a nerve calling me stupid when you come out with crap like that," said Aric. "I haven't a goddamn clue."

"Right," I said. "Whereabouts did you get the Klathican implant, anyway?"

"Valeria," he muttered. "Offworld market."

Didn't expect that. Though it made sense, given his family had so many connections there. I made a mental note to ask around. The two worlds were linked, had been ever since they'd formed the Alliance years ago. I needed to check the files for more information, but I'd definitely look into those implanted magic sources.

As for the kimaros…

"Your family weren't involved with KimaroTech labs, were they?" I asked.

Aric pushed himself away from the wall. "My dad may have bought something from them. Why does it matter?"

"Because they might be linked to the Stoneskins," I said. "The people who created those bastards."

Aric exhaled. "So this is a revenge thing for you. You want to get them back for kidnapping Ada."

"I want to eradicate all threats to the Alliance," I said coldly. "Including you, if it turns out you're plotting something." But I didn't think he was. Whatever his reasons for remaining in captivity, he was clearly at a loose end. Maybe he'd expected the Stoneskins to kill him. A cage was apparently the better choice.

For a half-second, the walls appeared to be closing in again. I blinked, willing the image to go away.

"I'm planning nothing, Walker. You should be worried about what the guards are saying. About your father."

Not again. "I don't give a shit. If you have nothing useful to tell me about KimaroTech, the magic implant, or the Stoneskins, I'm leaving."

"Huh," said Aric. One step towards me. Then another. "I think you're hiding from your father."

I gave him my best mock-perplexed stare. Maybe I hadn't been as convincing as I hoped. "You pulled that one out of your arse, Aric. I'd talk to him, if he were here. But he's not, so…"

A roaring kicked up in my ears. *Get out,* said my rational side. *He's fucking with you, and you're letting him.*

I stepped back towards the door. "It's been delightful talking to you."

Somehow, I got out the room and slammed the door on his insults. I took the key in a shaking hand and had it in the lock when the door trembled, almost coming off its hinges. Aric had thrown himself against it. I shoved back with my shoulder and turned the key, then stepped back, panting hard.

You're losing the plot, Kay.

My hand was bleeding where the key had dug into my palm. I wiped both on my jacket and walked away, back to the guard office.

"I'd watch him." I handed the key over to Carl. "Bastard tried to get the jump on me, but I locked him in."

"Good," said Carl. "I admit I expected something like that. He didn't fight the other guards. I trusted you to handle it."

I'd thought the Stoneskin fiasco had blown his trust in my responsibility. "Cheers," I said. "He doesn't know anything, but I thought I'd check. Said his family has links to Valeria, Klathica… and Thairon."

"Right." Carl nodded. "I can't pretend I know too much about the council's situation, but they certainly seem to be taking it seriously. As for Klathica, I never liked the lax rules of those magic-implants. It feels safer to have a lower level, even though I know an offworlder would kill me in half a second."

I'd forgotten he was a genuine Earth-born magic-wielder. I'd got used to everyone having freakish abilities and enhancements.

After Valeria, he knew I was no normal Earth magic-wielder. So did everyone else—or everyone the rumours had reached, anyway. I didn't care to ask if he knew about the experiments.

"Are the council definitely not on Earth now?"

"I believe they planned to return tomorrow," he said. "They know what they're doing."

Yeah. Abandoning Central when Earth needs half-decent leadership.

"And Ms Weston? I've needed to talk to her all day."

"Good luck," said Carl. "I haven't been able to get hold of her either. The last thing she told me to do was ensure that every file with information on the recent missions is kept under lock and key. Anyone would think there's an enemy inside the building."

There might be. Soon. Those files confirmed Ada's heritage and powers, and my own abilities as well. Sure, most people knew, but I *really* didn't want my father to get his hands on the information. Did Ms Weston know?

"Keep everything hidden," I said. "We have enough enemies without anyone else finding out what Ada can do."

I only hoped I could get through to the council before anyone else got hurt. Because if this whole fiasco made one thing clear, when magic was involved, there *was* no middle ground. You lost everything, or you survived by the skin of your teeth.

I'd lost everything once already. This time I'd survive.

7

ADA

"Well, well," said Alber, as I unlocked the front door and let myself into the house. "She returns."

"Ha ha," I said. "Where's Nell?"

"Here." Nell put her head around the kitchen door. "So you decided to show your face here?"

"Yeah, I was gonna steal all your DVDs if you were gone another day," said Alber. "But I figured you'd need to come pick up spare clothes at some point."

"And see you guys," I said. "Sorry, I've been kind of neglecting you since I got back."

Alber shrugged. "You and Kay are serious. I kinda expected it. Besides, Jeth's living in the labs now."

"I thought he'd be here."

"No, he said he was working late," said Nell. "I'd say they're overworking him, but he probably volunteered for it himself."

"Yeah." And Kay was back there, too. Unless he was home by now. I sent a quick message to check. I had enough to occupy my mind tonight. What Amanda had told me. Her brother, Kay's mother, and Thairon. Not to mention

Lawrence Walker. So that was what had been bothering Kay. He never talked about his father—according to Simon, who'd known Kay since he'd joined the Academy five years ago, he'd never even mentioned him by name, even though everyone knew who he was. I'd researched the Walker family once, but there had been a lack of information unsurprising for an Alliance council member. The obvious option would be to ask Kay himself, but he didn't know what his father had been doing the past five years. Now the council had gone to join him on Thairon, leaving Central up in the air.

"Hey, Ada," Alber called upstairs, to my room. "Jeth's here."

I climbed down the ladder to the landing, where Jeth waved at me from outside his room.

"You're back," he said in tones of surprise. "There I was thinking we'd have to adopt a new sister."

I rolled my eyes. "I've been here more often than you have, with the time you spend in the labs."

"She's got you there." Alber grinned from the doorway of his room.

"Have you told Nell?"

"Told me what?" Nell appeared in the hallway.

Oh, crap. "Er…" I explained how Kay and I had taken down the kimaros at Covent Garden. Nell listened without much change of expression, and I couldn't figure out if she was going to jump into lecture mode or not. I really didn't want to make Nell mad, especially not now.

"So I was wondering," I finished. "Might they have got the Klathican enhancements from the black market? I didn't see anyone I knew there at Covent Garden."

I looked at Jeth. He'd been the one to scour the markets for pieces of offworld tech.

"I suppose," he said slowly. "Wouldn't hurt to look into it."

"I can go," I said. "My boss is hardly around at the moment, so I can probably do it tomorrow."

"Not alone," said Nell.

"I'll ask Kay. We're more than capable of taking care of ourselves. This is Earth."

"And magic's unstable," said Nell. "I'm no magic-wielder, but even I can tell."

"Yeah… seems to be a permanent thing now." I pulled out my communicator.

Jeth cleared his throat. "Did the gloves help?"

"When I fought the magic-creature today… yeah, they did," I said. "The gloves kind of blocked the magic. I could still use a stunner, but it wasn't out of control like it normally is."

Nell's eyes flashed. "That doesn't mean it'll ever be safe for you to risk going to a high-magic world, Ada."

My heart dropped. She kind of scared me a little when she used that tone. "I know. Just saying."

I typed a message to Kay, Nell still watching me.

"Be careful with him," she said.

"We're not going to have that argument again, are we? You and Jeth both know he's on my side. He risked everything to save me from the Stoneskins."

"That's part of the problem," said Nell. "He was willing to lay down his life for you, yes, but he's a magic-wielder. Not a natural-born one, either."

"That doesn't mean anything." My heart sank, all the same. He was the first, and only magic-wielder injected with lustre, but magic didn't define us. And like hell would I let it divide us.

I was tired enough for an early night, but the look on Kay's face when I'd woken him yesterday morning flashed before my eyes as I tossed and turned, even more insistent than my usual nightmares. I wished I was by his side right now, not just because I missed him, but because I was afraid for him. Afraid the tide rushing towards us would sweep us both away.

～

"You sure you want to go to offworld district?" said Jeth as we crossed the car park to Central the following morning. The day had dawned cold, wet and miserable, and with no message from Central or Kay, I'd opted to wear guard uniform. It made me feel safer.

"I haven't heard from my boss," I said. "I might even go check the council's office, because the message yesterday was just *weird*. But if I can get permission from Ms Weston, I'm heading to the market."

"If you're sure, sis. Be careful, and let me know if anything comes up, okay?"

"Sure." We parted on the stairs, him heading for the second floor. I took a couple of deep breaths. Maybe I *should* go straight to the council and figure out once and for all what they were doing, and why they'd decided to deprioritise the Stoneskins. Better than hanging about in admin all day. Kay hadn't responded to the three messages I'd sent, so I'd look for him first, then...

It took a minute to realise I wasn't alone on the stairs. I was jarred back to reality when the end of a stick struck me across the leg, and I spun around in shock. An old guy was behind me, and he'd freaking *hit* me with the end of the cane he leaned on.

"What the hell?" The words slipped out before I could stop them, because I was so stunned. He was lucky I hadn't put him in one of Nell's chokeholds.

"Get out of the way," said the man. "I've no patience with

you snivelling novices. This place really has gone to the dogs."

What?

"You're one to talk," I shot at him, rubbing my leg. "Might want to try some manners?"

Jesus. He wasn't that old, really, though grey streaked his black hair. His angular face had the wasted, sunken look I associated with drug addicts, but his hand on the cane was steady. Dark eyes squinted at my name badge. "Ada Fletcher? *You* can't be the person they're all talking about."

I stared at him. "That's lovely. Who are you?"

He looked up from his communicator screen, one eyebrow slightly raised. "Clearly, the novices are kept ignorant these days. You don't know who I am?"

I took a step back, then another, as a horrifying familiarity struck me like a blow.

"No," I said, half to myself. "You can't be—"

This man… was Kay's father. Lawrence Walker.

"I'd thank you," said Walker, "to show me some respect."

Oh my god. So he was back from simulation. Was that why he walked so unsteadily? I supposed being in a coma for five years would have some pretty major side effects.

I glared to cover up the fear seeping through me. "Only if you do the same to me. That's not how you're supposed to speak to your employees."

"I don't show respect to abominations."

I stood rooted to the spot as he passed me by, before my thoughts clicked back into place. I all but flew to the first floor, spun around the corner to Ms Weston's office, and ran smack into Kay.

"Ada," he said, eyes wide. "You—are you okay?"

I nodded. My throat had gone dry. He didn't know. Did he?

"What happened?"

"Why didn't you answer your phone?" My voice trembled.

"Huh? Sorry. I was making a few calls, I didn't know." Kay glanced towards the office, then back at me.

"To who?" My mind was in freefall. At a distance, I'd never have said he and Walker were related. Maybe because Walker had an aura of absolute entitlement, like he'd expected me to lie down at his feet and worship him. Even when Kay was giving orders to people or facing down an enemy, his manner wasn't like Walker's at all.

Now, he wrapped an arm around me. "I'm sorry, Ada. What happened?"

"I—" *Just say it, Ada.* "I ran into your father."

For an instant, Kay's eyes showed the blank, unguarded horror I'd seen when I'd woken him in the night. Then he blinked and it disappeared. "About bloody time he showed his face," he muttered. "He didn't hurt you, did he?"

"He whacked me with his walking stick and called me an abomination," I said. "But—never mind."

"Bastard," said Kay. "He never needed a walking stick. I'll bet he's just trying to garner sympathy. He likes playing the victim."

I shook my head. "Do you think he was the one who sent out that message? Putting us off investigating the Stone-skins?" Now it made sense. Horribly so. If *he* was the one giving the orders, if he thought I was an abomination… no wonder the council had deprioritised investigating the creatures which had kidnapped me.

"Without a doubt," said Kay. "He must have just got back. I already checked upstairs. So the rest of the council must be here." He pulled away from me. "I have to talk to them."

"Me, too," I said.

He shook his head tightly. "He's making a move against us. He wants to reassert his power over the council."

"Doesn't mean I can't come," I countered.

"Ada… I don't know if he knows about your magic, but he'll want to get his hands on you if he found out where it came from."

"I—what?" I stared. "You do realise the whole freaking *Multiverse* knows?"

"No, they don't." He ran a hand through his hair. "They can only guess based on a handful of eyewitness stories, and half of them are wildly inaccurate. I've already hidden our accounts of what happened. I asked Markos to. There's nothing but our word, and we're *not* letting him find out."

"You're kidding," I said. "I'm Enzarian. It's obvious to anyone, with or without the contact lenses."

"He knows you're Enzarian. He doesn't know you're—"

The last of the Royals. "I get it, but isn't my name in all of your records?"

"Ms Weston has them."

"Oh." Could she have known? But why let me walk in here if she knew Lawrence Walker was going to show up? "He did call me an abomination…"

"That's his view on all magic-wielders," said Kay. "Ada, I know you can defend yourself, but one word from him can turn the entire Alliance against you. What if he decided you were single-handedly responsible for all the trouble? I can't stop him hurting you."

"I work here. The message was a threat against Central. If he wants to get us all blown to pieces, then that's his call, but I won't aside. Not if there's anything I can do to stop him."

"I never said we didn't have a chance." His tone suggested otherwise. "But you don't want to draw his attention any more than you have to. If you wait for him to call you to him, he'll think he has the advantage. Do whatever you can before he pegs you as a threat."

"What about you?"

"I'll talk to him," said Kay. "But Ada—you know people at

the shelters. From Enzar. There's a chance he might try to pin the blame on them. What you did—helping them behind Central's back—it goes against everything he stands for. He'll be furious when he learns I convinced Central to hire you even though you broke their laws."

"You're kidding me." *How* could the man be a council member?

"Sorry," he said. "I can't predict what Walker will do. His orders override everyone else's on Earth. He could knock Central to the ground if he thought the threat was inside the building."

My mouth hung open. I trusted Kay's word, but the notion that Walker wanted to bring down the Alliance was too much to take in right now. "All right. I was going to offworld territory to ask if anyone knows about those implants."

"Good call," said Kay. "I'm really sorry about this, Ada. I should have told you upfront."

"It's not your fault." I ignored the slither of doubt creeping down my spine. "If you're sure—we can talk later. I'll call you."

"I have a better way." He handed me a Chameleon and the earpiece to go with it.

"Sciras." I turned the device over in my hand and clipped on the earpiece with the other. "Are you sure you want to do this now? He doesn't know you're here."

"He will," Kay said. "He won't expect me to walk in there."

"Why's he even allowed onto the council, if he thinks magic-wielders are an abomination?"

"Because of his 'specialist knowledge' of offworld. He might have been kicked out of leadership by now if he'd actually stuck around. I'd wager the council doesn't know what to do with him. They didn't expect him to reappear out of nowhere after being off-grid for so long. He never showed up to meetings even when he was here."

"Charming," I muttered.

"Oh, he can be when he wants to," Kay said darkly. "Not as much as *his* father… but he was always so convinced his leadership was certain that he could treat everyone like shit when he worked here. I doubt being in stasis has helped."

"And—Thairon?"

"I'll get as much information out of him as I can, but I can't promise he'll speak up. He'll be thrilled to see me, I'm sure."

His tone was flat, but my heartbeat kicked up. I was leaving Kay alone with someone who'd turned him into a magic-wielder even though he hated magic. "Are you certain about this?"

"If he tries anything…" Kay revealed his own Chameleon device, complete with sciras enhancement. "I'd leave, before he realises where you're going. I wouldn't let him find out about the market, either."

I swallowed my anger at Walker and tapped the earpiece, feigning confidence. "I'll talk to you in a bit."

8

KAY

"*Allow me to lay it out in plain English,*" *said Lawrence Walker. "Tomorrow, you are going to come with me to Thairon and do something useful for once in your life—or you're going to die."*

A pause. I said nothing, letting him think the effect was sinking in.

Then I smiled. "I won't be coming with you."

For an instant, Walker looked almost surprised. "You would rather die?"

"You just answered your own question, Walker." Oh, my heart beat far too fast, my pulse raced as though knowing its hours were numbered, and I didn't care, because he knew, beyond all shadow of a doubt, I meant every word.

I kept on smiling. He kept on staring. Shook his head. "After all this, you want to die?"

"Go right ahead. Do your worst."

A dark flush spread across his face and elation made me grin wider. I was winning. Sixteen years and finally, I was beating him at his own game.

"Where did I go wrong with you?" Walker said, quietly.

"Are you asking me to make a list? Because we might be here a while, and I thought you had an urgent appointment tomorrow."

He moved from behind the desk and his hand shot out. But I'd dodged long before the blow would have hit. He didn't even make an effort, because he still saw me as a helpless child. Not an adult. Not an equal.

He had no idea what I was capable of.

I blocked his next strike and hit back, adrenaline singing through my veins as my fist caught him in the jaw. I'd spent years fighting back against opponents far more powerful than I was. Nothing scared me anymore.

I'd caught him off guard. He rarely hit me—usually he left the job to his bastard servants—so the satisfaction of landing a hit on him made my blood ignite.

Pain exploded up my jaw as his fist slammed into the side of my face, and the back of my head met the door with a crack that sent stars sparking before my eyes. He shoved me sideways and stepped over me, out the door. I gasped for breath, the pain finally setting in.

He'd gone.

I laughed, then coughed, uncontrollably, my whole body shaking. Pushing myself to my feet with one hand, I checked the damage. I'd have a wicked collection of bruises and my head rang with one blow he'd landed, but nothing was broken. He'd left me in one piece.

I'd pay later.

The truth hit me like a thunderbolt, the breath catching in my lungs, the room suddenly too small, too tight. I always paid, even when I thought I had nothing left to lose.

I breathed in and out, my fists clenching, scanning his office in an attempt to find something to distract me. He never let me in here alone, but a piece of paper lay on the desk, folded up. A map.

I picked it up, unfolded it. This was no Earth map. It showed the Passages... all the Passages. Part of it had been ripped away, but *all the worlds in the Multiverse, even the non-Alliance ones, were marked on the map.*

My eyes traced the corridors, the doors to offworld.

The vice clamped around my chest loosened, my heart lifting for the first time in what felt like years. This paper in my hand was worth more than my life. It was worth risking my life and running.

I would run. And I'd live.

I couldn't suppress the thought that I walked to my own execution as I climbed the stairs to the upper floor. Even the knowledge that I was more than a match for him now didn't stop the memories beating at the door. I might not be a kid any longer, but Walker could unleash the full extent of his power against me. Who would take my word over his? If he'd shot down the investigation into the Stoneskins, he could discredit anything I'd ever said and paint me as an unstable traitor.

The council's meeting room was unoccupied. But the room next door had two guards stationed outside. They wore uniforms in the style of Valeria's enforcement officers —shell-like suits with built-in adamantine protection. Even through the distorted glass on the door, I saw the outline of his reflection as he watched me.

"I'm Kay Walker," I said, my voice carrying in the deserted corridor. "I'm here to talk to my father."

They parted without speaking a word. Creepy as fuck. His style.

I opened the door to the familiar oil-like scent of Klathican drugs. Fear clawed into me, rooted me to the spot. I didn't let any of it show on my face.

"You," he said.

"Nice to see you, too," I said. "I heard you attacked my girlfriend."

There was no point in hiding anything. He'd know, no matter what. All I could do was pretend it made no difference.

"That Ada girl?"

"What happened on Thairon that's urgent enough to remove the council from their office? I don't know if you're aware, but there's a high chance Earth will be drawn into warfare in the near future."

"I don't know what you're talking about."

"I think you do." It gave me no small measure of satisfaction to regard him with the same look of disdain he used on everyone else.

"I'll be honest with you, Kay, I've just awoken from five years of stasis. I'm extremely tired and not inclined to talk politics with you."

"Pity."

"Don't try and be smart with me, kid. I noticed a substantial amount of credit was recently removed from the Walker accounts. You wouldn't happen to know anything about it, would you?"

"That? I bought a limited-edition chameleon car from Valeria."

For the first time, he really looked at me, one eyebrow raised. "A *car*? You spent my hard-earned cash on a *car*?"

I let the corner of my mouth lift. "Hard-earned?"

"You insolent little shit," said Walker. "I never should have trusted you alone."

"Trusted me?" I smirked at him. "Is that what you told yourself, rather than admitting I got the best of you? Did you tell yourself it was just like every time you left me shut in your worthless house while you went offworld?"

"Worthless? Is that why you burned it down? Don't think I didn't hear about it."

"I'm glad you kept on top of things," I said. "Someone has to act in the interests of the Multiverse."

"You've been busy," said Walker. "Over thirty requests sent to the council? For an underling, it's a record. How long have you been employed here?"

"Two months, since I graduated from the Academy."

"The Academy." His eyes darkened. "Should have known Elizabeth would go behind my back."

"It must be so horrible for you." I rolled my eyes. "To be betrayed like that."

"Don't try me," said Walker. "The Academy. It explains where you got your arrogance."

My communicator buzzed faintly. Casually, keeping my expression blank, I took my communicator and flicked the touch screen. A message from Ms Weston—she wanted to see me. About damn time.

"What is it?" Walker asked, eying my communicator with an irritated expression. "What are you planning?"

"Absolutely nothing." He'd never allowed me to have my own phone at home because of his paranoid streak about outsiders finding out where we lived. He'd shut the house up for weeks at a time because he was convinced offworld assassins were coming after him.

"I have an appointment with my supervisor," I said, "and as touching as this reunion is, I think my time's best served in the interests of the Multiverse. If you have nothing to tell me about what you've been doing the past five years, I'm sure the rest of the council will be more than willing to update me."

A muscle twitched in his jaw, and I held back a smile.

"Yes," he said slowly. "You certainly *have* been busy. I hear

Central was attacked in August, and you were in the middle of it."

"Your point being?"

Dammit. I hoped the rest of the council hadn't had chance to tell him the full story about Ada. It was a long shot that they wouldn't tell him at all, because they'd never met the bastard. They'd all been elected three years ago, after he'd left Earth. They'd have been scrambling to update him the minute he'd set foot in here.

But where are they?

"I confess myself surprised." He gave me a sweeping look. "It may be that the other council members exaggerated your achievements. You, defending Central against terrorists? Taking down the Conner family? Interfering in a war on Aglaia? And these ridiculous stories about a living god and creatures made of adamantine. Almost as absurd as the idea of Kay Walker as the magic-wielder defender of Central." His expression changed, from mocking to icy-cold, calculating. "Magic-wielder. Now that rumour has some truth to it, doesn't it?"

Shit. He knows.

"Oh, that?" I feigned innocence. "I forgot to thank you. It's saved my life half a dozen times, and helped save the Multiverse, too."

My father looked incredulous. "What?"

"Don't thank me. It's almost got me killed a few times as well, but seeing as it's the only present you ever gave me, I suppose it could be worse."

"You're here to beg for what I deprived you of as a child?"

I laughed this time. "You don't know the first thing about deprivation, Walker."

"You dare to mock me?"

"Don't pull that one on me," I said. "I think it's about time you were straight with me." I paused, long enough to give him a reflection of his own expression. "Were you involved with the project which made the Stoneskins?"

A moment passed.

"What do you know?"

"I'm here to ask you questions, Walker. Not the other way around."

"Is that so?" Walker stood. "You might think yourself at the centre of the Multiverse because of a few heroics, but you're just like Elizabeth. I've no doubt you'll meet the same fate—small pity I almost believed the rumours about your death were true."

"That's still going around?" I shook my head. "Anything else? Other than a deep regret for my continued existence? Or are you going to be straight with me about your involvement with the creators of the Stoneskins?"

"Stoneskins?"

My right hand clenched. "You hated magic. Why would you be involved with magic enhancements?"

He said nothing for a full minute. I couldn't tell if he was thinking or just trying to unsettle me, like usual.

"You are out of your mind." Walker shook his head. "How disappointing. I almost thought you'd become something worthwhile."

"Yeah? That's high praise coming from you. If you don't give me answers I'll find them another way. Your choice, Walker."

"So that's how it is?" he said.

"Yes." I didn't look away. He was the one who'd taught me to hold eye contact even as I wished I was anywhere but here, looking at anyone but him. The one person I'd hoped against hope I'd never see again.

"Yes," said Lawrence Walker. "I don't know anything about these wild accusations, but I'm sure the rest of the council will put you straight. Given your record, I highly doubt it'll work out in your favour." Walker's eyes bored into mine. "I really don't want to hurt you, Kay. I suggest you keep out of what doesn't concern you. It would be a pity if Central's hero were to meet with an accident, wouldn't it? And the girl, too."

The blood froze in my veins. He'd never threatened me directly before. He hadn't needed to.

Meet with an accident.

Just like Elizabeth.

It was all I could do to keep my face blank as I met the depthless eyes that had followed me around all my life, even the past five years.

"Yes, it'd be a shame if any of us were to meet with an accident, Walker." I let the tiniest spark of magic dance across my palm as I opened the door.

He said nothing. Just watched me. I'd met his challenge. The game was on.

9

ADA

Nell's warning about not wandering off alone rang through my head, but after half an hour had passed and Kay still hadn't come back, I couldn't deal with being stuck in the office any longer. So I took the train to Covent Garden again. The mess from the magic-creature's attack had somewhat been cleared up, though a large portion of the market had been cordoned off where the magic-wielders had dug the hole in the floor. The broken glass had gone and the main entrance was open. I hesitantly walked inside, not sure if the people who staffed the so-called 'black market' would risk showing up after yesterday. I was certain nobody *I* knew had been responsible for the kimaros or the magical device.

A winged man walked past, followed by a girl with scaled hands. Offworlders. Inside the market, I peered around and saw the 'black market' area had moved to another alcove. But the usual staff were there. Including Cynthia Knight. Skyla's former adoptive sister. Our eyes locked, and her stare froze me in my steps. We hadn't spoken since Skyla's betrayal, but the way she glared at me made her thoughts clear.

Another Enzarian girl stood at her side, while Hiera, the

Zanthan woman who usually staffed the place, talked to a pair of avian men handing cash over for something. I'd been here a few times but back when I'd been Nell's assistant, my specialty had been the Passages. It wasn't uncommon for me to go months without visiting… but one look at Cynthia's expression told me she wouldn't accept that excuse. As for the Enzarian girl at her side, I recognised her as one of a group of half magebloods from a village which had been lucky enough to escape mass slaughter by the Royals. It had been four, five years since then.

Even in my guard uniform, there was no way they wouldn't recognise someone from their homeworld. Almost everyone from Enzar had the same tan skin and delicate features. They also had lilac eyes, but covered by contact lenses like mine. The other girl frowned at me, tilting her head as I steeled myself and walked up to them.

"Hi," I said, conscious of their stares. "I'm Ada. I worked at the shelter."

"You helped us in the Passages," said the girl, while Cynthia looked at me stonily.

"I work at Central now. I wanted to know if you'd seen anything out of place around here. I don't know if you heard about the attack."

"Yeah, thanks to you." Cynthia's eyes were pure venom. "First you get my sister killed, then you try to destroy London. Now you're strutting around in your fancy uniform like you own the Earth."

What? I stared, lost for words. I should have spoken to her about Skyla, but Nell had told me Cynthia didn't *want* to talk to me about it. We'd never been close. She'd disapproved of Skyla's habit of taking risks.

"You're mageblood, right?" asked the other girl.

I nodded, though the lie tore me up inside. Not even the

Enzarians on Earth knew I was Royal, and normally nonmages didn't have any magic at all.

"I'm sorry for what happened to your sister," I said to Cynthia. It wasn't enough, not even close, but I hadn't expected to see her today. I'd been to hell and back since Skyla's death, and the words wouldn't come.

"I thought we were supposed to be safe," said the other girl. "People are getting hurt. Two guards blamed *us* for the attack here."

"Shit," I said. "I'm so sorry. Most people here aren't like that. We're doing our best to deal with the situation."

"Yeah, right," said Cynthia. "I saw you here yesterday. That was some trick you pulled."

Her challenging look told me she knew something was up with my magic. She'd probably seen the news reports from Valeria the other week, too. She wouldn't know the doors to Enzar had literally opened, but... damn. How to get the message across?

"Did you see those guys burying the bomb?" I asked instead. "They used illegal magi-tech. Lucky the guards and I dismantled it."

"That creature?" said Cynthia. "It wasn't magi-tech."

"No, it was a monster from a high-level magic world." I willed her to understand the hidden message in my words. *They're coming here. Maybe soon.* Had Nell told them yet?

Hiera noticed me and walked over. To my relief, she wore the same friendly expression as usual. Like, for a minute, nothing had changed. "Ada?"

"Hey."

"I haven't seen you around here in a while, Ada. I thought you had joined the Alliance."

"Uh. I'm working for them now..." As if the uniform wasn't enough of a clue. "I just came to say hi, since I haven't been here lately."

Great one, Ada. That doesn't sound like a lie at all.

"I wanted to ask… have there been people buying tech from Klathica in the last few weeks?"

"Klathica?" Hiera frowned. "Not that I know of. Why?"

Still conscious of the others' stares, I said, "Did you see what happened here yesterday? There was an incident with some people using magic-boost implants."

"I see." Hiera's expression turned into concern. "There isn't anything like that at the market—it's not only illegal, it's dangerous."

"I know," I said. "But I figured if anyone knew, someone here would. Those implants shouldn't even work on Earth."

"That's true," said the other Enzarian girl, and Cynthia glared at her. "I felt the magic level shift. I haven't seen anything, but I'll let you know."

I nodded. "Thanks. It's not just an Alliance issue. The creature got out of the Passages somehow." I paused, feeling a prickling sensation in my spine. "The Alliance will probably be sending more patrols down here. I'd… I'd relocate, maybe. Just to be safe."

"So now you're taking away our livelihood, too?"

I winced. "Someone targeted this place already."

"She's right," said Hiera, giving me an assessing look. "Some strange reports are coming out of the Alliance lately. They're making their own magic-based weapons?"

I shifted uncomfortably. Nell had made it clear we weren't to alarm anyone when there was no proof Enzar would be knocking on the door any day now, but it was hard to resist the impulse to scream it from the rooftops sometimes. I wanted my family, and the people we'd risked everything to save, to stay safe. But with someone targeting the market and offworld tech malfunctioning, they might easily end up at the centre of the next attack.

"Where's the last batch of tech?" I asked.

"Don't tell her," snapped Cynthia. "She'll rat us out to the Alliance."

"I haven't said a word about any of you," I retaliated. "I'm sorry about Skyla, but the people who brainwashed her were involved in offworld smuggling, too. I'm not the villain."

"It's here," said Hiera, showing me a box underneath the table. "We stopped selling the tech after what happened yesterday, but this is everything that came in last time. The hidden Passage has been closed off for weeks now."

I crouched down to sift through the box of metal parts, wishing I'd brought Jeth with me. "Doesn't seem to be anything off here," I said. "The guy with the bomb might have brought it in another way. And the kimaros, they've escaped the Passages before."

"Was that the magic-creature?" asked the other Enzarian girl. "I saw… sparks."

"Yeah. Keep away from them. If you see anything, call Nell."

"Not the Alliance?"

I chewed my lip. "Best to go through Nell first." If Lawrence Walker was really here, in control of Central… damn. Who knew what he'd do to this place?

My communicator buzzed in my pocket. I took it out.

Ms Weston's voice barked in my ear, "Where have you been?

I didn't bother with excuses. "You weren't in the office and I had an errand to run."

"You did what?" Her voice turned static, like she was calling from somewhere with bad reception. "You should be here. You're wanted as part of an Ambassador delegate to Klathica's Alliance branch for a meeting."

"Now?"

"In half an hour."

Damn. She hung up before I had the chance to explain. "I

have to go to a meeting," I told Hiera and Cynthia. "It's urgent. Check all the magi-tech before it arrives here."

"So you *are* shutting us down," said Cynthia.

"That creature came out of the Passages through the old smuggling tunnels," I said. "If we cooperate with the Alliance, we won't have to risk our necks anymore."

Unless the war comes here. Guilt rose, thick and choking. Magic-wielders like Cynthia would be first in line if Enzar came here. In another life, we'd be fighting on opposite sides of a war.

I shut the thoughts off. Thanks to Nell, that life would never be mine. If it came down to it, I'd always thought there was only one side I'd fight on: against the Empire. Things were a hell of a lot more complicated than old tales of Enzar had led me to believe.

"I'm sorry," I told her. "For all of this." I turned my back and left the market behind.

~

By the time I got back to Central, the group of Ambassadors had gathered in the entrance hall. Raj, Iriel—and Kay.

There was no sign of Lawrence Walker or the rest of the council. But I made straight for Kay, relief flooding me as he gave me the look he reserved for me alone—*it's all right.* Whatever had happened between him and Lawrence Walker, we were okay.

"Hey," I whispered. "Just went back to the market. What—"

"C'mon," said Raj. "We're running late, and I don't want to get on the bad side of Klathica's guards."

Dammit. Of all the times for the council and Ms Weston to start doing their jobs again. I'd wanted to see the boss before going offworld, though maybe Amanda had talked to her after what I'd said yesterday. Maybe the rest of the council would be able to override Lawrence Walker, considering he'd been away for so long.

"What's this meeting about?" I asked Kay in a low voice. "Why Klathica?"

"They want us to talk to the War Division at their Alliance branch," said Raj, as we walked to the Passages.

"*War* Division?" I echoed, heart plummeting. "Is this about Enzar?"

"Thairon, apparently."

"Shit. We're really going through that way?" I indicated the Passage entrance. "With Cethrax in there?"

"It's only two corridors down." Kay handed me a stunner. "That's all I could get."

"Yeah…" Raj shifted. "You sure we're safe? Because no offence to the council, but they haven't exactly been reliable lately."

"If it gets impassable in here, the Alliance are prepared to use the emergency doorway ports," said Kay. "Like the one in Valeria."

"So they can link up to several worlds at once?"

He nodded. "I reckon that's what the council's doing. That's how they got back so quickly without anyone seeing them."

So where's your father? I didn't want to bring the subject up in front of the others. But for once in my life, offworld was the place I least wanted to be.

Logically, I should have taken Nell's advice and stayed on Earth, were it not for the link between Klathica and the Stoneskins, and the burning curiosity to find out what they had to do with Thairon. Ms Weston must have pulled strings to get me on the mission. If the answers were on Klathica, I had to know.

Kay opened the door to the Passages, the metal door

sliding aside. Cold, quiet blue-lit corridors. Too quiet even for the Passages. A lot of worlds must have closed their doors.

I edged closer to Kay. "Are you sure about this?"

"I think Klathica knows something," he said, quietly. "We're meeting the other Earth delegates, and there will be people from Valeria, Alvienne—all the allied worlds, at least the main ones. You do speak Classical Klathican, don't you?"

I nodded. Nell had taught me, because it was one of the simplest languages to learn. As most Alliance members spoke it, it came in handy.

The corridors were deserted, and when we reached the main one, we found no one outside the twin lines of doors except guards. Klathica's guards were armed with what looked like the magical equivalent of assault rifles—which seemed to be growing out of their arms. *Jesus Christ.*

In my head, Klathica had always seemed a less-interesting version of Valeria crossed with Earth—urbanised, corporation-driven, and formed of a mishmash of other cultures from various worlds to the extent that it didn't really have anything of its own to offer. Aside from cyborg-style human enhancements and drugs.

To get into Klathica, we were subjected to no fewer than *six* rounds of security checks, including full-body scans. I was surprised they didn't catch Kay's Chameleon device, but he told me in an undertone as we left he'd had the foresight to hit the switch while it was in his pocket. The effect didn't transfer without skin contact, so it seemed to be invisible. Our jackets had so many hidden pockets even the security team didn't check them all—their eye-scanners picked up anything illegal. So clearly, whatever was in the Chameleon devices wasn't illegal here. As for our stunners, they were checked for bugs and then handed back to us. Weapons were a basic right on Klathica, apparently.

Once we'd finally passed through security, we found ourselves in a large, wide room. The Embassy, Kay told me. I couldn't help staring at the robots—mechas, they were called here—scattered throughout the room. Even though they were human in shape, their eyes were silver and flat. The humans in the room had just as many enhancements. Every other face had two eyes that didn't match—the right eye was replaced by one with a neon-blue iris, and which rotated unnaturally in its socket.

"What can you do with that?" I whispered to Iriel, unable to help myself. "You can't really see through walls?"

"I wish," said Iriel. "No, but I can read and process a page of information in five seconds flat. It stores data and transmits it to my communicator when I plug it into the wrist-port." She pushed up her sleeve to show a square-shaped slot on the underside of her wrist, like a USB drive.

Two mechas waylaid us and clamped metal wristband-like devices around our wrists to stop us wandering off while we were here.

"They implant us with an ID chip at birth," Iriel explained.

"Wait, they can track your every move?" I said.

"Only here," she said. "Doesn't work offworld."

It seemed pretty intrusive to me. But now probably wasn't a good time to mention it.

"It's in the interests of safety," Iriel explained. "I'm an Alliance member, so I have license to go wherever, but they'll have forewarning if I leave this world."

We left through the back door and found ourselves in a long, sloping corridor plated in blue glass-like material. The corridor became a bridge over a city, and I stopped to stare a moment. A river snaked below the bridge, weaving between warehouses—or that's what I assumed they were. Beyond were towering buildings. The view looked less fantastical than Valeria without the hover-cars and skyways around the buildings. The only transport was a large boat moored at the river's side, but I stared when a glass-walled lift-like capsule moved down the building on the outside.

"C'mon." Kay gently tugged on my hand. "If we're lucky, we get to have a look around later."

"No thanks," said Raj. "I'm pretty sure their police department still know who I am."

"You got arrested here, right?" asked Kay. "What was this one for?"

"When I first found out I could do magic." He grimaced. "Accidentally zapped someone, and they had two mechas strip me down and put their guns right up my—"

"Quiet, we're being watched," hissed Iriel. "We almost got arrested on the last drug operation, too. A group selling illegal offworld drugs on Earth," she added, for my benefit. "We tracked them here. Major cross-world operation. We got dragged in in case it had to do with magic."

"Turns out it wasn't," said Raj. "The authorities sent us packing."

I glanced sideways at Kay, whose hands were clenched, shoulders tense. "Yeah, after wasting our time in Venn's security unit."

"Venn? That's where we are now, right?" I asked Kay, who nodded.

I'd barely skimmed the files on Klathica, but Venn was the capital of the Klathican Republic, which covered half the planet. The other half was fragmented into islands connected by bridges from one major city to the next. The rest of the land had been turned to wasteland, and they relied on trade with low-technology worlds to get most materials. Like Valeria. Except where Valeria's innovations were for convenience, Klathica's were for fashion. Including magic sources. Klathica had named the world after their largest country, also like Valeria.

"Except Klathica has twice the ego and half the appeal," Kay muttered when he was explaining this, as we walked along the endless bridge until we reached the inside of a building with long windows overlooking the river.

The blue glass had made it all look alien, but without it, the city had a drab, grey appearance. Smog hung low over the opposite buildings. Inside, though, it smelled like a pharmacy, with a hint of something like flower oil. The scent made me slightly dizzy. Armed guards covered each door. This building was one of many Alliance branches here in Klathica, and we had to ride the elevator twenty-two floors up to reach the meeting room. Every time I glanced at Kay, he seemed tenser, and the strained attempts at conversation lapsed into silence. Partway there, we met with a group of other people who'd come through different doorways, including some from Earth's other Alliance branches.

The meeting room overlooked the river, too. A number of people were already there, some I vaguely recognised from meetings at Central. They were Ambassadors for the other allied worlds. The Klathicans were easy to pick out by their shiny, scale-like clothing. One was more cyborg than human, half his face plated in silver metal and with two cybernetic arms. I fidgeted in my seat, feeling more like an outsider than ever.

"As I'm sure you know," said the leader of this branch of Klathica's Alliance, a man called Zan Izen, "we're here to discuss the worrying situation in Thairon. Many of you have only been in the Alliance a short time, so it is possible you may be unaware of the history of the Alliance's relationship with Thairon. I feel it is beneficial to recount this, particularly to the delegates from Earth's Central London Alliance branch, who have not deigned to volunteer any of their own council members to attend this meeting."

I glanced sideways at the others, a little shocked. If it was important, why had the council decided not to come? Even if they were involved with Thairon, it wouldn't exactly have been hard to leave one of them behind to attend the meeting.

Impatience burned beneath my skin. I wanted to know what was going on with Thairon. I wanted to know what was so important that the council had decided to digitise themselves in virtual reality rather than dealing with the very real issues knocking at our door. I'd thought they were back on Earth by now. So… had Lawrence Walker come back alone?

"Klathica, Valeria, and Thairon were once closely aligned," said Izen. "Our creations were the envy of the Multiverse and have shaped the structure of the Alliance itself. But our original alliance was founded on a lie. Thairon betrayed us, stole the source of our power and took it for its own."

I stared, open-mouthed. Most of the others looked stunned, too, except Kay, and he hadn't completely managed to hide his shock. *He didn't know.*

"Thairon was once closely linked with the Enzarian Empire," Izen went on. "Like many worlds, it was progressive, high-magic, and set on innovation. Regrettably, the core world of its empire was also torn from within by deep-seated conflicts which only worsened with time. You all know, I'm sure, the two major sides to the conflict are those with magic, known as magebloods, and those without—the ones who call themselves Royal.

But the truth is there are more than two sides, and our Alliance was involved in the inception of the war. As representative of Klathica, I believe it's our duty to give you the truth, however distasteful you may find it. Some of you may wish to question our place in the Alliance—understandable, I'm sure. You see, Klathica had a complicated trade relationship with the Empire for over a thousand years. I regret to say many of our innovations were used to wreak destruction in their war. A hundred years ago, we once worked with the greatest inventors across the Multiverse to create energy sources to ensure our future. Those sources were sold across the worlds, including Enzar. But the same inventions meant to ensure its future destroyed it instead. The magebloods used our sources to power weapons, rebelled against the Royals and assassinated the leaders."

I couldn't breathe. It felt like I was pinned under the stare of the whole world. Klathica had traded with Enzar. And the magebloods had used those weapons to kill my family.

I didn't even know what to think right now.

"Three worlds once allied were now divided. Thairon itself fell under tyranny, its population caught under a spell, and we never did recover the source that rightfully belonged to us. But it is past the time for grudges, especially where Thairon is concerned. We received a message from Earth's council... I'm sure some of you did, too."

"Yes," said a guy I recognised as working for the New York Alliance branch. "We did. The council said the leaders of Thairon actually died—years ago. It's been running on automation ever since."

Exclamations filled the room. Kay had gone deathly pale, his clenched knuckles white.

"They're dead," repeated the Klathican leader.

"That's beyond wrong, if it's true," said Valeria's council member—Alexis Greene, her name was. "They're living a lie."

"It's all they've known," said another council member.

"More than that," said Izen. "It seems the leaders locked the population into a simulation designed to train them for war."

"But why in the stars' name did Earth's Central council go there?" said Greene.

"Very good question," said Kay quietly, "seeing as I don't believe they informed the senior staff of their intentions."

"They didn't?" asked the leader of New York's Alliance.

"We didn't know either."

Kay shifted beside me. I wished I could ask him what he was thinking, because I was stumped. If Thairon's leaders were dead, who were the council meeting with? And how in hell did Lawrence Walker fit into all this?

"Well," said Klathica's leader, "there is little we can do for Thairon. The terrible tragedy of the Empire is what concerns us now. It isn't the Royals who are winning the conflict, not anymore. No, the magebloods have taken their power, using weapons sold to them... by us. By Klathica. I wished to be honest with you all. Our world has been involved in terrible things, and the Alliance itself has never been entirely blameless. The Empire crisis may have been averted, had events played out differently. If any of you have questions, I would be happy to answer them."

There was a minute of stunned silence, punctuated by whispers. I didn't particularly want to draw attention to myself, not when they'd been discussing my homeworld, so I whispered to Kay, "Do they know about the Stoneskins?"

He gave a slight shake of the head, then said to the others, "Are you aware the group calling themselves the Stoneskins claimed to have been taken from Klathica to Thairon as experiments?"

As predicted, more whispers broke out. "These were the creatures you fought in Neo Greyle?" asked one of Valeria's council members.

"Yes." Kay didn't seem perturbed by all the stares. "They claimed someone from Thairon kidnapped them. They were from many different worlds, not just Klathica, but their leader was from here."

The StoneKing.

"I see," said Izen. "Thairon is a highly dangerous zone. The ground is poisoned and the population live on a satellite. There certainly is no evidence of such activities, and there are no doorways there. Until the past week, no one has entered or left that world in twenty years."

No. That's not true. The mission thirteen years ago. And five years ago, when Walker went there... But Kay didn't say anything. Amanda had said the mission her brother had died on was a secret, and illegal, so Klathica probably didn't know about it either.

But how had the Stoneskins got in and out of Thairon? What about their creator?

Kay's hand was clenched on the table. "The same year Enzar was cut off, correct?"

"Yes. You're Walker's son, aren't you?" said Izen.

Kay inclined his head sharply, his jaw tense. "Yes, I am. I think it seems a little too coincidental to assume Enzar and Thairon's situations had nothing to do with one another. The Stoneskins claimed to have been created on the orders of the magebloods, on Thairon."

My pulse kicked up. Did he really think it was safe to tell him? I supposed Izen *had* confessed to his world's involvement with the war. But where in hell were the council? They were the ones who needed to know, in case Enzar really did attack the Alliance. Based on what Kay had told me, I wouldn't trust our future in the hands of Lawrence Walker.

Izen paused. "I can assure you Klathica has no knowledge of these... Stoneskins. We have never shared any information on anything relating to magic, sources or otherwise, with anyone outside of the Alliance. We have had absolutely no connection with Enzar in twenty years—or Thairon." Beside him, an older Klathican guy exchanged glances with the woman at his side. My spine prickled as a distinct current of magic ran through the room.

I opened my mouth—whether to shout a warning or not, I didn't know—and the window exploded in a shower of glass. I ducked, arms raised to shield my face.

"What in the hells is that?" someone yelled.

Lowering my arms, I took in the scene—stunned council members and Ambassadors, glass sprinkled across the floor, and a rectangular metal object had clattered into the centre of the desk. I'd seen one before—

The market.

"It's a magical bomb!" someone shouted.

Panic erupted. Communicators were drawn, orders shouted, and Kay grabbed me by the arm and dragged me to the shattered remains of the window. People were already jumping for the narrow bridge below.

"Wait!" I pulled back. "I can counter it."

"Dammit, Ada—"

No time. Kay swore and squeezed my hand, then let go. I lunged for the table, magic searing my palms as they closed around the device. The charge sparked against my skin but didn't burn, and I shot magic of my own into its foundations, breaking it apart with the amplified sciras Kay had transferred over to me. The magic from the device flooded me, shaking me to the core, but I kept standing. The tingling sensation faded away, leaving smoke, and magic sparks, and shocked silence from the fifteen or so people still near the window.

"It's all right," I said shakily.

The remaining council members crowded around the table. "That's a pure source," one said. "Did anyone see where it came from?"

"Looked like one of our drones flew past," said a Klathican woman. "But nobody outside the Alliance knows this place even exists."

"Let me look at it," said one of the Valerians. I warily

handed over the metal pieces, and the cracked, lifeless remains of the source which had been encased inside them.

"How can you hold this?" the Valerian man asked me. "The device is made of pure magic."

"She has a magic-blocking implant," said Kay quickly. I glanced at him, an apology in my eyes. Disabling the danger had occurred to me first, before the question of what people would think when they saw me holding the inside of a bomb. He probably figured they'd assume I had a Klathican implant or something similar.

"We'll dispose of the remains," said the Klathican woman. "The source can't have come from our world. This isn't a Klathican source."

"That's Valerian technology," said Valeria's leader in a shocked voice. "And—it's part of the source we sold to Central, London, Earth."

10

KAY

The Klathican head had ordered a drone-copter to evacuate the building, a bullet-shaped hovercraft-like method of transportation reserved only for the elite. We climbed to a landing dock on the roof, surrounded by a security force. While we waited, guards searched each of us, checking for everything from cyber-enhancements to hidden weapons.

The landing dock offered a clear view of the main road cutting through the centre of the city like a blade. On either side were grid-like lines dividing the streets. I focused on that rather than on the guard intrusively running his hands over Ada. Throwing a punch at one of the mechas would not be a good plan. The cyborg-like security force weren't particularly gentle even searching Klathica's own council. Maybe they thought one of us had arranged the attack. Or someone outside. Venn's population was in the hundred-millions. At least security had taken what was left of the bomb to be safely destroyed.

"It's unheard of." Izen shook his head. "We carefully

monitor all of our sources. We should be able to check the Alliance's records and see who last purchased one."

"You sell them?" asked Ada, eyes wide. "In pure form like this?"

"Certainly not," said Klathica's leader.

"You are far more lax than you should be," said Greene, Valeria's council head.

"I should say the same of you," he countered. "Only in Valeria are sources like this encased in *batteries*."

"That's enough." Typical of Klathica and Valeria to start blaming one another. They were the two worlds which had almost kicked off a war, and only other worlds' intervention had formed the Alliance instead. But I sure as hell hadn't known they had any links with the Enzarian Empire. I kept one eye on Ada, but she seemed more freaked out by the bomb. I didn't blame her.

"While we're bickering, whoever threw that bomb is getting away," I said, looking out over the city.

"I sent drones to search the city from the skies." Izen tapped the screen built into his cybernetic arm. "If they're a resident of the State, they won't be able to hide—everyone has an ID chip implanted in their arm, logged with certain pertinent information. Even the people who disappear off-radar. It's how we check who leaves through the doorways."

"Do you track people you give temporary implants to?" I asked.

"Why do you ask?"

"Because some people on Earth reacted badly to the rising magic level," I said. "They all had magic-based implants, and the technology matched Klathica's."

"All state-approved implants meet our regulations," he said, "but we cannot control what happens to them after they leave the KimaroTech labs."

"That name again," said Ada. "Are all your labs called KimaroTech?"

"The Klathican Republic's are, yes," said Izen, with a meaningful glance at me.

My father might not be the CEO, but our family still owned every single KimaroTech lab. I'd never quite grasped just how far the influence stretched. He couldn't be aware of everything they'd been doing, especially as he'd been off-radar the past five years. I'd not told Ada yet, but now someone had just tried to kill us, we had bigger problems.

"I realise this is a bad time," I said, "but would it be possible for us to visit the labs?"

Ada shot me a look that said, *what are you doing?*

The whir of a drone interrupted as it descended from the sky, a ramp hitting the side of the dock.

"As it happens, staff from KimaroTech are operating the doorway port," said Izen. "The Walker family owns the lab, don't they?"

"Yeah." That was answer enough for him. They wouldn't know what I was thinking. What I suspected. But from the look Ada shot me, I had the sinking feeling she'd made at least one of the connections I had.

We boarded the drone, and the rest of the council sat in the slab-like seats we'd been assigned. Ada and I sat side by side, mercifully not next to the still-bickering council members.

The drone flew low over the city, revealing people with all manner of enhancements from extra limbs to cat tails, bat wings, and some accompanied by mechas. The robot servants were mostly reserved for the elite. Grey clouds gathered over the sharp metal tips of skyscrapers and mingled with the smog from factories. Now we'd entered the lower-class district, visible not only from the houses, which were more like shoeboxes stacked up high as the skyscrapers, but by the grim-faced enhancement-free humans walking the streets. No mechas here.

Ada was pressed to the window of the drone, her eyes wide. "I only heard about Klathica in passing. I didn't realise it was so… divided. Guess it's the bird's-eye view."

"Yeah, I have to say I prefer Valeria's hover bikes," I added, as the drone dipped down headfirst causing everyone to grab onto their seats to keep from falling into one another.

Ada's gaze turned downwards. "Kay… what was that about KimaroTech?"

I paused. "We probably shouldn't discuss this here." And not just because the council were still present.

"The *Stoneskins* came from here," said Ada quietly, and my heart sank along with the drone.

I lowered my voice, and said, "I should have told you… the Walker family founded KimaroTech. But no one in my family has set foot on this world since my grandfather did. At least, I thought not."

Her eyes were round. I stopped breathing. I'd really blown it.

"I thought I'd heard the name before…" She trailed off.

"It's the biggest brand on Klathica," I said. "But even though the Walker family technically owns it, my father never showed an interest." Part of me wanted to say I was just a kid and hadn't paid any attention, which was true. I closed my eyes for an instant, shook my head. "I did check the records just in case, but I didn't find anything. If I had, I'd have told you."

She exhaled. "I know you would have." But I caught a flicker of hurt behind her eyes all the same. The same hurt I'd seen when she'd asked if I trusted her.

Making sure the others were occupied in their own conversations, I leaned in closer. Looked her in the eyes. "If there's anything I can do to stop whoever targeted us, I will."

Ada nodded. "I trust you." Those words all but destroyed me. How many more lies could I tell before that trust broke? If I'd just told her before we'd come here… but that'd have opened another hundred questions.

"We'll have to go through the other Passage entrance," said Greene from the row in front.

"There's no need," said Izen. "We've recently reconnected the doorway port."

"You've done what?" I asked.

"That was what I was going to tell you before the interruption," said Izen. "Klathica and Valeria were once inter-linked—of course, all connection to Thairon has been removed, but we believe a connection between Alliance branches can only be beneficial in these times of discord and danger. The Passages have never been practical for use, especially now. Using the doorway ports would mean the council can meet in person in times of crisis without traversing the between-world."

"Valeria moved the doorway port from the lab after it was destroyed, right?" I asked Greene. I'd heard, and considering the lab in question was owned by KimaroTech, I was glad of it.

"Yes. We also relocated the scientists to the same place, as their skills are needed."

"Good," I said, "but the council are currently on Thairon. Would Earth be included in linking to the doorway port?"

"Not Central, if the council aren't there," said Greene. "We need a higher-up Alliance member to authorise it."

Damn. One person had that level of authority, and I sure wouldn't be mentioning it to *him.*

Izen tapped the computer in his wrist. "They caught the man who planted the bomb," he said. "You're all clear."

"Good," said Raj. "I've been in a holding cell here before and I honestly thought I'd die there."

The drone landed outside a building indistinguishable from its neighbours. Not flashy like Valeria's, but dull steel-framed structures with wire snaking down the walls which proved they were plugged into simulator tech.

Inside, several officers held down a rough-looking guy whose eyes had the dilated appearance of someone into both drugs and sim-tech.

"They promised they'd fix me," he was whining, waving the stump of an arm. "I can't afford cyber-tech, but they promised to pay me."

"*Who?*" demanded the enforcement officers.

"These guys from KimaroTech."

Hell. I stopped dead, unable to stop myself from staring at him. Lucky for me, the others did, too.

"Someone from KimaroTech ordered the attack?" Izen approached the officers.

"I don't know, man. I just needed the money. They gave me the bomb, put me on a drone. They wore masks so I couldn't see their faces, but they had KimaroTech uniforms."

"Masks?" said Izen. "Lab masks?"

"No. Black masks. Hard as rock. Dunno how they could see."

"They may have stolen uniforms," said Izen. "We can't rule that out. I want a full questioning of all the staff here. But you," he turned back to us, and the rest of the council members and Ambassadors, "you should leave before you're implicated in this. Offworlders are more likely to be prosecuted."

"That's ridiculous," Ada said.

"If Ada wasn't here, we'd be dead," I added.

"Be that as it may, I'd leave before you're delayed further."

"Who is authorised to give orders to KimaroTech?" I asked him. "It is Klathica's Alliance, right?"

"If you're suggesting *I* had anything to do with this atrocity, Kay Walker, you're mistaken."

"I just wanted to clarify who has authority to enter the labs. Seeing as the criminal said he was working for KimaroTech. I've never actually been here," I explained, as his eyes narrowed again. "Not until I became Ambassador. I'm not in charge of the Walker family's offworld finances."

My father had left me no information when he'd gone to Thairon. I hadn't *wanted* to know what twisted crap he got up to on other universes.

"It is my hope the answer will become clear in time," said Izen. "Once we question everyone. But nobody has the power to override the orders of the Alliance."

Yeah. Nobody but the Alliance itself.

"Come on," said Raj, as Ada and I left Izen and headed down the corridor with the other Ambassadors. "Trust me when I say you don't want to end up in a holding cell here."

"The ungrateful dick," Ada muttered under her breath. "Not so much as a thank you. How could any of *us* have ordered the bomb?"

"Because you don't have trackers." Iriel said from in front. "It's unfair, of course it is. We're all grateful you saved our necks, Ada."

"Yeah." Raj shuddered. "That was a close call."

Damn right. We climbed into the elevator, and the confined space instantly set my nerves on edge. Izen didn't suspect me, but I was fairly sure he knew KimaroTech—and my father—were interested in magic sources like the one in the bomb. Here on Klathica, it somehow seemed more real even than when I was in my father's company. Because he lived a lie so complete, you could only see the cracks from a distance. When you laid eyes on the damage he'd done. Given what Izen had revealed about Klathica's connection to Enzar's war, if the bomb hadn't interrupted us, Ada might have guessed the truth I'd long suspected… that KimaroTech itself, and my father, had funded the war on Enzar.

As the glass lift rose, the city revealed itself. No one walked on the streets of the impoverished district where those who could scrape together a few pennies signed into the simulators and lived a life inside their heads. Maybe they were better off than we were.

"Kay, do you think we should question the scientists about the Stoneskins?" asked Ada.

"Hell, no." Raj shuddered. "I want to get back to Earth before someone throws another bomb at us."

"I can't say I feel safe here," said Iriel.

"No, but…" Ada looked down at her hands. "I'm glad I had those gloves. If I'd held the device longer, it'd have burned through them for sure."

"Even that kind of protection isn't permanent," I said. "They might have caught the guy, but I think it was an impostor. Every native here has one of those ID chips. There's no hiding evidence."

"You think someone in KimaroTech's really working against the Alliance, though?"

"Hard to say." I spoke in an undertone. "They won't be taking orders from Earth, if they are. Walker's only been back a couple of days and Thairon had absolutely no contact with any other world."

"Right." She fidgeted. "I just… hope you're right. The last thing we need is enemies within the Alliance itself."

She must know almost as well as I did there was someone at Central who, for all intents and purposes, *was* an enemy of the Alliance. But most of these guys would have followed the orders left by Robert Walker, not his son. My father had taken no interest in KimaroTech—at least, I'd thought not. Now I didn't know what to think.

We had to walk through another seven layers of security

before we actually reached the main part of the Alliance headquarters. The area was divided into meeting rooms and labs, and more than a few bore the logo of KimaroTech. A line of armed guards stepped aside to let us into the room containing the doorway port. It first appeared like an ordinary meeting room, set up with a table and chairs and various tech devices to enable communication. But the back wall was given over to a device identical to the one I'd seen in Dr Helm's lab on Valeria—a box, plated in blue auros, glowing faintly. It opened up, and the walls lit up, too, as the door closed behind us.

The walls gleamed blue, as did the floor and ceiling, like an isolated section of the Passages. A man in a padded suit manipulated a series of dials on the side of the machine, rotating through symbols.

"Alvienne," he said, and two men stepped forward. He was sending us back to our homeworlds, one at a time.

"Holy shit," Raj said under his breath. "I've never seen anything like this before."

I had—the doorway port was just like the one we'd used on Valeria to short-cut from the lab to their Alliance headquarters. I watched the symbols, making a mental note when I saw one I recognised. I'd memorised a list when I was using the world-key.

"Earth's isn't activated, right?" Ada watched, wide-eyed.

"We're going through Valeria rather than through the Embassy again," said Iriel, examining the list of symbols etched on the machine's gleaming exterior. "I didn't know this port was linked to Zanthar. Where does that lead, the bottom of the ocean?"

"Many of the original doors are closed. This doorway port has been in use for over twenty years," said Izen. "It's still linked up to some worlds that are no longer inhabited. We've blocked some connections—like Thairon."

Thairon. I recognised its symbol, too. I'd seen it in my mother's notes before she'd left.

"Valeria," said the operator, and this was our cue, along with Valeria's own leader and three others. We said goodbye to Klathica's council—Izen gave me one last searching look, but didn't comment again. At least his face was easy to read. He wasn't pleased, and doubtless he'd make our lives difficult if we tried to come back, but he hadn't known about the bomb. The others hadn't betrayed any obvious signs either. But I'd let my ability to read people go lax in Walker's absence. I should know better. Ada might have died back there.

Inside the doors of the port were more blue panels, and the back wall shimmered red, then went transparent. On the other side was the interior of another building, with glass windows overlooking a skyway. I'd have known it for Valeria even without seeing the hover cars.

"Damn," said Raj, once we reached the other side and the transparent doors closed behind us. We stood in a spacious office, the entire back wall taken up by windows looking out onto a row of sleek hover vehicles.

"Right," said Greene. "I don't suppose one of you would care to tell me why you could handle a live bomb?" She addressed Ada, who froze.

Oh, hell.

"Because," Greene went on, "to the best of my knowledge, Klathican implants don't stretch to opening doorways half a world long, to high-magic places that are supposed to be inaccessible, like the two of you did in the attack on Valeria. Both of you have abilities that shouldn't be possible."

"Do we have to do this now?" I asked. "We're Alliance employees. Our *abilities* are perfectly legal on Earth." Mainly because no one had thought to make laws against something supposed to be impossible. Nobody actually knew the truth about what had happened to us. We were entitled to our secrets, and I intended to keep it that way.

"I am certainly not accusing you of breaking laws—either of you. But I would advise you to be careful when travelling offworld."

No kidding. Armed guards covered every corridor in the Passages, and we were scanned twelve times before we got to Earth's door. By the time we'd finally reached Central again, it was early evening, and we made right for Ms Weston's office. She'd have heard about the bomb by now.

"Kay, a word," she said, as I opened the door.

"Don't you want our reports?" asked Iriel from behind me.

"Later," said Ms Weston. "I would like you to compile them individually, but not on Central's property, and keep an electronic record, too."

I stared. Was she implying what I suspected?

"And me?" asked Ada.

"I'd call your family."

Ada paled, but she nodded, leaving the office with Iriel and Raj.

"You think someone's going to destroy the evidence," I said outright, once Ms Weston and I were alone.

"I trust no one here," she said bluntly.

That makes two of us. "Where's the rest of the council? They can't still be on Thairon."

"It's a difficult situation to explain."

"I'd really like an explanation. We almost died today. Valeria's head said the tech came from Central."

"We authorised nothing," said Ms Weston. "I've been in contact with every department, and I can assure you that no offworld substances left our stores."

Unless someone didn't want you to know.

"Kay," said Ms Weston, "I would advise you against leaving Earth again in the near future."

"I'm fighting on behalf of the Alliance. It's my job." Or, it was, back when the job description made some kind of sense.

Did she seriously think I was the target? It might have been any of us. Logically, Ada was the most likely target. And it made me really fucking mad.

"Is Lawrence Walker still here?" I asked, quietly. A horrible suspicion had rooted inside me, and I needed confirmation. Even if it wasn't what I wanted to hear.

Even if it was what I *least* wanted to hear.

"I believe he's upstairs, yes." Her face was tight, angry. "With no concern for the Ambassadors he sent out to Klathica or otherwise."

"I don't suppose you know what he *is* doing?" I asked.

Ms Weston shook her head. "I was hoping you could tell me, Kay. He refuses to give me access to the council's meeting rooms."

"I tried asking, but I don't know why he came back from Thairon and not the others. Whatever the situation is over there, couldn't it wait until the madness here on Earth is over?" *If it ever is.*

"Unfortunately, it seems the council saw fit to give me as little information as possible before leaving Earth," she said in her sharpest tone. "Once Walker contacted them, they left almost immediately."

"They didn't even tell you…"

"The directive from Walker is that I am to remain here in admin, and not influence the council further."

I had no idea what to say. Walker had deposed her? Ms Weston might as well *be* on the council, for all the influence she'd had since transferring here. She'd been in charge of all communications on Vey-Xanetha. But if anyone would see her as a threat, it was Lawrence Walker.

"Kay, you have to promise me you won't do anything reckless."

"Bit late," I said. "Seeing as someone just tried to blow us up."

"Thairon," said Ms Weston. "I want you to promise you won't interfere on that world, no matter what you may hear. Earth needs you."

"You think I'm going to head over there and forcibly drag the council back the office? What do you take me for?"

"You can't head over there," said Ms Weston, "because every world-key on Earth has disappeared. There is no doorway in or out."

I stared. "The council don't have one."

Her expression said it all. *Hell.* So Lawrence Walker had returned to Earth leaving the rest of the council with no way out.

"How do you know?" I asked quietly. "Nobody else does, right?" No, because if the council were gone, it only left her and the other senior staff. Ms Weston had never been friendly with the other departments.

"No," she said. "After Vey-Xanetha, and the Stoneskins… I suspected something like this would happen. Central is a weak link in Earth's Alliance, and it's up to us to defend it."

Not if it's poisoned on the inside. "And Thairon? Does no one in Earth's other Alliance branches know? Because it's a case for Ambassadors if I ever saw one."

"That may be, but there's too few of you and Earth needs defenders more than ever. The risk of war, whatever Lawrence Walker says, is imminent."

"Yeah, but he seems set on making people believe the opposite," I said. "Don't know why he thinks he can wave a magic wand and everyone will suddenly forget every magic-related catastrophe of the last few months, but without the council, we're lying down and asking Enzar to take over."

Right now, Enzar wasn't the imminent threat. Nor even Thairon. Lawrence Walker was. Ms Weston *must* know that.

Ms Weston's expression tightened. "I was shot down when I offered my perspective on the matter, as I did with Thairon. Walker informed me that the negotiations are taking a long time. He sent the same message to the other Alliance branches. As he's been ranked as the highest influence in Earth's Alliance's records for five years now, nobody will believe any different."

Goddammit. "Whether Earth is in danger or not, Thairon's at the centre of something bigger than any of us. The Stoneskins were created there. They were linked with Enzar, too—Klathica's head told us as much. It's all tied together, I know it, and Enzar has power enough to bring the Alliance to the ground. If a doorway opened there again, could we survive it? I'll bet Walker hasn't even considered the possibility. He hasn't even asked about the Stoneskins, so he won't know they're linked with Enzar at all."

"I sent in a report on the matter—abbreviated," said Ms Weston. "Unfortunately, Walker's authority overrides mine. I certainly won't be able to authorise an investigation."

"If I went to Thairon—"

"That's not what I meant," said Ms Weston sharply.

"Not even if there's evidence of the Stoneskins there? Ada deserves to know. And the population should be set free from the simulation, whether the council's there or not."

She closed her eyes, her hands clenched into tight fists. "I'd have thought you'd know better than to consider abandoning Earth at a time like this. Thairon is a lost cause. I know, because my brother died there. He broke Alliance code for a futile mission behind the Alliance's back, and the mistake cost him his life. Are you willing to make the same choice?"

Ice-cold hands gripped me all over. Her words lodged into me like throwing knives.

"Maybe I am." I didn't even realise I'd said it aloud until Ms Weston looked away, almost guiltily. Like she regretted losing control like that.

"I don't doubt Walker has ensured nobody will follow the council. My brother didn't tell me a thing, the fool. He just left and never came back. He left no evidence behind."

Neither did she. The only material thing my mother had left me was her will. One piece of useless paper.

Wait.

"They must have considered the possibility that they'd fail," I said. "Or that someone might follow after and need a clue, something…"

Ms Weston's expression turned glacial. "Stephen had his communicator with him, which contained all the details of the mission. According to the Alliance, his tracker disappeared at the same time as the others' did."

I couldn't speak. The logical, practical part of my mind said that meant Thairon had some way of disabling communication, probably with their high tech.

The rest of my mind instantly filled with images I'd tried to block out for years. I'd never found out exactly how she died. Back then, just a confirmation might have given me some sense of closure.

The two sides fought for dominance. I spoke through clenched teeth, "So the Alliance told you? You asked the council?"

For a long minute, I thought she wouldn't answer. The battle raged on. I didn't need this. I'd put even the smallest memory of her behind me because it was the only way to hang onto my plan to join the Alliance while knowing I'd be implicitly supporting the people who'd erased what really happened. Even if the current council at Central hadn't been in office at the time.

Ms Weston looked away, appearing diminished, weary. "The medical division told me. I was an intern there for a brief time."

I was barely aware of backing away until the cold metal of the door handle dug into my back. I'd known she'd been in the medical division when the experiments had taken place thirteen years ago. But it hadn't occurred to me that the medical division would have had to authorise the official death records. Or their version of the story.

My communicator buzzed, as did Ms Weston's. She hit the touch screen. Her hand noticeably shook. "Kay… you should leave. I'd suggest you not come into Central tomorrow. Tell Ada, too."

"Is that it?" I asked, only now becoming aware I was shaking with anger. "You're giving up? You used to work for the Law Division."

"You of all people should know there are some individuals who consider themselves to be above the law."

Did I ever. "Yes, I do," I said. "And you of all people should want to stand up to him and not calmly sit by and let him get away with fucking up any more lives."

As Ms Weston's eyes blazed, I knew I'd gone too far. But white-hot fury replaced the numbness flooding my body.

"I want to keep this city safe," she said. "I'm aware this Alliance branch has an appalling history of cover-ups, and almost all of them can be traced back to a single name."

"How long have you known?"

"A long while." Ms Weston's hands were so tightly fisted her knuckles turned white. "There's little an individual can do, but the system was flawed, even in the Law Division."

"So you moved into admin…"

"Because it was clear another cover-up had taken place."

"And you stayed because…" Of me? No way. Admin wasn't exactly influential. Though our department was half made up of Ambassadors these days.

"Go, Kay," said Ms Weston, quietly. "I'll write you off for tomorrow. You have a distinct ability to disappear at convenient times, don't you?"

I blinked, totally disarmed. She'd never witnessed me use the amplifier.

"Kay, I've read enough reports from witnesses both on Vey-Xanetha and to the events when the Stoneskins attacked to guess the nature of your abilities," she said, as if she'd read my mind. "I'm not quite the imbecile you apparently believe me to be."

Damn. I stared at her for a few seconds. Really, I was the imbecile. I hadn't given her enough credit for being able to see through my explanations.

"Fine," I said. "I won't come in. Are the Passages still off limits?"

"Sadly, no," said Ms Weston. "There have been a number of attacks in there, and the guards will not be driven out of their own territory. As for me, I'm going to stay here, and defend Central with everything I have. The tech team has been setting up cross-world communications for quite some time. We have backup systems in place in case Central falls."

In case it falls from within. If I wanted to stop Walker, I had to trust Ms Weston had the situation in hand. Central was out of my control—but Thairon might not be.

"You seem certain I have a plan," I said.

"Do what you have to do. But remember the risks."

Was she giving me permission to go to Thairon? Her words followed me out of the office and upstairs, reverberating around my head. She knew what happened to my mother. That was why she'd railed so strongly against me going after Ada. But now…

As expected, Walker was still in the office on the third floor. Now I knew the rest of that sector was empty, every sound seemed amplified. My footsteps on the polished floor. The slam of the door as I wrenched it open so hard it bounced off the wall, and my father looked up, cane held up like a weapon.

Lucky I was too angry to be scared of the consequences.

"I don't suppose you'd care to tell me why you just tried to assassinate Klathica's war division?" Fury punctuated every word. "Unless it was a cover-up so no one would realise you locked the council into a world in stasis."

Walker blinked at me. "If you're trying for attention, it's a poor effort. Not one the council would appreciate."

"I wouldn't know, seeing as the council's conveniently absent right now. Odd how that happened just as you made your dramatic return to Earth, isn't it?"

"What are you saying?" Walker's voice was quiet.

"I'm saying you wanted the rest of the council out of the way so you could push ahead with your plans for world domination. Starting with extortion and murder, I don't doubt, once you've convinced everyone on Earth the stories about the danger to the Alliance aren't true."

Walker's expression was flat, unreadable. "I will not stand for these ludicrous claims."

"Then tell me the truth."

"The truth is a dangerous thing, Kay. I'm sure you know the consequences of people knowing you opened a doorway to Enzar would be far reaching. You must understand. To keep the public's faith in the Balance, certain information must be concealed. *Especially* on Earth."

"People already know about the Stoneskins. Anyone with knowledge of magic can fill in the gaps. And then what? They can accuse you of whatever they like, because you've already proved you're a liar. Trapping Earth's council offworld won't solve a thing, and neither will throwing bombs around. The council have faced worse in your absence, Walker. You'll have to do better than that." I stopped before I said anything else I'd regret. My only edge was to make him think I knew more about what was going on than I actually did. If he thought his plans were pointless, he'd abandon them like an old coat—like the first magic-based experiments.

It didn't mean I had a freaking clue how to stop him if he really did assert his power across half the Multiverse.

"You don't understand. You're a child."

I almost laughed. "I was never a child, Walker. You took care of that. I'm telling you your little scheme is going to blow up in your face, not to mention kill all faith in Earth's Alliance and leave us vulnerable to an attack. What's your plan when *that* happens?"

"You think this is a joke?"

"You know, most people don't react well to betrayal by the people who are supposed to be in charge. It tends to lead to awkward things like rebellions. Trust me, the Alliance will react when they find out you concealed the truth, and not in a good way. There were two dozen eyewitnesses on Valeria who saw the Stoneskins. The whole Alliance is on alert in case Enzar attacks us. You can't discredit me, Walker."

"I think I can," he said, with the closest I'd seen to a smile. "The information on Enzar's current situation leaves this building only when I say so."

"You aren't the centre of the goddamned Multiverse," I said. "Maybe being in simulation messed up your head, but it doesn't give you the right to drag Central down with you. Your own father was the one to reveal the truth about the Alliance on Earth."

"You think he told the truth? Robert Walker was even more of a liar than I am."

I ignored his words—he wanted me to beg for information. "I wouldn't know. I never met him. But trust me, this won't end well for you." Honestly, I didn't have a clue what I was going to do. But it was worth it to see his eyes narrow at my use of his own bullshit speech against him.

"Is that a threat?" Walker took a step towards me, and I instinctively tensed. "You think you can walk in here and threaten me? You never did have any respect for authority."

"Wonder where I learned it?"

"Enough," said Walker. "That's enough."

"I'm glad we agree on something. So, what about Thairon? Did you plan to leave it in stasis forever? Don't the other people there have the right to know it's your fault they'll never escape?"

"They have no rights. Their own world's laws come first. It might have escaped your attention, but the Multiverse doesn't have a tendency to play fair, Kay."

"Yes, you taught me that, too," I said. "Was that why you ordered the noninterference stance against Enzar?"

"That," snarled Walker, "was to protect the interests of the Alliance. My fool of a father's actions almost destroyed us. His grandiose statement to Earth almost unleashed anarchy. You know nothing about sacrifice, Kay."

I laughed humourlessly. "I think you're the one who doesn't know a damn thing, Walker. I do have another question, actually. Is our family connected to Enzar's war?"

It was my darkest suspicion. I didn't know if it was true. The thought might just be the paranoia born of watching the bastard systematically destroy people's lives.

"Our family *is* the Alliance, Kay," said Walker. "I'm disappointed you still don't realise it. We all have our regrets."

That means it's true. But with every question I asked him, I revealed more of what I knew myself. Did he know Klathica had funded the war? Probably. The Stoneskins… whether he'd created them or not didn't matter. War was coming, and Walker would rather the world sat and looked the other way while he built his empire.

"What's yours?" I asked, before I could help myself. "Thairon? Do you regret killing their council?" Considering he'd been stuck there for five years even after they'd died… maybe.

His eyes narrowed a little. I almost expected him to deny it like everything else. "My only regret with regards to Thairon is not ensuring their backup systems were destroyed as well."

My breath caught, though I managed to keep my face blank. He'd never directly told me he'd been the one to kill their leaders—I'd inferred as much from whispered conversations in the corridors of the Walker house.

"So they got the best of you even in death. What a shame."

"Thairon is no concern of mine," Walker said. "Now… Ada Fletcher. I confess I was too preoccupied with Thairon to listen to the reports when I first returned to Earth. She's not Earth-born."

You're way behind the times. A flicker of triumph mingled with dread. If he had so much as a hint she was from Enzar, I didn't like to think of the consequences. He'd already proved he didn't care if I got caught in the crossfire. But I'd die before I let him hurt Ada.

"Few magic-wielders are. Does she have to do with your attempt to blow up Klathica's offices?"

Walker's eyes narrowed. "What are you accusing me of now?"

"Being the only person on Earth with exclusive access to our technology, and the means to override anyone else's decisions." I didn't bother feigning ignorance. Nobody else here had the knowledge or access to Klathican tech *and* the branch of the Alliance we were meeting in. I was certain he'd either been trying to get Ada and me out of the picture, or he'd been testing us.

A new suspicion took root in my mind.

"Abomination," I said slowly. "You hate magic-wielders. Is that why you tried to plant a bomb at Covent Garden and frame the offworlders for it?"

Walker gave me a perplexed look. "Do I look like I've had time to create elaborate schemes against London's offworlder population?"

"I wouldn't know," I said coldly. "Seems like you've been doing a whole heap of jack shit."

"If I were you, I'd stay out of offworld politics. Unless you want to go the same way as Elizabeth. It'd be a shame if your girlfriend was presented with a weapon she had no defence against, wouldn't it?"

Fuck. He knows she can counter magic.

"Yes," I said, my voice distant. A familiar roaring in my ears blanked out everything else. "If Earth lost their best defence, I can't imagine the consequences in the war. It's a very good job Central's in such safe hands."

I turned heel and left before he could reply. I was only half-consciously aware of walking downstairs. *It finally happened. He really tried to kill me. And Ada.* This was exactly what I'd been afraid of, and it was no consolation whatsoever to know my paranoia had been on the mark. But we were no closer to figuring out what the bastard was up to. He'd got rid of the council in the most convenient way possible short of killing them. He'd deposed the only staff who might have challenged him. He'd taken over Earth's biggest Alliance branch, and nobody at the others—nobody in the Multiverse, aside from me—knew what he was really capable of.

If Lawrence Walker was good at anything, it was masking the truth.

You've got that much in common, then.

Fear alone had stopped me telling anyone, even when he wasn't around to contradict me. Even if Ada accepted me as I was, I couldn't tell her I hadn't consciously believed Lawrence Walker was a twisted human being until he'd proven I was expendable by volunteering me to a pointless experiment after my mother died. No one other than me would ever know. The past was done. Trodden into the fucking dust.

Except he was back. And he'd nearly killed us.

11

KAY

I came to my senses when I reached the entrance hall and found Ada in conversation with Saki, of all people.

"Hey," I said to Ada. "You all right?"

"Kay." She gave me a tired smile. "Yeah. I'm okay. Did you get the latest message from the council?"

"What this time? The council aren't even here."

"Someone's been busy denying every report you've ever made," said Saki.

I rolled my eyes. "Incredible. I thought you didn't believe me about the Stoneskins, anyway."

"After Valeria? I saw those creatures on the news."

"Good," I said savagely. "That makes one person on the goddamned planet."

"Not just one," said Amanda, who'd just come through the doors. "I believe you. So does my sister. You'll have support from others at Central."

"Exactly," said Ada. "He can't deny what's happened when he wasn't even on this world. He doesn't know shit, Kay—and you know it."

Yeah. I did. I just didn't want to believe it. There was

something to expecting the worst of people. It took away the shock when it came true. God only knew I'd spent enough years playing mind games with Lawrence Walker.

"So a handful of people believe the truth. But who has the power here?"

"You do," said Saki.

"I'm not on the council. I'm not authorised to make decisions on behalf of Earth's Alliance, and thanks to Walker, the two of us are listed as unreliable and unstable."

"I can take care of it," said Saki. "I have… experience in falsifying records. Learned it from Walker himself, actually."

"You what?"

"Walker wanted me to fake certain documents to hide the cause of death of operatives in an offworld mission. More than once."

"He told *you* to do it?"

Saki glared at me. "If I wanted to keep my job, I had no choice."

Ada made a choked sound. "That's twisted. He can't have…"

"He can." Of course he could. All my worst fears were slamming down on me, and there wasn't a thing I could do. "Did… did you happen to see the records of Thairon?"

I had to know. Never mind that Ada and Amanda were here, watching. Never mind that a significant part of me didn't *want* to know.

"Of course," said Saki, in tones that suggested I was an idiot for asking. "When I was an intern here, six years ago. He picked someone who didn't dare report a superior."

The world tilted under my feet. "You do realise his *wife* was killed on that world? What about the version told to the victims' families? Was that a lie?"

"All the records say is that the team went offworld and

never came back. The official records say "cause of death unknown". Nobody else went after them."

I took a calming breath, wishing the tight feeling in my chest would go away. She didn't know any more than I did. I only knew my mother had died on Thairon because she'd told me herself where she was going, before she left on the mission. That was the last time I'd seen her. "Thairon's records are entirely falsified?"

"Not entirely," said Saki, giving me a wary look like she expected me to fly off the handle. I guess I understood why she hated Walker so much now.

"That's what Amanda was telling me," said Ada. "The team left a record of basic information, but it'll be out of date. What Izen told us on Klathica is more likely to be the latest."

"I didn't know the council over on Thairon were dead," said Amanda. "I... I'm not sure even my brother did. He didn't say so, anyway."

Damn. I wished I'd worn a recording device when I'd gone to confront Walker. I'd never expected him to admit that he'd killed them so easily, without any half-lies. Maybe he knew I could see through him now. Or maybe he didn't care who knew. Not now he had the power he'd always craved. The clever bastard knew people on Earth were disinclined to accept what they couldn't see with their own eyes. An invisible war they didn't have to be involved with. He might have been planning this long before he'd gone to Thairon.

I addressed Amanda. "Did your sister tell you why the council haven't come back?"

"No. What happened?"

I drew in a breath. "According to Ms Weston, Walker came back alone, and took the only world-key. All the others on Earth have disappeared."

"No." Amanda shook her head, paling. "He can't have done that."

"He speaks on behalf of all Earth's council now," I said.

"Why can't you go to Thairon?" asked Saki, eyeing me suspiciously.

"I'm not saying we can't," I said. "Just the last people who did ran into a trap and paid with their lives. We don't know what's out there, and I doubt *he'll* tell us."

Amanda's face was milky white. "What did my sister say?"

"She told us to avoid Central tomorrow."

Ada nodded. "To be honest, I'm starting to think we can do more good on our own. If the council's really gone… Nell will have a fit if I tell her."

Damn. "I don't think he'll target your family, but you might want to advise them to go to a shelter or somewhere. Just in case."

"Al can go stay with a friend." Ada's fingers raced across her communicator screen. "And Nell's more than capable of defending herself. She's in less danger if I'm not there." She looked up at me. "What a freaking mess. Is there nobody else who can get onto Thairon?"

"It's not a question of whether they *can*," I said. "Think about it. It's a world ravaged by natural disasters which has already killed a whole team of Ambassadors. Most people think it's been closed off entirely for years, and they don't even know anyone tried to liberate it. We're the only people who know the whole picture."

Ada took a deep breath. "Yeah. And it might have answers about the Stoneskins." Her voice grew stronger with each word. "If you can think of a way to get us onto that world and free the council without running into a trap, I'm in."

"I can help," said Amanda. "My brother—he kept journals. I'll see if he left any clues."

Clues. "Thank you," I said. "Anything might help."

Dragging Ada into danger was what I least wanted, but maybe she'd back off when I told her the full truth. We were on the brink of no return, and whether Ada was with me or not, I'd walk into Thairon in the same way my mother did. We might not know what we were up against, but I'd take Thairon, and an unknown enemy, over Walker's tyranny.

Better hope luck was on my side this time.

~

ADA

"What *happened to you?*" Nell demanded, yelling at me through the phone as I waited for Kay outside Central. He'd gone to warn everyone he could—a depressingly small number of people. I'd told Jeth, but ordered him not to spread panic through the departments. Nobody in the building, not even Ms Weston, had the power to take down Walker alone. If he knew we planned to go to Thairon, he'd close off the Passages and we'd lose our shot of rescuing the council.

I winced. "I'm all right. We were in a meeting offworld. I didn't have chance to tell you beforehand."

"And Walker's back. Jeth told me."

"Yeah. He is."

Guilt swirled inside me. I didn't want to abandon my family. But Kay and I were the only magic-wielders who knew what was going on. The simulation couldn't be escaped from the inside, apparently. Which meant someone had to go into Thairon and unplug it, just as Kay's mother's team had tried to do. If we saved the council, we might just be able to salvage Central from whatever Walker was planning.

Hatred burned in my blood, like the horror infecting Kay's life was seeping into mine. I'd stand by his side even if we were the only two people left against the Multiverse.

I'd never let the council die on Thairon, or let all those people live out their lives in a lie built by tyrants. Whether we found the truth about the Stoneskins or not, if I let this go, I'd never forgive myself.

"Ada Fletcher. When you go quiet like that, it's never good news. What are you planning?"

"I don't want you to panic, but it's not looking great for Central. The council's trapped, offworld. On Thairon." I swallowed. "If I went there, would you try to stop me?"

"If you *what?*"

"Kay and I are the only people who know, except our supervisor, and she can't do anything to challenge Walker without losing her ability to help anyone at Central. I promise I'll be careful. It's no different to any offworld mission."

"Ada Fletcher, on what *planet* would you think I'd ever allow you to leave?"

"It might be our only choice. Kay has a plan." *I think.*

"Of course he does. That man will be the *death* of you, Ada. His father—"

"Tortured him as a child," I said, in a low voice. "I don't know all the details. But Walker's not looking out for Earth, only himself. If he gets his way, Enzar will be able to get at us without interference. The rest of the council are gone. We're on our own."

"Ada… I can't let you do this."

"Don't," I said, my voice breaking. "Please, don't guilt-trip me. I'm going to Kay's, all right? And I'll come see you tomorrow if you promise not to chain me to a chair, but you can't deny there's something seriously wrong at Central."

"Ada, this is *none* of our business. It never has been. You worked for them, yes. I could see it helped you, but now all it's doing is placing you in danger. Do you really want a repeat of the Stoneskins?"

I ran a hand over the sciras-chameleon. Kay had given one to me. "That was different. I know how to fight them now. And I can turn invisible. It's not like we're mounting an all-out assault on Thairon." Though if we were, I wasn't sure I'd say no. Staying out of the action went against my instincts. God, I was scared—of course I was. But the future of the Multiverse might depend on us recovering the council and deposing Walker.

Eventually, I convinced Nell I wasn't going to get murdered at Kay's apartment. Luckily, I still had my stunner, so she couldn't argue I had no defence. Kay, meanwhile, returned from the guard office with a handful of weapons.

"Apparently, Carl thinks we're likely to get killed, too," he said, once I'd hung up the phone. "I think our odds are better than his, with Cethraxians running around the Passages again."

"Don't say that."

"Cethrax broke through three doors today," said Kay as we crossed the car park and headed down the road. "The attacks seem random, but I don't believe it for a second after all the other crap Cethrax have pulled."

"Me neither." Was anyone on the Alliance's side? Cethrax definitely weren't the ones who'd ordered the attack on Klathica's council. If I hadn't been there on Klathica, our own council's disappearance would be the least of our problems.

The bomb came from Central. As for what Izen had said, about Klathica supplying weapons to Enzar... I hadn't told Nell. Whatever Klathica had done over twenty years ago, our real enemy was right here. On Earth.

Kay looked at me. "All we can do is wait until the Passages

open tomorrow and talk our way through one of the doorways."

"You know how to get into Thairon," I said. "Don't you."

He drew in a breath. "Yeah. I think my mother hid a map of the satellite. Obviously, to actually get to Thairon itself, we'll have to go offworld and use a doorway port or world-key."

He didn't say another word until we reached his apartment. Then he hesitated, turning his key over in his hand. "You don't have to come, Ada. We're both targets. It wouldn't at all surprise me if people were watching this place."

"Who's *they?*" I asked. "Kay—what is it?"

"We can talk inside." He glanced over his shoulder before entering the building and again when we reached the fourth floor. My heart beat fast, and not just from the exertion of climbing the stairs.

"Kay," I said, as the door shut. "Who do you think's after us?"

"My father." He bolted the door from the inside and then started pacing the room. "Walker wants control over every-thing. We're in another power game, and he knows you're important to me, so you'd be on his list even if he didn't know about your magic. He ordered the bomb. He knew you could stop it."

"No." I shook my head. "No way. Why would he want to assassinate the offworld council? He's *on* the council. Right?"

Kay turned to me, his face tight, drawn. "He already has Earth prime for the taking. Central's council members are gone. I suppose trapping them on Thairon would draw fewer questions than killing them."

"Why? Why kill them?"

"I don't know," he said. "I'm not sure if he wants the power for himself. Maybe he knows the Empire's a threat and wants to challenge them, and he thinks the council's in the way of doing that. God only knows what his logic is this time. The point is, he has the means to kill anyone who stands in his way. I know for a fact a number of his opponents have suffered mysterious accidents before."

I stopped shaking my head and stared in horror. "No way."

I'd said the wrong thing. His jaw clenched and he looked away from me.

"Who?" I whispered. "Who did he kill?"

Kay's gaze remained on the wall. "For one, Thairon's council was murdered thirteen years ago, and their new leaders locked the population in stasis. I know for a fact my father visited them shortly before. He must have had a world-key hidden, behind the Alliance's back. It's not illegal for council members to own one, but he might have been doing anything over there and nobody would have been able to find out."

"You don't think…"

"He did it," said Kay. "He just confirmed it, but I knew. Back at the Walker house, he talked about *arranging accidents*. Frequently."

"Oh, god." I couldn't even imagine what it must have felt like to live in the same house as a murderous despot.

He looked at me slantwise. "It's okay if you want to leave, Ada."

"You're kidding," I said. "You think I'd ever dream of blaming you for what he did?"

"Some people would," he said quietly, rubbing the back of his neck. "I knew what he was doing and did absolutely fuck all about it. Tell me how that doesn't make me just as guilty."

He sat down on the bed, not looking me in the eyes. His had blanked out, like he'd shut down inside. I didn't blame him a bit.

"Your mother," I said, hesitantly sitting beside him. "She

didn't know?" I wished I could take the question back almost instantly.

Kay shook his head. "My mother took care of me when I was younger, and he was rarely around. The dick showed up every few weeks, yelled at everyone, and disappeared offworld. My mother stayed because she had nowhere else to go. Guess it didn't hurt to have access to the council's information. That's how she knew about Thairon. She and her friends plotted against Walker to set Thairon free. Then she was killed. Because she went against the Alliance's rules, the whole thing was covered up." He paused, and I heard the hitch in his breath. "He took away every trace of her existence and made me swear never to talk about her again."

"Tell me," I said softly. I was sure he'd never spoken it aloud before. I didn't even know if it helped in any way or made things worse.

His eyes hardened. "He showed his true colours after she died. He acted like I was some strange kid she'd left on his doorstep, but he couldn't get rid of me. I was the only heir to the Walker name. The others—his brothers and sister—died when I was a kid."

"Really?"

"The Walker name isn't exactly a blessing. Anyway, I assume the experiment was an attempt to turn me into his pet magic-wielder, only it didn't work. So he went back to ignoring me and left his servants in charge. When they weren't pushing me through tutoring, they were telling me being a Walker gave me the right to walk over anyone in the Multiverse. In the same breath they told me I wasn't worth shit." His hand clenched over mine. "I'm sure he was losing his mind by the time he left Earth. Last thing he ever did was tell me I was going with him to Thairon, or he'd kill me himself. I fought back because I expected to die, and at that point, I didn't care anymore. But apparently he didn't think I was worth the effort, because he left."

He'd kill me himself. A lump rose in my throat. Wariness flickered behind his eyes and I knew I had to trust him. He still didn't think I believed him.

"He left you? Alone?"

"First decent thing he ever did."

"Kay, I believe you. Why did he decide to go to Thairon on his own, without the council?"

"Because he's been paranoid about it ever since my mother died," he said. "He was convinced they had a master conspiracy to take over the Multiverse. My mother left a note in her will. It said, if he goes to Thairon, he's not coming back." He pulled away from me, walked to the desk drawers, and unlocked the top one with a key. "There has to be some kind of a clue in there somewhere."

He took a single piece of paper, crumpled around the edges. "I guess she thought he'd screw me over. She even contacted the Academy so they'd let me in early, given the chance. She knew I'd want to get away from Walker as soon as I could legally move out. Obviously, I didn't know about it, and when he did finally leave, I managed to screw things up and get arrested."

"None of this was your fault," I countered. "You were a kid, he was your guardian…"

"I can think of a million things I could have done to stop him, but I never did. Not until it was too late." He pulled his hand out of mine. "He fucks up everything he touches, Ada, and I'm the same way."

"Kay, you know that isn't true."

He drew in a breath. "You're too damn *decent.*"

"I'm selfish," I said. "You think I don't have regrets? Nell was younger than me when she fought her way out of Enzar to save me. She gave up everything for me, and I repaid her by running around the Passages when I didn't have to, and bringing down our whole business. You've done so much for the Alliance since you've joined, not to mention Enzar. Never mind stopping the freaking *Stoneskins.*"

The corner of his mouth twitched. "That was hardly altruism, Ada. Yeah, they'd have wiped out the Alliance, but it was you I was thinking of."

My heart missed a beat. "That isn't selfish, Kay. It's human nature. You aren't to blame for anything he's done."

Kay said nothing for a long moment.

"I have to go to Thairon," he said. "I think I'm the only person on Earth who knows how their systems work."

"Their—what?" The change of subject disarmed me. "How?"

"I know," he said, quietly, "because I was Earth's only test-subject for custom simulation."

Huh? "Custom simulation?"

"A simulation of his own making, adapted for home use. The tech was being used on Klathica and Thairon, but Walker got around the Alliance's usual rules by pretending he needed the simulator for research purposes after my mother died."

My heart sank a little at his words.

"What—what did he do?"

"He shut me in there every time I so much as challenged him. He didn't have to go to the bother of training me as an obedient soldier if he could just plug me into a machine that would do it for him. He was continually disappointed I didn't turn out to be a remorseless killer like him, but being thrown into the middle of a simulated war zone was a handy incentive to take his threats seriously."

I gasped. Kay's expression was as carefully blank as ever. If I was squeezing his hand too hard, he didn't say.

"I figured out how to get around the simulations after a

while," he said. "I think he wanted me to go to Thairon with him originally, but only as an obedient servant. I kept defying him, and when it came down to it, he snapped and left me behind. Probably saved my neck, considering what happened to the others who went with him."

"Kay…" I moved closer, rested my head against his shoulder. "I'm sorry." Words were inadequate, but what else could I say?

"It's all right," he said. "I know how Thairon's system works, and I have to go there. If it's true…" He turned over the paper in his free hand. On the side facing me was a handwritten letter. The other appeared blank from this angle, but Kay focused on it intently. "I knew it."

"Knew what?" I said hoarsely.

"This is bloodrock."

I jumped as magic flared from his hand holding the paper. The side facing me shimmered, faint glittering dust sliding off it. "I should have realised before. Bloodrock wears off when you get hit with magic, right?"

I blinked at the total change of subject, scrambling for a ledge. "Uh. Guess it does."

"Yeah… it's like an advanced illusion." He shook the paper. More glitter slid off it. Faint lines began to appear on the side I'd thought was blank.

"What is that?" I stared, momentarily distracted from the horror of what he'd just told me. "It looks like a map."

"I thought so," he said. "This is the missing piece of the map I took from my father's office when he left Earth. She wrote on the other side. And…" He flipped it over. Now the side with text faced me, only faint lines had begun to appear around the edges of that, too. "It looks like some kind of… code."

"But what *is* the map?"

He flipped it around again so I could see. "It's the

Passages. This is the missing piece. It shows the hidden Passages—all of them."

"What? That's…"

The entrance to Earth's hidden Passage in London. The one near my old house.

Impossible.

"The map was my grandfather's, originally," he said. "Guess he never noticed that door. But it shows the doors on the upper levels. And the lower levels."

"Why—why would she want you to have it?"

"I've no idea," he said. "There *is* an entrance to Thairon there, but it's closed off. Either way, I memorised the symbol already. It's on the doorway port on Klathica, and probably Valeria's too. I'm going there tomorrow."

"Kay…"

"I know it's a fool's crusade. I know getting the council back won't stop him, and neither will setting that world free. But their leaders are dead. They aren't real, they're simulated. If we shut them down, the people of Thairon are free, as well as our own council. I'm going. I don't expect you to come with me, Ada, but I thought you had the right to know."

I wiped my eyes. "I—I understand." And like hell was I letting him go alone.

"So you understand why I can't ask you to come with me."

"Don't you try to push me away," I said. "Seriously. I'd follow you to the end of the Multiverse, Kay."

His eyes widened. He said nothing for at least a minute, as we were suspended there, silent.

"Ada," he said, his voice uneven. "I don't want to throw the burden on you. This is more than you deserve to deal with."

"And you deserve one person in your life who knows who you really are," I said. "Fuck the rest of them. Fuck Walker. You're the best thing that's happened to me in a long while." I almost laughed at his perplexed expression, though moisture gathered in my eyes again. "You're forgetting I've spent my whole life helping people who've given up hope. I'm not about to give up on you, Kay."

"You're incredible, you know that?"

"I do my best." I gave him a shaky smile. "I can disable a bomb and take down a Stoneskin. Isn't that a good reason to have me with you on Thairon?"

"I'm not doubting your ability," he said. "Not for a second. But Thairon shut down at the same time as Enzar was cut off. I don't believe in coincidence. Not when I know what Lawrence Walker can do."

"If it's to do with Enzar, then it's to do with me. Nell always tried to shelter me from the truth and being blind-sided almost got me killed. I want to know, Kay. I want to help get the council back and free the people of Thairon. And the Stoneskins—I want to know how they knew about me. Only someone on Enzar could have told them I existed."

"All right," said Kay. "We'll figure that part out once the Passages are open again. I'd like to know how Walker got hold of all the world-keys. Probably terrorised whichever poor fool was guarding them." His hand clenched around the paper in his hand. "The goddamn letter made no sense when I first read it. *I have given a copy of these codes to the Alliance...* I guess she meant whatever this text is."

I pulled back so I could see the text scrawled around the outsides of the page. I didn't recognise the symbols.

"That's not from Earth," I said.

"No," said Kay. "It isn't. I can't read it, and I've compared it to every recorded language on the Alliance's systems. If it's a code, I've never been able to crack it. I actually did try a few times, but obviously I couldn't tell anyone what it is…"

"It must be important, though, if she left it you."

"Not necessarily. I was a kid. Not like I could apply for an offworld permit. She locked the letter in a safe he couldn't open. And it's hidden by magic—I wasn't even a magic-wielder when she left." He read over the text again, frowning. "It looks like she made a backup copy of some kind of information. Maybe she wanted me to give it to the Alliance. But it *says* they already had the information. He traced the lines of the map again, tilting it on its side.

"No… it carries onto this side."

"It's not the original map," I said. "What happens when you put them together?"

"Good point." He drew away from me, back to the drawer again, and pulled out another, more crumpled piece of paper. When he unfolded this one, it was at least four feet long. He laid it out on the bed, slotting the missing piece into place.

"Nah, it's just the Passages—but on the other side's a map of Central."

"That's what it is." I took the torn-off piece again and handed it to him without looking at the words on the other side. "Is the extra map part of Central?"

"It's underground," he said, eyes wide. "There isn't supposed to be a basement at Central, but… I can actually read this part. There's a space underneath Central big enough to turn into a shelter… in case of an attack on Earth."

He looked back at me. "She sent a copy to Central in case Thairon attacked Earth, but they didn't. The Alliance covered it up along with everything else. But just in case…"

"She left you a copy."

A pause. He read the text again, forehead creased. "She knew I wanted to join the Alliance."

"She trusted you."

"I seriously doubt it. I was just a kid."

My heart hurt. The damage went so deep, maybe even I couldn't reach it.

"We're going to bring him down, Kay. He's one man. We have the Alliance. Has no one ever challenged him before?"

"Not directly," he said. "But if he perceives anyone to be a threat, he eliminates them by any means necessary."

"Couldn't every magic-wielder just team up and overpower him?" I asked. "He's not a magic-wielder, right?"

"Unless he has Klathican implants, no. I didn't sense anything from him, anyway. He never trusted magic. Went against his perfect world-view. Then again, so did my mother, and he married her."

"Did she really not know what he was like?"

"Maybe." He paused. "I didn't realise until after she died she was playing *him* as much as he played her, if not more. She was an orphan, she came from nothing, and when she joined the Alliance, she needed his connections. I don't think a kid was part of her plan. Her goal was to liberate Thairon, and she cared about it more than anything."

"She cared about you more."

He stared into space a moment. "Maybe she did," he said, "but she's gone."

I wrapped both arms around him, and he buried his head in the crook of my neck. "I love you," I said, "and I'll say it as many times as it takes you to believe me."

12

ADA

"So that's it," I said, looking around at the table. Kay, Amanda, Raj, Iriel and Jeth wore expressions varying in degrees of incredulity and confusion. We'd agreed to meet in a coffee shop, a weirdly ordinary setting, considering we were as good as plotting against the government. Even stranger was that our fellow Ambassadors had come along. Both Raj and Iriel were off-duty and had thought something was wrong at Central, so we'd decided to forewarn them. Jeth had promised to tell the tech team, who were in charge of all communications in and out of Central. But as for Walker himself, we couldn't challenge him directly. And if we told *everyone* at Central the truth, word would get to him before we reached Thairon. If Walker could make an entire council disappear, he could easily convince the world Kay and I were deluded liars. I could only imagine the lies Walker had concocted in the past, to preserve the image of himself as the model council member. Earth's saviour.

I hated Walker with a steely rage that took my breath away.

"That's…" Iriel shook her head. "How would the rest of

the council have no idea Central's staff are trapped in hostile territory? It's completely off-book."

"Walker's powerful," said Amanda. "He erased all evidence of the last mission."

"What's that even mean?" asked Raj. "This is making me seriously uncomfortable. Don't get me wrong, I know there's trouble, but I don't see how we're supposed to take down one of the most powerful guys on the planet. In the *Multiverse.* Are you sure you didn't just misinterpret what he said?"

Kay stiffened. It had taken me a while to convince him we couldn't go in alone, that we needed to contact people who might believe us. Amanda had told her sister, but Ms Weston's priority was keeping Central safe. God knew someone had to.

But someone also had to go offworld and stop this madness before Earth's Alliance fell into anarchy. Before Enzar showed up and obliterated everyone. It went beyond Walker, whatever his plan was.

"I'm quite certain," said Kay. "I know Walker's ways. I'd never force any of you to help, but I wanted to spread word to anyone who's witnessed anything he's done. That bomb yesterday was his work."

"About that." Iriel shifted in her seat. She'd taken the news much more calmly than Raj had. "Whether Walker was responsible or not, Klathica's hardly the safest place at the moment. But you said you wanted to go back?"

"No," said Kay. "Valeria, actually. Their Alliance branch is under armed security—for what it's worth. Walker hasn't been there, so I figured we could talk our way through. I know someone who works in tech on Valeria. I'm still planning to take precautions. And like I said, none of you are under any obligation to come along. In fact, it might be best if some of you stay on Earth. Maybe keep an eye on Walker."

"Spy on a madman or go offworld into danger?" said Raj. "Damn, we're spoiled for choice."

"Quit it, Raj," said Iriel. "I'll help, if there's anything else that needs decoding."

"Actually… there is something." He passed her a piece of notepaper, on which he'd copied the code Elizabeth Walker had wrote on the map. We'd discussed possible ways to decipher the meaning, but even Jeth hadn't been able to.

"Is this the code you sent me?" asked Jeth. "I couldn't crack it."

"I'm almost certain it's the codes to get onto the satellite," said Kay.

"I can check," said Amanda. "I found something… in his journal. They used a code to communicate with one another."

Kay looked at her sharply. "Can you solve it?"

Amanda nodded. "Let me see."

Iriel handed the notepaper over while Amanda pulled a thickly bound journal from her bag. It looked like Elizabeth Walker had thought of everything. Kay hadn't shown me the rest of the letter, and I hadn't asked to see it. Though it hurt to admit it, he hadn't wanted to tell me the truth yesterday. Circumstances had pushed him into it. I hadn't asked any more questions about what his father had done. We'd both been exhausted last night, and held onto one another through the nightmares. After this was over, we'd figure out what knowing the truth meant for us.

"What language do they use on Thairon, anyway?" I asked.

"Classical Klathican," said Kay, grimly. "I should have guessed the connection. They shared a language once. Not the only thing they shared, it seems."

Oh. The Stoneskins' possible connection to KimaroTech. Kay didn't know if his family had been involved with the project, but it still left us with no answers. It was like trying to assemble a jigsaw with half the pieces missing, and I had the sneaking suspicion the missing pieces were on Thairon.

"We have these earpieces," said Kay, "but only three. Ada and I will need them in case we get separated. It'd be best to give the other to the person who volunteers to keep an eye on Walker."

"Who *what?*" asked Raj.

"I'll do it," said Iriel. "But he has guards, right?"

Kay nodded. "Yeah, two of them. I reckon they're wearing adamantine-enhanced armour. Like the guards on Valeria."

"They are?" I asked.

"I think magic could take them out, but I can't be sure. Don't let him see you. In fact, take a Chameleon."

"Good plan," I said. "I spoke to Nell, and she's going to watch offworld district. They've upped security over the other doorway near West Office, right?"

"Let's hope so." We couldn't be in several places at once. We needed allies. We'd sent messages to all Earth's other Alliance branches, but they had problems of their own to deal with. Malfunctioning magic-based devices. Attacks from Cethrax around the Passages.

"Did anyone offer a verdict on who was responsible for the magical device at the market?" I asked.

"No, and that's what worries me," said Jeth. "Nell said there were ten arrests over in the offworld district yesterday. I think people are panicking. Ada…"

"Jeth." I gave him a stern look. "No arguments. But come on." I turned to Kay. "Anything about how we're going to get in? Whereabouts does the doorway port lead?"

"To Thairon's old Alliance headquarters, I guess. If not, we can get a world-key from Valeria or somewhere."

"You mean, steal one," said Raj. "Have you any idea how much trouble we're going to get into if we get caught?"

"A damn sight less than Earth will be," muttered Kay. "I know it's not a perfect plan."

"It's a bloody terrible one," said Raj. "Sorry, Kay, I know your old man's messed-up in the head, but we don't have enough clout between us to talk down every Alliance member. We're supposed to be on the same side."

"Don't I know it." Kay's hands had clenched around his communicator again. "But I do know how to get the people out of that simulation without killing them."

I didn't need to ask how. His tone was flat, but emotion burned behind his eyes. Too many years of silence. Too many years of pain.

Amanda cleared her throat. "According to my brother's journals, Elizabeth made the plans. She was in charge of getting the team onto the satellite and figuring out how to stop the simulation. It's impossible to escape from the inside, and as I understand it, what each individual experiences in simulation is coloured by their own subconscious, to some extent. It's what makes the experience feel real."

"Like Klathica's plug-in simulators," said Kay. "Yeah, I'm not planning on going *into* the simulation unless we have no choice. For one thing, there's no way out."

"What's controlling it?" asked Iriel. "There must be a source."

"Yeah," said Kay. "That's what the Klathicans were talking about, right? They said Thairon stole their power source. I reckon they used it to keep the simulator running so it'd never switch off. Everything else on their planet burned to the ground. There's nothing left but the satellite, and an unending virtual matrix imprisoning everyone."

"So the simulation's powered by a magic source?" I said. "I have to go, Jeth. You know I'm the only person who can drain the magic out of a source without dying."

It was the first time I'd said so in as many words.

"Well, damn," said Raj, and the others murmured in agreement.

"The simulation's self-perpetuating," said Kay. "The source can't be infinite, but as there's no other way out, we have to stop it ourselves."

I stared. "Wait, so thirteen years ago... who exactly stopped the group from switching it off?"

"I have no idea," said Kay quietly. "Maybe guards, maybe a trap. We have invisibility, sciras... it ought to get us past most obstacles, but getting onto the satellite? I spoke to Dr Helm, he said the doorway port opens on the ground. And that's if the old Alliance headquarters is still standing."

"How bad is it?" I asked. "Like nuclear wasteland bad?"

"The worst," said Kay. "Picture Cethrax but with the aftereffects of a magical apocalypse. There'll be kimaros and worse. The magic level will be unstable and the air's unbreathable. The satellite's in orbit above the smog."

"What... how can we even go there, then?" I asked, more sure than ever I was missing something.

"Hover boots." Jeth spoke up for the first time. Everyone stared at him.

"Uh... what?" I gaped at him.

"We're adapting Valeria's hover-tech for cross-world use. You'll be able to take them through the doorway port. They have oxygen shields which activate automatically so you can breathe."

Ah. "And you didn't think to mention it before because..."

"I wanted to see your face. I'm joking, sis," he added when I glared at him. "I'd rather help with this than make weapons, to be honest. But it's risky. Really risky. Ada, I know Nell's a bit over-concerned with safety, but there are no doorways *on* the satellite. The Stoneskins, if they really did come from there, must have come from the ground."

"I was never sure the Stoneskins needed to breathe," I

muttered. "But there's no way they used a doorway port to escape. All the links to Thairon are blocked, right?"

"Right," said Kay. "There's the hole in our plan. My theory is the StoneKing must have got hold of the auros there, opened his own doorway, and escaped. Unless someone opened a doorway from elsewhere and smuggled the Stone-skins out, and from what the StoneKing told you, that doesn't sound like what happened."

"No," I said slowly, "it doesn't, at all. So they had auros… there could be other doorways?"

Kay paused. "There might be, but the land's ninety-nine percent wasteland. Except one area—the place directly below the satellite, the old Alliance headquarters. It's entirely made out of adamantine, so it should still be standing. But it sounds like that's the place where the doorway port used to connect to. What's left of it, anyway."

"All right." Raj sighed. "So what do the rest of us do?"

"Keep out of Walker's way if possible." Kay's gaze passed over the group. "If you want a part in this and you want to risk watching him, don't let him see you."

Iriel leaned forward. "The problem is, I can watch Walker, but I can't watch our cross-world communication channels at the same time. I was trying to scan all the files in the office."

"What for?" Kay frowned.

"Because knowledge is power," said Iriel, "and we're sorely lacking in that department. I can use this—" Her eye rotated in its socket—"To hack into the Klathican Embassy's records."

Everyone gaped at her. Kay was the first to speak. "You what?"

"What I said." Her eye spun again. "I've always wanted to do it."

"I'll spy on Walker," said Raj, to everyone's surprise.

"You sure?" asked Kay.

"I'm good. I'll be invisible, right? The others are master hackers and translators. My only skill is getting arrested. Better hope I don't get caught this time, right?"

"Thanks, man." Kay tossed him a Chameleon. "Hit the button. It's ten minutes only, so change the battery when it dies down. You don't have to get too close—just follow him if he ever leaves the office."

"I'll have some spare batteries on standby," added Jeth. "Amanda…"

"I'll tell as many people as possible not to trust Walker," she said. "Use all connections. New York already knows?"

"I told Simon," said Kay. "But no one on Earth outranks Walker."

"Not for much longer," said Amanda. "We'll get Central back where it belongs, under Alliance control." She handed Kay the notepaper with the codes on it. Kay pulled out his communicator and began scanning the pages.

"And we're going to Valeria." I nodded to Kay with more confidence than I really felt. "Jeth, tell Alber and Nell I love them and I'll definitely be back by tonight, okay?"

"Gotcha," he said. "I'll call Helm and tell him you're on the way and to get you some hover boots."

This didn't feel like a goodbye. But it might have been. There really was no way of telling, and whatever anyone said, we *were* at war. Any day might be our last.

I couldn't let go. I'd fight to the end. Not just for Kay's sake, but for the Multiverse.

We left the coffee shop. Kay let the others walk ahead, eyes on the sharp outline of Central. It looked the same—alien, and yet so familiar. How could things have gone so wrong?

"Why do I feel like he's still playing me?" he asked, quietly. "If he wants something, he'll do anything—lie, manipulate, bribe, whatever, to get it. Look at the evidence. Who are they going to believe?"

"They'll believe you, because they've known you for months, and they know everything you've said has been the truth." I squeezed his hand. "The Alliance are on your side, Kay. You're the one who saved Central. You're the one who stopped a war. He's nothing. Your father's been AWOL for five years—he has no proof to back up his claims. You do. Everyone at Central knows what you've done for the Alliance. No matter what lies he tells, he *can't* undo that, and if he tries, we'll stop him."

Kay closed his eyes, and nodded, once. "Sure. Right."

I leaned in and kissed him. "It'll be okay. Kay."

He smiled against my mouth. "If we ever get out of this alive, I don't know how I'm ever going to repay you. I'm glad you're here, Ada Fletcher."

"Me, too." I drew back. "All right. We've got this."

13

KAY

I expected to have to talk our way past the guards to get into the Passages. I didn't expect Ms Weston to block our path.

"There's no other way offworld," Ada told her.

"I'm aware of that," said Ms Weston. "Are you absolutely certain about this? I covered for you at Central and marked you as on leave of absence, but it's possible Walker has his own people amongst the guards."

Yeah. He probably does. His personal guards at Central, for one, which he'd most likely brought back from Thairon with him. Maybe he'd used them to divert attention at West Office's Passage entrance to let the kimaros escape. I was almost certain the incident had his name on it, like everything else. But that paled in comparison to what he'd done to the council.

"This isn't like when the Stoneskins took me," said Ada. "We have every protection possible and we won't even be travelling on the ground. Thairon's less dangerous than Enzar, and we both survived."

"Barely." Ms Weston spoke through clenched teeth. "If

you willingly leave Earth, there's little I can do to stop Walker from following. He took all the world-keys and the trackers."

"I have my own tracker," I said. "I know. Believe me. I thought the council would have had some kind of backup— or evacuation. Especially after what happened last time."

"I have no doubt they did," said Ms Weston. "No one could have guessed an enemy would walk right in the doors."

"It's no one's fault but Walker's," I said, quietly. "I know—I should have told you. But without proof…"

"Your word is enough for me. I understand your position, Kay, and I will do what I can to ensure Walker does not have access to any confidential information. But he has the world-keys, and his guards… I suspect they aren't entirely human."

I'd suspected the same since I'd seen those guys wearing flat black masks outside his office. Klathican hybrids, maybe.

"Carry a weapon," I told Ms Weston. "Tell Markos and everyone else at the office, too. This isn't the time to play by the rules."

"No…" Ms Weston moved aside, leaving the Passage door open to us. "I would have to agree with you there, Kay."

"Ask Amanda about the plan," Ada said. "Raj is spying on Walker. Invisible. Someone has to, but he might get hurt. And what if Walker *is* working with people offworld? Like the Stoneskins?"

"Central has precautions," said Ms Weston. "If it comes down to an attack, they will not find us undefended. Earth may have the lowest level of magic in the Alliance, but we are far from helpless. If Walker lets his guard slip, he will find no mercy from me."

"Yeah. Might get lucky." I didn't expect another miracle. But I wasn't alone this time. And I was damned if I'd let him do any more damage.

Ms Weston moved aside to allow us into the Passages.

"Thanks," I said, and we entered the blue-lit corridor. Cethrax's swamp-smell filled the air, and vox-kind blood clung to the walls. I kept one eye on Ada and the other on the shadows in case anything crept out of them. We were armed, of course, as well as carrying the sciras-chameleons. I had a tracker, too, in case I needed to focus on a particular magic signal. I'd covered all the bases. I just hoped it was enough.

The main corridor was under more guards than I'd ever seen. Every door was closed and guards lined every inch of the walls. Some carried guns, some daggers, some were mecha-style soldiers, and one door was even guarded by a clawed distant cousin of a wyvern. I looked around, but didn't see any of the flat black masks worn by Walker's guards. Ms Weston would have said if she'd seen any, but the old paranoia sat on my shoulder. Though if Walker had every world-key at Central in his possession, he didn't *need* to use the Passages.

Luckily, Valeria's guards and I were well-acquainted and Ada and I got through without a hitch. I'd said I was visiting the Alliance headquarters, which was true. We made for the hover-depot to pick up my bike for a faster route through the city. Not much faster, but while guards and enforcement officers interrupted pedestrians every few steps, the high skyways were more difficult to police due to being a hundred feet or more in the air. Ada clung to my back as we ascended to the skyway.

Below, enforcement officers swarmed the streets like shelled insects, and occasionally, the traffic would grind to a complete stop while they searched vehicles. I parked the bike on the seventieth level of Alliance HQ, in one of the designated zones, switched on the invisibility, and rather than using the heavily-guarded side entrance, climbed in through a window with Ada close behind. Dr Helm was expecting us, but it would take all day to get through security, to say nothing of gaining clearance to use the equipment as we planned. For once, Central being cut off worked in our favour, because if we ended up getting caught and questioned, there would be no response from Central. My father would only interfere if he suspected we were directly challenging his plans. Hiring hover boots didn't fall into that category. At worst we'd get a caution.

Down three corridors, up some stairs to the top floor. Dr Helm had relocated his lab to the science division of this Alliance branch, which, like everything else, sat behind adamantine-reinforced doors and walls. Helm and his assistant Lynn watched us through a camera-like device, which scanned us from head to toe, highlighting our weapons on a screen built into the door. The doors slid open and Dr Helm peeked out. He wore his usual lab-wear, reinforced against any potential accidents.

"You have two hours." He let the door slide closed behind us. "The council and most of the other staff are in a meeting, but the Klathican Ambassadors are coming soon and they'll be using the doorway port."

"That's fine," I said. "I hope we won't take too long."

And I hoped Central would still be in one piece when we returned. I'd half-expected to arrive here to find Walker had taken over the labs. He definitely had connections on Valeria.

"I don't suppose," I said to Dr Helm, "there's the slightest chance there might be a world-key around here—or even just auros."

"I don't know if Neo Greyle's Alliance has any in this building," said Dr Helm, "but if you wanted to get into the stores, your invisibility trick wouldn't fool our security. There are sensors which pick up on magic of any kind."

"Ah, crap." It was worth asking, if just because having our own means for moving between the worlds would be easier. But it couldn't be helped. Now my father had locked Earth down, there was no other option than the doorway port. Lynn tapped buttons on the side, shooting us wary looks. Well, we were armed to the teeth. Not to mention going into a world which nobody aside from my father had walked away from alive in over thirteen years.

The doorway port's side ran through symbols, one after the other. I took out my communicator to check the notes, while Ada looked around the lab.

"So we're going in on ground level?" she asked.

"These will help." Dr Helm placed two pairs of hover boots on the cluttered desk. "They have the oxygen shield enabled." He indicated a switch on the back. "That button deactivates the hover function so you can walk normally. That—" He indicated a second switch on the inside of the heel—"is the accelerator. It responds to the slightest movement. Want to test them out first?"

"Probably a good idea," said Ada. "I didn't do great last time, but I *was* only wearing one boot."

"You need both for balance," said Dr Helm.

The boots were metal-plated, and when I put them on, the insides moulded to fit to my feet.

"Huh, must be a new feature." Ada experimentally bounced on her heels. "I nearly fell out of it last time. But I did steal it from Delta." She bit her lip. "I never thought I'd be doing this again."

"Me neither." I flashed her a quick smile. I still didn't know how to talk to her now she knew the worst of me. But she'd seen me act like Walker before, and chose to stick around anyway. After everything we'd been through, she was willingly walking into danger at my side, again.

I took her hand and dug my heel into the boot, levitating a few inches off the ground. Ada yelped as I pulled her into the air. The acceleration was faster than I'd anticipated and we both narrowly avoided colliding with the ceiling. The lab spun around us as we flipped over in mid-air.

"Watch the equipment!" Dr Helm shouted from the ground. "They have impact shields, but it'll hurt if you hit that wall."

"Kay, cut it out!" Ada half-laughed, trying to tug her hand free, but I hit the accelerator again. This time we shot back towards the ground and spun, then accelerated to the ceiling. I let go, and Ada ended up hanging upside-down in mid-air, laughing helplessly. "You dick."

"Think I could get used to these." I tapped the heel of the hover boot. "All right. We have two hours, right?"

"Give or take," said Dr Helm, serious once again. "You should hurry. But I don't know what awaits on the other side. Are you absolutely sure you have a plan? Because if I get caught, they'll close the doorway port and possibly stop it ever reaching Thairon again. There's no way back."

"That's why I'd prefer to have a world-key," I said. "But there's no other way. We have to get the council out of the simulation before things get any worse."

Honestly, our plan had 'last straw' written all over it. But challenging Walker head-on would only make things worse both for us *and* the council. Trapped in a simulation, they wouldn't be able to stop Walker if he went back to finish them off.

However… we weren't alone. Both Ada and I had cameras and recording devices clipped to the inside of our guard jackets. There was a chance the technology would burn out on contact with a high-magic world, but if eyewitness testimony wasn't good enough anymore, we'd reach the people of Earth via the next best method. If there was any proof that the Stoneskins had come from there, and that Walker had imprisoned the council himself, nobody would be able to deny it.

The doorway port opened. Ada looked warily into the blue light. "You sure we can breathe out there?"

"The hover boots were tested in zero-oxygen zones," said Dr Helm. "I tested them myself, actually."

"Well, that's something," I muttered.

And I took the first step through the doorway. The world on the other side looked no different from the lab, but right away, the change in the magic level rubbed against my skin. It was high here—higher than I thought it had a right to be.

"What *is* that?" asked Ada, in a whisper, walking to my side. We stood in a corridor, windowless and made of black adamantine. Just like the lab. Except there was no equipment here. Nothing at all.

This was the Alliance's old base. Of course it would look like any other base on a high-technology world. Thairon might be dying, but its technology had been one of the most advanced in the Multiverse. Simulations. Satellites. Cyborgs.

"Kimaros!" Ada shouted.

Sparks shot towards us and we ducked. Lucky the ceiling was high enough they sailed right over our heads, absorbed into the adamantine ceiling. Minor sparks. I took Ada's hand and turned invisible, waiting. No other attack followed, but Ada's hand trembled with the impact of the magic thrumming in the air.

"See anything?" I asked her in an undertone.

"I can't sense where it is," she whispered.

The corridor dead-ended at the doorway port. Only one way to go—towards the kimaros, wherever it was.

I activated the hover boots and Ada did likewise, and we sped to the corridor's other end. No sign of the monster. But I'd sensed it, and those sparks had come from somewhere nearby. I hadn't expected to run into a kimaros right out of the gate. Guess that answered the question of whether the events which had destroyed the planet had been magic-related. The ceiling, walls and floor were entirely made of adamantine, so the kimaros surely couldn't be *inside* the building…

The magic level sparked without warning. My skin buzzed, even with Ada's glove blocking the worst of the static. I'd felt this strong a charge once before—on Vey-Xanetha, faced with a living god. My teeth rattled in my skull, and if not for the layer of adamantine built into my uniform, I suspected my skin would burn to touch whatever caused this level of static.

Luckily, the rising magic didn't knock the hover boots out of action, because the floor was uneven and cracked in places. We flew into a hall-like room, where human-sized capsules littered the floor, wires thick as tree branches tangled together between the capsules and a series of dust-covered monitors at the back of the hall. I dropped to ground level to peer through the nearest capsule window, my breath frosting the glass in an exhale of relief that there was nobody inside.

Every capsule appeared to be empty, and no lights shone from the computers hooked up to the monitors. Only dust remained. The council weren't here. They must be where the simulator was located—on the satellite.

"Don't touch anything," I whispered to Ada. "It wouldn't surprise me if there was some kind of trap."

"There were… people in there?" She stared at the inter-locking wires leading from the capsules to the machinery underneath the monitors.

"A while ago. The population isn't here. This was prob-ably a sim-room."

The next door led to a corridor made of glass all over like a greenhouse, or one of Klathica's bridges. Outside, black-scorched ground stretched to the horizon, the skeletons of buildings rising through thick grey smog.

"The air's toxic out there," I said. "I read somewhere that thousands of people died literally overnight. They never did find out what caused it." I squinted through the smog, up at where the sky should be. "The satellite's somewhere up there. We might not be able to see it from here."

I pulled out my communicator to check the map. I'd saved the whole thing, as well as all the codes.

"This building's totally out of use," said Ada. "But—how did your father know where to go? Has it been like this for thirteen years?"

"Longer. The council relocated before. But this old Alliance HQ was kept as the only viable place to build a doorway—the air in here used to be breathable, but I guess the oxygen ran out. They could have migrated to another world—that's actually what the majority of the population voted to do. They went to Klathica instead. But too many became addicted to the simulation programme. The government had no trouble moving them to the satellite without them even being aware of it. If anyone did wake up and try to get down to ground level, I imagine they either fell to their deaths or suffocated."

"That's… twisted." Ada's face paled. "These people who programmed the simulators… even if they're dead, they're still dangerous."

"Yeah, but when we switch it off, they'll disappear." And the population of Thairon… I didn't know where to start with them. Some had spent nearly their entire lives in virtual reality. We needed to set the council free first, then work out a plan on how to evacuate the satellite and help everyone escape their virtual prison.

We passed through more deserted rooms and corridors. The building might have been a mirror of Klathica's headquarters, on the inside. But the burned-out landscape was bare of life. There didn't seem to be a door, but a skylight on the ceiling led to a landing dock on the building's roof. There, we found the rusting remains of old sky-craft, probably spares for the building's evacuation. I assumed everyone must have got out somehow. Or been thrown into the wasteland. No traces of human life were visible below.

"Where's this satellite?" asked Ada, staring through the smog.

"Higher up," I said. "We could cross the ground a bit, see if we can get a better view from further along."

There didn't seem to be anything on ground level, anyway, other than the occasional skeletal remains of an old building. The place was long dead.

I activated the hover boots and glided down from the roof. Ada followed, somersaulting in mid-air.

"That was deliberate," she said.

"Sure it was." The smile faded from my face when I spotted the logo on the side of the building. *KimaroTech.*

"That place was owned by KimaroTech?" Ada frowned.

"The whole Alliance on Thairon was." Even now, it was difficult to find the words. "It was Walker who financed the simulators in the first place."

"Your father?" Ada faltered. It still hadn't sunk in. Not all of it. But she believed me. That was more than I'd ever dared hope.

"No. My grandfather. They've had the sim-tech for over thirty years."

"Wow." Ada shook her head, looking up at the sky. "I see something up there..."

So did I, now I looked. The outline of a disc shape hovered above the smoke. "That's the satellite. It's lower down than I thought." I kicked the hover boots into action.

A shower of sparks erupted from the sky. I swore and backtracked, the hairs on my arms rising.

"The hell was that?"

"Kimaros!" yelled Ada, and I turned to see a shape unfold from the fog, a red cloud with half-formed teeth and claws.

"Shit."

I briefly let go of Ada's hand and shot a jolt of power at the creature. The beast shrank back, screeching. I was willing to bet it hadn't been challenged before—but there might be any number of the bastards here, considering the magic level.

Adrenaline spiked. I wasn't aware until now how much I wanted to hit a willing target, and I dug my heel into the accelerator, shooting towards the creature at a speed that lifted the hair from my head and stirred up a nonexistent wind. The kimaros swiped at me with a claw, still half-hidden in smoke.

"Come and face me. Come on…"

"Kay, watch out!" Ada shouted, and I kicked off the acceleration before it carried me right into the smog—a good job, because two more kimaros had risen from the smoke in a hail of red sparks to join the first.

A presence brushed against me with the suddenness of an electric current. Though it didn't communicate in words, it felt unfriendly. I cursed, shaking my head before the presence took over as Veyak had. Couldn't be one of the smaller kimaros. There was something bigger, more powerful, hiding in the fog.

Sparks shot out and I swore again, forced to accelerate higher to avoid them. In a blur of movement, Ada was above, firing magic-shots down at them. The creatures shrank away, but an angry screech told us one of them had been hit.

I reached out a hand and let the charge build under the surface. Level two. No way was I risking level three in a place like this. But it was enough. The sharp bolt of lightning I fired speared the smog, and as the backlash hit, Ada and I were already a mile up in the air.

"I could get used to this," she said breathlessly, diving

once again to fire magic at them. "I'll mention it to the tech team when we get back."

"Long-range fighting? Yeah." Adrenaline buzzed through my veins as I threw another magic shot at the kimaros. They might be powered by the level of magic, but then, so was I. Purple-red light blazed across my vision, and a cracking noise rent the air as two of the kimaros exploded into smoke.

I glanced up. We'd risen higher than I'd thought, and now I clearly saw the shape above the smog. It was curved, metal, half-moon-shaped. The satellite.

"Damn," said Ada, noticing. "How do we get in there?"

"There's a hatch near the back."

My heart beat fast, too fast, and not from the hover boots. I fired one last shot at the writhing kimaros as we flew higher, to the floating satellite.

I had the codes memorised from Elizabeth's will. My hands shook as I keyed them in, my fingers stumbling on the buttons. It took three attempts to put the code in.

Then the hatch slid open. A narrow, tomb-like corridor waited ahead. Suddenly, there didn't seem to be enough oxygen in the shield. I closed my eyes and willed the images to go away. She might not have died here. I didn't know if she'd ever made it onto the satellite.

Breathe, Kay. Remember to breathe.

More corridors. More security codes. Ada and I stayed side by side, invisible, hover boots above the ground, moving swiftly yet carefully to avoid triggering any traps.

And finally… the main room, shaped like a giant cocoon with no windows. It was even worse than I'd expected. Thousands upon thousands of human-shaped capsules hooked up to life support machines, thick cables covering the ground. I couldn't see the faces behind the fogged glass. They might have been sleeping.

An army, ready to awaken.

Humans, trapped in a web.

"Follow the cables," I said, in a faint whisper. They would take us to the source. The machine powering the simulators. The door had sealed itself behind us, and a series of blue lights on the ceiling proclaimed the oxygen levels were normal. So the air was breathable in here. Fluorescent white ceiling lights bathed everything in a bright glow at odds with the utter lifelessness of the place. Silence pervaded, apart from a faint humming which seemed to come from everywhere around us. These were the most sophisticated systems I'd ever seen. Thick glass capsules linked up with wires to machinery that presumably kept their captives alive.

The cables ended at a bank of monitors at the back of the room. I followed the lines with my hands, figuring it out. Freeing the council was paramount. Once we got them back to Earth, we'd come back later with a world-key to get the others out. There might only be a handful of people who even knew this was happening, but we wouldn't be alone once we'd revealed Walker's lies to the Multiverse. Once we'd deposed him.

As for freeing the trapped people, they'd be disorientated once they woke up. They might even attack us. I didn't have a clue how we were going to get them down to the ground and off this godforsaken wasteland. We'd need to bring backup first, then bring the satellite down to ground level to get everyone out. Saving tens of thousands of people seemed less insurmountable than knocking Walker off his pedestal. But I couldn't afford to accept an alternative.

Ada made a strangled noise. "They're here…"

I joined her beside a set of three capsules. Anger surged through my veins at the sight of our three council members, locked in stasis. Wires ran from the capsules to a single monitor, one of many in banks amongst the numerous capsules.

"I'll wake them," I said.

I instinctively squeezed Ada's hand before laying my other palm flat on the monitor beside the three capsules, firing magic right into it. Cracks spread across the shiny coating, and as Ada joined her power to mine, we sent it right through the core of the machinery. Screens cracked, wires split apart like severed veins, and the resounding noise echoed through the eerily silent chamber.

Ada pulled her hand out of mine, turning visible and peering into the nearest case. "He's not awake."

Neither were the others. The wires to the council members' prisons ended at the monitors we'd destroyed. Ada tugged on the door to the capsule containing one of the council members, but it wouldn't open.

"Let me try." I dug my hands into the door and pushed, but it didn't give. Locked? No, there were no keys. The capsules had automatic doors in place. They should have opened when the simulation switched off.

Which meant it was still active.

Magic remained, pulsing through the air like a beating heart.

"They're not waking up."

"Because that's not the source controlling them," said Ada, and at the same time, the cold, dark presence pushed against me again. My hands tingled in response.

No. "The kimaros," I said. "There's a stronger magic force here. It's not just out there... it's in this room." The source controlling the simulator was *living.* Like Veyak.

Ada's eyes rounded, her face pale under the flickering ceiling lights. "But where is it?"

"Not in here." I led the way through the room to a door at the end, using my hover boots to clear the space as quickly as possible. All we found was a small, dusty engine room. That was it. No living sources, no presence of magic. The source must be outside somewhere. Ada and I looked at once another.

"All right," I said. "I can pilot this thing, but we don't want to leave it on ground level with those monsters out there."

"Good point." Ada looked over her shoulder at the capsules, biting her lip. "It feels like we're abandoning them."

"We don't have much choice. I'd rather avoid waking everyone at once."

We headed back into the main room. Row after row of capsules filled the space. If not for the hover boots, we might easily become lost in the dark labyrinth of wires and glass cases. As it was, within a couple of minutes, we were back in the main corridor again. After checking the demolished machines wouldn't be a danger to the people left behind, we made for the hatch.

The knot in my chest loosened a little as we emerged from the satellite. Even though we hadn't achieved our objective. If another creature like a living god was responsible for keeping the simulator running, there was no way in hell we'd get out of here without some serious backlash on the magic level. And we still hadn't found evidence of the Stoneskins.

As we descended, Ada took aim and fired a bolt of magic through the centre of the smog. Even the bright light didn't penetrate the gloom. Not so much as a sound disturbed the darkness. But I still felt the magic pulsing from below. We reached ground level again, this time more than a mile out from the building on the ground.

From here, the smear of grey obscuring the view suddenly looked more like mist than fog. Almost... like the ledge of a cliff.

The blood froze in my veins.

Not that.

My mind was playing tricks on me. It couldn't be...

The hover boots deactivated and I dropped a foot in air, the sudden motion startling me back to life. *Shit.* I wasn't standing on a cliff. The greyness spread like fog, and I looked up to where Ada still hovered, eyes wide.

"Hell," she whispered. "That's the void."

14

ADA

I'd recognise the smoke-covered cliff anywhere. I'd nearly died when I'd thrown myself over the edge of the void between worlds to stop the magic burning in the source the Stoneskins had pressed on me from blowing up the Multiverse. Kay had saved me—with adamantine.

The grey smothering the air wasn't smoke, it was a doorway. Just like the ones the Stoneskins had opened. The void looked impenetrable, impossible to see which world lay on the other side.

I shivered. Kay had descended a foot or so, his feet skimming the charred ground, and I dropped to join him. "The void. How can it be here?" My voice sounded impossibly small. "The void might lead anywhere in the Multiverse. Besides, what's even powering it?"

"Auros?" He shook his head. "I have no idea. But it must end somewhere." He snapped the hover boots to life. I hit the heel of my own boot, and followed.

"Wait!" I caught up to him. "The source might not be on the ground."

At least, I couldn't see anything. But light shone from within the fog, faintly grey tinged with red. With hover boots, we could actually cross to the other side without falling into the abyss like I almost had last time. But no way would I go near the void without having some idea which world hid over the edge.

I had a few suspicions, and none meant good news.

"Ada, look out!" Kay stared at something behind me. I spun on the spot and almost lost control of the hover boots again, but caught myself just in time. Lucky I did, because I'd been inches from colliding with what looked like a tall, shimmering wall.

Kay, at my side in an instant, grabbed my arm and yanked me back. I yelped, tugging my hand free. Some kind of magic forcefield? Damn.

"Sorry—wanted to make sure you were out of range." He shot a bolt of magic at the wall.

The shimmering tower lit up in a fireworks display of red sparks. They didn't stop there, but rose higher and higher, into the smog—easily ten storeys tall.

I stared, speechless, as a tower-like black-walled building appeared where nothing had been there before—sleek and imposing, like a windowless Central with no other features. Flat and black, it stood like a dark shape cut out of the world. When I dropped a foot or so in the air, the building's surface shimmered black-blue.

"Bloodrock," said Kay. "I thought it looked familiar."

"Damn." I shook my head and gaped up at the towering structure. Just like the lab, the new building appeared to be made of adamantine. But it couldn't be, if bloodrock had kept it hidden. Again, that odd blue light passed over the surface.

"It's made out of auros," I said. "That must be what's powering the doorway... somehow." I couldn't see every angle of it. But the building covered one side of the void. The other was lost in the fog.

"Hellfire. You're right." Kay approached the building warily. "But if it's made out of auros, it's not magic-proof. We should be able to find a way in…"

A shiver curled around my spine. There was something eerie and unnatural about the sleek building stabbing upwards from the decaying, wasted earth. If it wasn't magic-proofed, I could get us in.

But what if there were more kimaros inside? I was as vulnerable to magic burn as anyone else, and going into a strange building on a hostile world fell into the category of life-risking decisions. Then again, so did coming to this world in the first place.

There were no windows, but there *was* a door on the ground. I dropped to the ground, hover boots skimming the cracked earth, and tentatively tried the door with my re-gloved hand. It swung open.

"That's… suspicious." I peered into the gloom, distinguishing nothing except a dark corridor.

"Tell me about it," said Kay. "All right. I'd say we go invisible."

"Good move."

I took his hand, briefly, and when he brushed the skin of my wrist under the glove, we both turned invisible. Drawing in a breath, I followed him into the building.

More dark corridors awaited. More doors either side. A clicking sound told me Kay was testing them to see if they opened. Only one did, and it led to a deserted meeting room.

Through a combination of coordination and luck, we covered the ground floor without colliding with one another. There was no sound, at all. Nothing living in here. When we came to the final corridor, I whispered, "Are we seriously going to check every floor?"

A sound in the darkness made me spin around again.

"That's the side facing the doorway." Kay indicated the corridor ahead.

The corridor ran parallel to the side of the building facing the void, and there was a closed door. The buzzing sensation of the magic became unbearable. My hands clenched inside the gloves. The door clicked, though neither Kay nor I had touched it.

Hell. Someone was on the other side, directly from the void. I held my breath. What world could be outside? Surely, if it was Enzar, I'd feel it. I'd know my homeworld.

The door opened, revealing a strip of light from the void, and a dark shape crawled through. I recognised the short, hunched outline of a dreyvern. Cethrax's goblin-like monsters.

And behind it was a human-sized shape. Human, but not human. The light fell on its marbled grey skin and confirmed my suspicion: it was no ordinary person, but one of them. One of the Stoneskins.

Impossible... they died.

Kay tugged on my hand, alerting me that they were coming this way. We moved back along the corridor, deactivating the hover boots so the faint whirring sound wouldn't give us away. The Stoneskin took the lead and unlocked one of the doors. I crept closer, staring over its shoulder.

Every drop of blood in my body turned to ice.

It was a lab, full of human-sized capsules. Inside each was one of them. A Stoneskin. At least fifty of them. Human-sized figures trapped behind glass.

Not all the Stoneskins had died. There was more than one lab all along.

I couldn't move. These Stoneskins hadn't escaped with the StoneKing. They'd remained here, at the mercy of whoever had created them to be used in Enzar's war. I was willing to bet that void, the doorway, led into Enzar. But the goblin…

Cethrax must be linked with Enzar, through the void.

Kay let go of my hand, a whirring sound telling me his hover boots had reactivated. But the Stoneskin was already leaving the lab, the goblin on its tail. They spoke, in Classical Klathican but too quickly to make out the words, then the Stoneskin struck the dreyvern hard enough to send it head-over-heels down the corridor. The Stoneskin walked through the door without looking back.

Snap. The door shut, and the goblin staggered to its feet, blood dripping from its nose. It yelped, a gurgling cry, as it lifted off the ground.

"Who do you serve, goblin?" Kay spoke Classical Klathican flawlessly.

I switched my hover boots on and flew to join Kay. My heart beat frantically against my ribs as every survival instinct flared to life. *The Stoneskins. Enzar. Cethrax…* What in hell *was* this place?

"Who in the under-grounds are you?" screeched the dreyvern. "You speak in the human tongue."

"So you do speak," said Kay. "That means you're from the Vox Grarl's territory—or what used to be his territory. Who do you serve now?"

What's his plan? But it was a clever question, really. The Stoneskins had never been created with a will of their own—and like so many others in this game, they'd been created to answer to Enzar. It all came back to the Empire in the end. To the war.

"Grarl," snarled the goblin. "Let me go, or he'll kill me."

"So you still serve your Vox," said Kay. "And who does *he* answer to? Who controls Cethrax?"

"And the Stoneskins," I added. "Is it the same person? People?"

"We all serve the Undergod, human," snarled the goblin. "He watches us. Always."

"Spare me," said Kay. "A *human* brought you here. Right?"

"The magebloods," choked the goblin. "Walker was wrong. The magebloods are going to win the war, and win us the Multiverse."

"Walker?" Kay's voice was deadly quiet. "How do you know that name?"

The goblin sobbed and didn't answer.

"Tell me the truth or die," said Kay.

"They say the name, they all say the name," cried the goblin. "The mageblood humans. They say Walker is finished."

"And why's that?" asked Kay.

"They're going to kill him," moaned the goblin. "He got away before, but they'll find him. The Undergod watches everyone."

What? He couldn't be right. But if they really meant Kay's father, that meant…

They're coming after Earth.

"When are they planning to do this?" demanded Kay. "And how?"

"I know not! I'm only here to watch the slaves. Let me go."

"What do the magebloods want with Cethrax?" I asked loudly.

I moved back a few steps. We needed to go back to Earth *now,* and warn everyone. I doubted the magebloods would care who got in the way of their attack. Even if Walker *was* their target. I didn't for a second trust the word of a goblin.

God. I can't believe this is happening. Just when I thought I'd shaken off the Stoneskins, the bastards had come back. More to the point, the *magebloods* were behind it? They had *Cethrax?* So that's who the Vox had been speaking to. Enzar. The bloody monsters were in league with my homeworld. To top it all off, that was what the Stoneskins had been created for in the first place. To fight on the side of the magebloods. The Stoneskins here weren't fugitives searching for revenge, led by the StoneKing. They were an invincible army created to dominate my homeworld.

I couldn't even take it all in. There was no time to think. Only act.

"Whoever you are, you are going to die," croaked the goblin. "The Undergod spares no one."

"You're deluded," said Kay, "and I'm about done with you. Tell me everything you know about the masters you serve and their plans, and I might just leave you alive here."

The goblin groaned. "The magebloods have Cethrax. They have other worlds. All are united under the Great Undergod. They will destroy the Alliance with their slaves."

Every word hammered into me like a rock. The three most dangerous worlds in the Multiverse—Cethrax, Enzar and Thairon—were allies. The Alliance lay under the control of a madman. And nobody on our side knew but the two of us. I shakily tapped the hidden camera inside my jacket, hoping to god it was picking the goblin's speech up. This was all the proof we had. Who the hell would believe it? Certainly not Walker.

"The Stoneskins," said Kay. "They were KimaroTech's project here? Right?"

"Walker tried to stop it. But it was too late. We answer to the magebloods. He was trapped in the humans' games, and the Multiverse moved on."

Tried to stop it? But I'd thought Kay's father had been responsible for creating the Stoneskins.

"The hell does that mean?" Kay's voice betrayed nothing.

The goblin choked. "I don't know! The Great Undergod told me. He whispers it to me every minute of every day. He's coming for the Alliance… leave the humans to their games…"

A presence brushed against me, magic sparking in my veins, and Kay reappeared. By the look on his face, I must have become visible again, too.

The kimaros. It must be controlling the goblin somehow.

Oh, no. He'd said 'the Great Undergod'... was he talking about the *kimaros?*

Never mind that. Cethrax, the Stoneskins *and* the magebloods were after the Alliance. And we'd walked right into the middle of it.

I stared dumbly at the goblin, which screeched as it saw me. "Enzarian! Traitor—"

There was a horrible *snap.* It fell limply to the ground.

Kay's arms dropped to his sides.

"You killed it," I gasped.

"I was always going to," he said flatly. "We need to warn Earth."

Warn Earth there was going to be an attack... but from where? Surely not here. Cethrax, most likely, because they were the one link between the void and Earth. My head swum. The magebloods were supposed to be *losing* the war. Yet that wasn't the important thing here. What he'd said about Walker...

"He was working against them?" I asked Kay.

"Don't trust a word the bastard said." Kay moved unsteadily on the hover boots, but his grip on my arm was firm. "Come on."

"Yeah." We hurried out into the corridor. "What he said about the Great Undergod, though—I don't think it was all nonsense. I reckon he meant the kimaros. It's one of them— like Veyak. The magebloods must be using it to convince the lower Cethraxians to work for them."

"Thought so," said Kay. "Figures, really. Wish we could knock this place down."

"I know." But we didn't have a way to destroy the Stoneskins themselves, even if we blew the building up. Earth might already have been attacked by the army waiting on the other side.

I picked up speed, and we found the exit, crossing the burned ground back to the base so quickly that dizziness made my head spin. I didn't dare slow down. If the army had attacked while we'd been gone…

"Goddammit," Kay said, as we went back into the first building through the door. He pocketed his communicator. "No signal."

I checked my own communicator. "We need to warn them. I hope the cameras didn't burn out."

I one-handedly typed a message, though it was beyond me to think of words to sum up the situation. *Someone's going to attack Earth, possibly Cethrax, and they're trying to kill Lawrence Walker.* It sounded convincing enough. But the council weren't even there, and the Alliance guards couldn't stand up to an army of magic-wielders, *or* the entirety of Cethrax's forces. Throw in the Stoneskins and we might as well let Walker finish us off. Even if we managed to convince the other allied worlds to fight on our side. Assuming Walker hadn't alienated everyone.

"I'm not gonna defend the bastard." Kay eyed the message on my communicator screen. "I'll throw him to the wolves if I have to. But unless there's proof, he won't believe us."

"Unless…" I couldn't say *unless we're too late.* Every movement threatened to paralyse me. The combined power of Cethrax, the Stoneskins, the magebloods… and the message wouldn't send. Damn. "No. We have to go back first."

Kay nodded, and we ran through the corridors of the base.

"Why *Earth?*" I burst out, kicking up speed until I was forced to stop inches from hitting a corridor wall. "Why is it always Earth?"

"No clue." Kay accelerated to my side. "This way."

We spun around the final corner and back through the doorway port. Dr Helm exclaimed as we shot through it, tumbling head over heels into the lab.

"What happened?" He jumped back, hurrying to close the port behind us.

"There's a threat to Earth," said Kay. "A big one. What's wrong with these boots?"

"They're reacting to the change in atmosphere." Dr Helm recovered himself. "Nothing to worry about."

"Good," said Kay, "because we need to get there *now*. Enzar are threatening to attack Earth, and they're working with Cethrax."

"Why?" Dr Helm gaped at us. "How do you know?"

"They sent a message. There's no time to explain. If you can, warn Central that Lawrence Walker's a target for an attack."

"Walker?"

Kay was already heading for the door, hover boots activated. I hurried after him.

"You can't take those with you!" Dr Helm looked scandalised.

"No time," said Kay. "I don't have a bloody clue how to control these things high up. We'll use the bike."

We pelted through the lab and out the side-door, where Kay wasted no time elevating the hover bike to the right level and hitting the acceleration the instant we were in the seat. I clung to him as we shot into the air.

"Where are you going?" I yelled in his ear.

"Shortcut!" he shouted back, pulling a lever. The bike righted itself, on a level with the rooftops. I closed my eyes against a wave of dizziness as the rows of hover traffic spun below me. A warren of streets and roads, teeming with countless people. If Cethrax attacked Earth, they might come here next. How in hell were we meant to warn everyone with the council gone and Walker casting doubt on our every statement?

A square-shaped outline appeared in the sky. This must be what Valeria's sky-doorways looked like from the outside. Kay steered the bike up to the edge and leaned right out of the seat to push the door open. On the other side, the Passages waited, a gleaming blue doorway in the sky.

It was too late to stop the bike, even as the shouts of Enforcement officers below reached us on the breeze. Kay hit the acceleration and we shot into the Passages.

"Jesus!" I yelped. He performed a U-turn around a blue-lit corner that almost took me out of my seat. I hung onto his jacket for dear life. "We can't take this thing to Earth!"

"I'm aware of that." He parked the bike at a Passage inter-section, and hopped down. I followed, wincing, and got out my communicator. Still no connection. *Damn.* We'd have to tell them in person.

Kay ran ahead, while I hurried to catch up. We'd come out of the doorway near Central's Passage entrance, which meant a patrol must be nearby. Kay didn't stop until we reached the doorway leading onto the streets of London.

"What the devil are you two doing?" Carl asked as we sprinted out, ignoring more exclamations from the other guards on duty.

"Has anything happened at Central? Or with Cethrax?" asked Kay breathlessly.

Carl's eyes narrowed as they fixated on our hover boot-clad feet. "No. Why?"

"We heard about a threat from Enzar. They're working with Cethrax, planning to kill Walker, and I doubt they'll spare anyone who gets in the way. This is urgent." Kay's foot tapped, still encased in the hover boot, which the guards behind Carl were eying curiously.

Carl's incredulous expression cleared, and he tapped his communicator. "Danica warned me something might happen… but you had better be right."

We ran back to Central—well, half-hovered, until Carl shouted something after us about offworld tech regulations. The guards at the back gate, however, let us in without a fuss, or even a glance at the boots.

It should have struck me as suspicious.

But the crowd in the entrance hall was what finally made me stop, gripping Kay's hand to warn him to deactivate the hover boots. Every Alliance employee seemed to be here. I'd never seen so many people gathered in one place at Central.

There he stood: at the head of the hall. Lawrence Walker. Along with the rest of the council.

I blinked, convinced I stared at a bizarrely detailed hallucination.

"The hell?" said Kay, eyes fixed not on Walker, but on Mr Shean and the others. The council was supposed to be *gone.* They were supposed to be on Thairon. I'd *seen* them, in those glass cases, locked in stasis.

"There you are," said Walker, loudly. "I'm glad you decided to join us."

"What's going on?" asked Kay. He shook his head, seeming to pull himself together. "If you haven't already heard, Enzar and Cethrax are planning to attack you."

"Oh, that?" Walker made a dismissive wave of the hand. "I took care of it. Their assassins are now in our holding cells."

My heart missed a beat. "What? Didn't they send the Stoneskins?"

"Those mythical creatures of yours again? They were human, sadly misled. They stand to await trial. Now the council has returned, things can proceed as normal."

The council. They were supposed to be trapped in simulation. I scanned the crowd for a familiar face and saw

Amanda standing beside her sister. Ms Weston looked, for the first time since I'd seen her, frightened.

"When did the council come back?" Kay demanded.

"You are mistaken," said Walker. "They have been here all along. I think it's time to call this meeting to a close. I saw one or two of you with recording devices? Feel free to send your videos to whoever you feel would benefit. I would hate for anyone to miss out on hearing my words."

What... the hell? They were nodding. Walker must have some kind of control over the crowd. I glanced at Kay, whose fists were clenched, his face white.

"Actually, you haven't," Ms Weston interjected. "What of Thairon? Until today, that was your priority. There are twenty thousand people locked into a simulation, and have been so for thirteen years."

My heart lurched. We couldn't have brought them all back to Earth without help. Not before we set the council free and brought Walker down... *but Cethrax is coming. Walker's lying to everyone.*

"That is sadly not our concern," said Walker. "Defending Earth is paramount. Besides, many of them will have lived in stasis for their entire lives. Disrupting it now will result in anarchy and bloodshed. The system is safe. It was tested and Earth-approved before it was fully put into practise and became permanent."

"Tested on whom?" Ms Weston raised an eyebrow. "Willing volunteers?"

No. Nobody in their right mind would volunteer. Nobody but a child punished for their faith in someone who was supposed to take care of them. Who was supposed to do the opposite of what Lawrence Walker had done.

Kay himself stared at Walker, fury etched on his face. I wished I could reassure him. But right now, I didn't see a way out of this situation without us either ending up arrested or dead. Assuming the army wasn't already on the doorstep.

"Enough about Thairon," said Walker. "We will revisit it once the Alliance, and all its worlds, are safe. You may leave."

The crowd dispersed. Walker beckoned Kay and I forward.

"I must have a quick discussion with the council," he said. "But I'd be very interested in talking to you next, Ada. I think we missed the chance to be better acquainted."

Yeah, because you hit me with your stick. I looked desperately from one council member to the other. Mrs Grey, Mr Shean... all their faces were blank. Brainwashed? They couldn't have been here the whole time. I'd seen them behind the glass.

Just for an instant, the air shimmered, and another face looked at me with Mr Shean's eyes. I stepped back, and Kay steadied my arm.

Bloodrock.

Walker and the council left the hall into a side room. I turned to Kay, panic bursting in my chest. "He—the council. They're not themselves. They're other people, disguised, with bloodrock solution." And only magic-wielders, if anyone, would be able to tell the difference. The rest of Central's staff mustn't have noticed. Raj and Iriel hadn't been amongst the crowd. Worry squirmed through my chest. Were they hiding, or had Walker found out they were watching him?

"He's duping everyone," said Kay. "Hear what he said about videos? The world's noticing by now. There's no way they wouldn't. So he's playing on that. Setting himself up as the hero."

"That's madness," I said. "And about the attack? He *can't* have known." We were protected here inside Central, but if someone attacked Earth—I didn't dare think about it. My *family* were out there.

"It's all a lie." Kay shook his head. "He's spinning a narrative to the people of Earth. In his mind, he's reassuring them the Alliance have the situation under control. Imagine the panic if Earth's entire seven-billion-strong population knew we had enemies like *that* out there."

"Fair point." I could barely wrap my head around it. I wasn't sure I wanted to, because just the thought was enough to make me want to curl up in a corner or run away. The Alliance was supposed to keep everyone safe. To most people on Earth, they were mythical figures that defended the world from monsters. In a world where people did a pretty good job of killing each other without outside influence, the Alliance symbolised hope. Now Walker was trying to ruin it all.

Kay leaned in close. "Don't let him play mind games with you, too. I don't believe for a second he doesn't know Enzar are a threat. He's aware of his enemies. He'd be dead otherwise."

I nodded helplessly, unable to think of anything else to do.

"Ada, don't let him know he's won. He thrives on the power he has over you, even over your emotions. Take that away and his confidence shatters."

"But—Enzar. Cethrax. Thairon. Doesn't world domination matter more to him than playing games with me? He won't have an empire to rule if Cethrax and Enzar trample us flat."

"I know," said Kay. "If it's any consolation, we have a world of proof that he's a deluded asshole now."

"That doesn't help. Sorry." I took a steadying breath. My hands curled into fists. Even being prepared didn't make it any easier to face Walker, now I knew the full extent of the twisted things he'd done. I wasn't sure I'd be able to restrain myself from ripping his face off. But getting arrested would do neither of us any favours. I clenched my teeth to keep myself from screaming to the crowd that they'd been fooled by a madman.

Walker parted with the rest of the council and beckoned me to follow him into the side room. Kay gave my hand a reassuring squeeze, then let go. As I walked towards Walker, two of his guards emerged from the room. He gestured to them to go back inside. *It's a warning. He wants you to know he has backup.*

With the adrenaline buzzing through my veins from our near-miss on Thairon, I didn't even have it in me to be terrified of Walker or his creepy masked guards. I followed him into the room, hiding my shaking hands behind my back. He indicated I take a seat. The door closed behind us, and I had to resist the impulse to check I still had my weapons. No one had taken them away. Which meant Walker thought he had nothing to fear from me.

I didn't know what to say. Emotions tore through me, flashes of anger and horror. This man had tortured Kay, and now he was prepared to watch a world razed to the ground. No words could encompass that. I was certain he knew I must hate him.

"So, Ada," said Walker. "I've wanted to talk to you for a while. I'm sure you have a great many things to say to me, especially concerning your... friend. And his mother, if he told you about her."

I gave him my most insolent look. "No. I don't have anything to say to you at all."

"The reports paint a picture of you as a little more mature," said Walker. "But I confess I had a little trouble tracking some of them down."

Yeah. Markos hid all the reports, and so did Ms Weston. Everyone's working against you, Walker. But in having everyone here under his power, he was still winning.

"Luckily," Walker continued, "I have detained a young Ambassador who claims to know the truth. You know Raj?"

My heart dropped. *No. You bastard.* "We went on a mission together. Where is he?"

"In the cells." Walker's mouth twisted. "Contrary to what you've apparently heard, Ada, I don't like to kill people."

"You just don't like to get your hands dirty," I said. "Like the Stoneskins project."

"What do you know of that?"

"Your family started it."

Careful. He might not know we'd been to Thairon. He wasn't psychic, but he might have had spies. I didn't trust what the goblin had said.

"My father." Walker's face darkened. "He started Kimaro-Tech to build weapons to sell to Enzar, and covered it up with humanitarian claims. I've spent my life trying to undo the damage—and the least I can do is reassure the population of Earth that their planet isn't about to go to war."

"You're lying." I winced inwardly at how weak I sounded, compared to him. "You're looking out for no one but yourself. You lied to the whole planet. Why would I assume you'd tell the truth to me? You don't even know me."

"You're like him," said Walker. "An idealist. Humans are selfish at the core. Do you think *my* father had Earth's interests in mind when he made that speech thirty years ago announcing the *Multiverse?* Did he not predict chaos, riots, would result from his announcement?"

"That's not true," I shot at him. I might have slept through half of school, but I'd paid attention to that particular lesson. "There wasn't mass chaos and anarchy back then. But there will be if the whole planet found out you're lying to them about the war. And the Stoneskins."

"I did not bring you here for a lecture, Ada."

"Then what?" I shot at him. "Were you going to tell me

who you've got posing as council members? Or where you got bloodrock from? Same place you picked up that bomb, I imagine. The Walker family's well-provided for, isn't it?" I stood, hands balling into fists. "I don't believe for a second you had nothing to do with the Stoneskins. Cethrax, too."

"Yes, I'm curious as to how you knew about that," said Walker. His tilted head challenged me to tell him where I'd been. A fresh wave of anger seared my veins. I wanted to pummel him into the ground.

"Cethrax are making mincemeat of the patrols in the Passages. I'd be a bit more worried for my safety if I were you."

"I have lived my entire life with the same," said Walker dismissively. "I don't fear death."

"Good."

My anger peaked. I launched out of my seat, immediately crashing into the two guards. They'd clearly anticipated my move. Hands clamped over my arms, pinning me down on each side. *Dammit.*

"So you do plan to oppose me," said Walker. "How disappointing."

"You deserve the worst Cethrax can offer for what you did to Kay. But I won't let the whole of Earth be sacrificed because you're too much of a stubborn asshole to tell me the truth. I killed the goddamn StoneKing, Walker." I twisted to glare at each of the guards who held me down. They were masked. Black masks. Adamantine? Maybe. The same masks the person who threw the bomb on Klathica had said the KimaroTech employees had worn. Of course Walker was responsible. "If you fuck with me, you're making a mistake. I'm not the Alliance's enemy, but *you* are."

"Take her to the cells," said Walker.

"You bastard," I yelled, as the guards lifted me from my

seat. "You need me. Earth's under attack, and you're locking *me* up?"

"You're a challenge, aren't you?" Walker shook his head. "I admit I didn't know just how involved you were with those offworlders."

"Go to hell," I spat, struggling. "You don't know shit about the threat you're ignoring. The Stoneskins are after you. They'll burn Earth down to get to you."

"They won't," said Walker. "Because I took care of it."

"Really, now? Or was that a lie, too?" I tried my old trick of pretending to go limp in the guards' arms, but they weren't fooled for a second. If anything, their grips went tighter, like they were trying to wrench my arms from their sockets. I bared my teeth at him to keep from wincing.

"Not a lie," said Walker. "Surely you understand why I needed to reassure the public I had the situation in hand? The threat *is* taken care of. I have many witnesses who saw my guards kill those *Stoneskins*."

"It's a lie, isn't it?" I burst out. "You fabricated it. I thought you were on their side, anyway. I thought you created them, including the ones waiting on Thairon. And you have enemies you don't even know about. Cethrax wants you dead, and so do Enzar."

"You don't understand anything, girl," said Walker. "As to the war, if Enzar makes a request for you, I'll hand you over without question. You'll remain in the holding cells until then."

"Like hell."

Magic waited under the surface. The guards holding me had magicproof armour... but I could absorb antimagic, too. They weren't like the Stoneskins. They weren't unbreakable.

I reached under the visible world for the antimagic in their armour, and dragged it towards me. Purple-red ignited in the air. The guards staggered, taken by surprise, and I fired the magic directly at Walker.

But he wasn't there anymore. The world shifted in front of me, warping… a doorway opening, edged in blue light.

How…?

He'd used a world-key. The bastard had opened a doorway. Which meant—

"Ada!" The door slammed off the wall behind me and Kay tackled one of the guards. Walker had gone, but the doorway he'd opened remained there. The burned black ground of Thairon filled the back wall from floor to ceiling. I cursed and spun around, running to the other guard—

Crash. Stars burst before my eyes. The back of my head throbbed. I fell to my knees, twisting to see Walker appear out of the air—*he has a Chameleon*—and then he was gone again. The two guards held Kay pinned down, blood streaming down his face.

"No!" I screamed.

One of them stabbed a syringe into Kay's neck. I crawled towards him, but another guard tackled me, knocking the breath from my lungs. I fought, knees driving into his thick armour, hands hammering against his mask. Out of the corner of my eye, I saw two guards drag Kay after Walker, through the doorway.

I yelled in fury, magic bursting from my palms. Sparks buzzed, and I kicked the button on the hover boot. Then I slammed a knee into the man's groin and flipped him off me. Another kick to his head took care of the mask. He slumped against the desk. I'd knocked him out.

But Kay was gone. The doorway was still open, bathed in the gleam of the auros that fed it. *Opening a doorway between worlds which aren't the same magic level can wreck both of them. I need to close it. God. Kay.*

"Ada!" Amanda rushed into the room.

"They took him. The guards took Kay… Walker took him."

"Ada… you can't go back."

"I have to. We needed to free the people anyway, and—and now Kay's there. His father's probably torturing him." My breath came short. There was no question. I had to go after him. He'd done the same for me.

"Warn the others," I told her. "Tell my family. Please. The war's coming here, maybe right now. I need to get Kay back." I paused and detached one of the cameras from my uniform. "Here's proof. Don't let Walker's people get hold of it. I'll have the other cameras switched on, but there's a really powerful source out there. Tell the rest of the Alliance…"

"I have," said Amanda. "My sister's on it. All we can do is make Walker think he's won, but there *are* others who will believe us."

"Thanks." I gave her a quick hug. "Really, thank you. I have to go."

I turned to Thairon. To Kay.

I'll find you. I promise.

15

KAY

I *can't move.*

    I'm trapped.

God. Not again.

My eyes snapped open, and I would have punched out the guards pinning me down if not for the drug—whatever he'd injected me with—paralysing my body. I slumped over a table, the guards holding my wrists and ankles. Cuffing me. Sharp metal dug into the skin of my wrists.

Fuck. I was in the lab, on Thairon.

And he was there, wearing the same blank indifference. The expression that flooded me with terror. He had me trapped. Right where he wanted me.

Move. Dammit. Move.

My heart raced. My skin tingled with magic, but whatever he'd done to me stopped me using it. He'd thought of everything. Once again, the bastard had come out on top, while I lost everything. And with the Alliance in his hands and an army on the way, Earth was screwed.

"You're too dangerous to keep nearby," said Walker.

"Fuck you," I whispered. If I could speak, I wasn't entirely paralysed. I fought against invisible bonds, feeling cold sweat beading on my forehead.

"I wish you hadn't driven me to this." Walker gave me a pitying look. "If you'd come with me here in the first place."

"What, so you could sacrifice me to whatever monster's controlling the simulator?" My head spun. I clenched my teeth, determined to stay conscious, and to stop panic from engulfing me. My life depended on it.

"Kay, don't try to fight. I'm doing you a kindness. The truth is, killing creates all kinds of complications, and I would rather our family's reputation remained intact until the end. The story of the youngest Walker, who valiantly sacrificed himself to save a dying world, tragically abandoned to ruin."

"Is that how you're gonna spin it?" I willed my limbs to come back to life. My head moved a fraction, tilting onto the side, and horror chilled me as I took in the sleeping forms of Stoneskins trapped behind glass.

"Earth needs stories like yours, Kay," said Walker. "I'll be closing the doorway outside, and it's time I returned to Earth. I thought you'd be pleased. You get to make an impression after all."

"So I get to be a prisoner like you? Like the council?"

If I could just *move...* I'd kill him. I wouldn't hesitate this time.

"The council?" Walker shook his head. "They'll die before they give up the Alliance's secrets. I'm not overly concerned about them."

"You're still living a goddamn illusion." Anger burned in my veins. *Come on.* Surely magic could overcome this drug? "Listen to yourself. You handed three members of Earth's council over to the enemy. The same enemy who want Earth wiped out of the Multiverse, and who already threatened to kill you. Now you're standing on their freaking doorstep like you're on holiday, gloating at me while Central falls into chaos. Tell me this is part of some plan that *actually makes a jot of sense.*"

While I spoke, I fought the invisible bonds with everything I had.

"My new council will keep Central safe," said Walker. "The original council know nothing the enemy isn't already aware of. They will not betray secrets they cannot know. I have a way out." He drew his hand from his pocket, and the blue-black glint caught the light. He had Earth's world-keys. Bastard.

"Never think I underestimate Enzar. I know they've laid waste to countless worlds. I will *not* let Earth be one of them. Not ever. And yes, that is more important than the council. It's more important than any individual Alliance member, however special they may think themselves." Walker stepped back. "As it is, Thairon will not be bothering us again."

"Because you've leaving them like this. Like the cowardly bastard you are. How much effort does it take to close a freaking doorway?"

"When the doorway in question is fuelled by a nexus," said Walker, "more than you can imagine."

"A *what?*"

"The nexus is the centre of all magic in the world it belongs to. Not all worlds have one, but they're considered a valuable commodity by both sides of the war. An unlimited magical source. Thairon's nexus runs the simulators here."

My heart raced. "An unlimited source. On a loop."

"Precisely," said Walker, "and it's that which fuels the doorway between this world and the Empire, too. There is no simply closing it now. The only way to cut Enzar off is to detonate the source at its core."

"*What?*"

"Thairon has outrun its usefulness," said Walker, "and as it has a connection with Enzar, I decided it would be best to take care of both problems at once."

"You're lying. Even you wouldn't be stupid enough to set a bomb off on a high-magic world."

"There's nothing left here, Kay," said Walker. "I'll detonate the bomb and sever all connections between this world and Enzar. From a safe distance, of course. From Earth."

No.

It was no use looking for sympathy. I'd learned that lesson long ago. He really was going to lock the door on this world and leave me to die. Just like in the simulator. But this time, for real.

I wouldn't let that happen.

My hand twitched, and the guards laid me down on a table. "No," I gasped. "You think closing one door will keep Enzar out? They'll come and kill you. They know who you are. They're with Cethrax—"

"That is no concern of mine." Walker's cold, indifferent face was the last thing I saw before the world faded to blackness.

ADA

I stepped through the doorway, the hover boots' oxygen shield activated again. Walker had opened it directly into the entryway of the KimaroTech labs—the hidden building Kay and I had unearthed, where the Stoneskins were sleeping and the link to Cethrax opened through the void.

Panic clawed below the surface, fear and helpless rage mingled together. I hurried down the corridors, heart beating fast. *Find Kay. Then... shut down the simulator. Get the council back*. The two of us alone couldn't take on the Stoneskins. But the ones in the lab had been asleep...

I clicked on the Chameleon as footsteps sounded ahead. It would only last ten minutes, but if I needed to, I'd use the sciras and fight my way out. I activated the hover boots and glided around the corner. The footsteps came from Lawrence Walker, and he paced in front of the door to the lab, tapping it occasionally with his stick. What the hell was he doing?

Where was Kay?

I waited for Walker to pace away from the door then moved into a position to see through the glass window above. *Oh, god.* Kay lay on a table, eyes closed, a guard on either side of him. A dozen Stoneskins were inside human-sized capsules hooked up to the walls. Similar wires snaked around Kay, and pierced him through the neck. Pressing a hand to my mouth to stifle the scream building in my chest, I took quick, careful breaths.

Magic sparked through the room, tingling under my skin, and I gasped as it hit every nerve in my body. Wherever the magic came from, the chameleon effect instantly disappeared, leaving me visible—vulnerable.

For a moment, Walker's guards stared at me. I stared at them. We moved at the same time. I hit the hover boot's switch and moved out of range in time to activate the sciras button on the Chameleon clipped to the inside of my sleeve.

"Give up, Adamantine."

I froze. One of the guards lifted his mask. Underneath was a Stoneskin's blank face. A familiar one.

The one I'd thrown into the void. The bastard who'd planted the source on me.

"You're alive..."

And he was working for Walker. Shit. He must have come

straight here through the void after I'd pushed him through. The void had linked to this world the whole time.

The StoneKing's dead. He's not the one you should be worried about here.

If this Stoneskin stood between Kay and me, then I'd mow him down. I leaped at him, the sciras numbing the impact when I slammed a fist into his jaw.

"You're working for that dickhead now?" I punched him again. No effect. "Walker's playing you. He doesn't give a shit—"

"You would interfere, wouldn't you?" Walker moved forward, shaking his head at me. "I suppose I should thank you for delivering the creatures that, technically, belong to me."

"So you *are* in charge of the Stoneskin project?" I indicated the sleeping Stoneskins, and swiped at the guard's neck. If he hadn't been made of rock, I'd have hit him dead on. As it was, he caught my wrist in his hand. I swore.

"Certainly not," said Walker. "But I was lucky enough to intercept these particular Stoneskins when I escaped this world through the void. Thankfully, they were receptive to my instructions, as they hate and despise the magebloods who ordered their creation. Enzar won't miss what they never had in the first place."

I slammed the heel of my hand into the elbow joint of the guy who held me, kicking at his legs with my hover boot-encased feet. His hold loosened enough for me to wrench my hand free and jump onto a table. Crap. My punch had knocked his helmet loose, but his face was covered, preventing me from jabbing him in the eyes like I'd done to the StoneKing. So Walker owned *these* Stoneskins, but not the original experiment that had created them. He'd just stepped in and taken control. Same as he'd done to Central.

Not anymore.

"You walked through the void? Seriously?"

"Yes. I heard you did the same yourself." His eyes glittered in a way that sent horror coursing through my veins. He'd known all along what the Stoneskins had done to me—but did that mean he knew their original plan? Did *he* want to throw me to the magebloods as bait?

"So what's your game?" I asked, keeping an eye on each guard. "You're challenging Enzar? I thought these Stoneskins were intended for the war."

"If you and my son hadn't tried to stop me, I'd have already closed the doorway," said Walker. "Unfortunately, I am unable to close the source keeping the void open while I'm here on this world. But you came here, so I assume you have a plan. I'll give you an hour, Ada. Find the source fuelling the simulator. If not, my son will remain comatose, as will Earth's council and the entire population of Thairon. I think that's enough of an incentive."

I stared. "What? The source running the simulation is keeping the door to Enzar open?"

"There is only one source," said Walker. "Thairon's nexus."

My heart missed a beat. The StoneKing had said each world had a nexus—a major magical source. There was one here? Was that the source I'd sensed, but hadn't been able to see? The reason for the constant low-level hum of magic here on this world?

"Nexus?" I feigned ignorance.

"The core of their power," said Walker. "The source keeping the link between this world and Enzar alive. Good luck, Ada."

My heart beat fast, too fast. "What the hell am I supposed to do with the source when I find it?"

"It's your choice. Let's hope you can find the source before my guards make you live to regret escaping Enzar."

And he strode from the room. Swearing, I hurled a bolt of

magic after him, but one of the guards moved in the way, his adamantine coat absorbing the attack.

Crap. This was bad. I had an hour. And then... what? I was willing to bet he'd close the way back behind him. We were stuck here now. Trapped on Thairon with a ticking clock.

I looked at Kay. His eyes were closed, his mind in a place I couldn't reach.

The guards, however, were within striking range. I jumped from the table, launching myself at the nearest. My body slammed into him in a move that knocked the breath from my lungs and probably hurt me more than him, even with the sciras. I ducked to avoid a punch and struck back with a blow that would have taken him off his feet had he not been a freaking Stoneskin. *I'm not playing this game again!* I hammered my fist into his jaw, but to no avail.

"Do you *want* to die?" I yelled.

"I can't die," said the Stoneskin. "We are unbreakable. But you, Adamantine, are not."

I pulled magic towards me, backing away along the wire-covered floor. The instant one of them grabbed me, my only weapon would be cut off.

I fired a bolt of magic at the ceiling's fluorescent-style light, which exploded. The room was plunged into darkness, and I ran, pulling the gun from my pocket, for all the good it would do. The faint glow led the way to the tables, and I grabbed Kay's limp hand.

I'm sorry.

I activated the sciras shield. If my plan went wrong, we were dead. But I didn't have time to think over it. I reached for the magic and sent a crackling wave of energy at the approaching guards. Even unconscious, Kay's amplifier built the charge higher, higher. The floor crumbled under the Stoneskins' feet, and they fell into the ground.

I dropped Kay's hand, breathing heavily, staring at the small crater I'd made in the floor. This kind of magic destroyed worlds. But would it be enough to stop the simulator? I hoped so. I needed to shut it down, rescue the council and Kay—and stop Lawrence Walker before he brought Earth crashing down with him in his quest for power. I had to do it before Enzar's army realised there was a link to Earth right here, and came through the void.

I backed away from the crater. Magic shook the building. *Oh, crap.* What was happening now? I hated to leave Kay here, but I needed to cut off the simulator or he'd never wake up. Walker wouldn't have made it easy. The nexus must be hidden somewhere near the satellite. We'd already figured it must be living… but neither of us had seen it last time we'd been here.

I walked, then ran for the back door, using the hover boots to raise my speed. *Run. Keep moving.* I didn't dare think of what Kay might be suffering in the simulator right now.

I came to an open door. On the other side, a reddish haze lay where smoke had been when we'd come here before. The presence of a powerful magic pressed on me again. An electric sizzle below my skin. Living. Deadly.

The smoke began to take form. Eyes like craters fixated on me from a reddish-purple shadow the size of a house. Pure magic, and chaos, rolled into one. The creature was backlash from third level magic in a living form. And given the level of destruction Thairon had suffered, it was beyond me to guess just how much power it contained.

I stumbled back. We watched each other. One source to another. No, I wasn't really a source. But I'd just almost levelled a building. I stared the creature out. *I'm not afraid of you.* Compared to Walker, to Enzar's armies, this creature was nothing.

Sure didn't feel like it, though. A nexus. I was looking at a *nexus*. Alive, primal, and terrifying. My breath stopped.

A gleam caught my attention. At the creature's feet lay a bomb. Identical to the one from Klathica.

Oh god. He never intended me to find the source. It was a bomb, and he'd planted it directly underneath the kimaros, right next to the void. If the bomb exploded, and took out the void… this must be how he planned to cut off Enzar's army. While he was safe on Earth, away from the aftermath. He didn't care if Kay and I were caught in the impact, too.

But he knew I could disable a bomb. There must be some other trick here.

"Nice try," I muttered, kneeling down and reaching out with both hands.

I pulled on magic, and the recoil knocked me flying. I tumbled head over heels, my back slamming into the wall. Groaning, I staggered to my feet, the hover boots objecting to the magical backlash.

"Shit." So the kimaros's power stopped me deactivating the source from a distance. But I didn't dare pick it up even with the gloves on, or it'd burn me. Or blow up. The adamantine wasn't strong enough.

Adamantine. Stoneskin.

There were a hundred Stoneskins sleeping back in the lab.

"You're controlling the simulation," I said to the kimaros. "So—can I wake them up?"

It *should* be possible. I searched under the raging current of magic for a thread I recognised. Nothing, of course. This wasn't the kind of magic I was familiar with. But if I kept drawing the magic away from the source… surely there'd be a limit.

Sparks leaped out, and I jumped. *The wires.* The wires criss-crossing the floor from the lab led right to the kimaros.

It didn't move. It was a prisoner here as much as everyone else.

I knelt and grabbed a fistful of wires. Magic flowed like electricity. Each wire led to a person, a Stoneskin. I couldn't tell one wire from another. But just one was enough. I'd done the same back on Vey-Xanetha. I pulled the magic into me, placing myself in the path of the current. The magic flowed through *me*, into the machines keeping the Stoneskins alive. Which meant...

I blinked, and suddenly I looked through eyes that weren't mine. The distorted view of a lab greeted me from the other side of glass.

I was in one of the capsules. I was controlling the Stoneskin's body.

And I was Ada, too, clutching the wires, barely containing the magic pulsing within her.

Holy shit. I can control the Stoneskin. Which meant... I could remove the bomb.

I pulled on the wire, through the current of magic, and felt the capsule slide open. The Stoneskin walked out, trailing wires behind. I almost stopped at the sight of Kay, still motionless, through the Stoneskin's eyes. *Carry on walking.* The Stoneskin army was so receptive to orders, I barely had to nudge to send the Stoneskin walking down the corridor towards me. They were conditioned from birth to obey, just like the inhabitants of Thairon's satellite.

I slipped back into the Stoneskin's perspective and froze when I saw my*self,* crouched down by the wires, eyes blank. *Walk.* The kimaros watched me curiously. I, or the Stoneskin, ducked down, and took the bomb in my unbreakable hand.

It didn't break. But I was a Stoneskin. I clenched my hand over the bomb, and this time, the plates snapped. Crumbled. Even the source died in my hands, its power drawn into the coat of adamantine encasing my skin...

I jerked back into my own body and leaped to my feet, letting go of the wires and drawing on the source's power instead, right from the kimaros. The Stoneskin stood blankly looking into the distance. I gritted my teeth and walked up to it, waved a hand. Its mind was a blank slate, waiting to be rewritten. Like the others. Like Kay... *No.* He'd told me himself. Walker had never been able to control him. That's why he needed to dispose of him.

Time to undo this spell, and wake them up.

I took one step towards the kimaros. A sound came from behind me.

The Stoneskin moved slowly. Its hands held a gun. Hell. Someone had woken it.

"I'm not your enemy," I whispered.

The gun fired.

~

KAY

I'd known it would be waiting for me all along. The edge of a cliff, surrounded by thick mist. The loading screen for a simulator.

Not again. I closed my eyes, struggling to keep my breathing even. I didn't live in that house any longer. I'd turned Walker's favourite way to torment me into an advantage, learned to fight my way out. But right now, I honestly couldn't tell if what I saw was real or an illusion. That was the point of the simulation. It rewrote reality in terms of your thoughts. And try as I might to bury those images, they always resurfaced.

"Then I'll have to beat you," I said quietly. I took one step towards the edge, then another.

The opposite ledge was masked by smoke. A figure waited there, but I never had seen who it was.

"Fuck this place," I whispered. None of this was real. I closed my eyes, concentrating not on my surroundings or even sensation, but on my thoughts. I knew who I was. Walker hadn't taken *that* from me. Though I did wonder: was everyone here trapped inside their own mind, or some collective illusion? Either way, none of them were capable of finding the way out. Or even unplugging themselves.

The smell of blood washed over me, and my eyes opened on a familiar sight.

Corpses scattered on torn-up ground. Broken bodies. Shouts ahead as the battle raged on, discordant and chaotic. But for me, there was only this patch of ground, rapidly dropping away into a cliff. My feet were inches from the edge. The enemy crept from behind a rock. Gun trained on me. I lifted my own weapon in a mechanical, practised movement. I was a soldier.

I was *his* soldier.

No. I was Kay Walker, and I was trapped in a simulation-room with a ticking bomb, and Ada...

Bang.

Just as the bullet hit, the enemy's face turned into Ada's.

"Kay," she whispered, blood streaming from the corner of her mouth. "What have you done?"

16

KAY

*G*od. *No.* Somehow, she was closer to me than I'd thought, and collapsed into my arms, blood streaming from her chest. She gasped a couple of times, then went limp.

I stood, transfixed in horror, a roaring sensation in my ears. Ada, bleeding in my arms. Because of me.

"Kay," whispered Ada's voice. "You knew this would happen eventually. You're a killer. You're his."

"And you're not real," I said, my own voice barely a whisper.

Pull yourself together. It's not her. You're imagining it. The simulator played on your deepest fears and made them reality. Back then, I'd thought I had nothing to lose. This time…

I closed my eyes, doing my best to ignore the sensation of blood dripping down my hands. Ada's blood. If I had to go back to where it all started, maybe—

A sharp jab in the back of my neck. I opened my eyes to semi-darkness. A room the size of a cupboard. Three padded walls. One door, closed. Locked from the outside.

My hands were too limp to pull the visor from my head, numb from pounding on the door, screaming though no one could hear me. The illusion played out behind my eyes even as in the real world, I tugged at the door handle.

How long had I been here? I'd stopped screaming after the first hour. I'd left my voice somewhere back in the simulation. I'd wanted to escape, but that was a lie. There was no escape.

His voice screamed at me on the other side of the door, telling me how pathetic I was, how I'd never be worthy of the Walker name—

"Walker didn't make you into a monster, Kay," said Ada's voice, as Walker's shouts faded to a dull hum. "You made your decisions all on your own."

"Who the hell are you?" I asked, aloud.

"They have the source. The Stoneskins. We'll all be theirs, soon." She spoke Klathican, in a non-Klathican accent. Nothing from Earth. Definitely not Ada this time.

My eyes opened. The speaker was another girl… at least, that's what she looked like. Her appearance changed every other second, making my vision blur—flitting between a small child and an adult. The same person? Maybe.

"The Stoneskins are waking us up," the girl-woman told me in Classical Klathican. "A few at a time. You're new here. But they'll want you… they need more magic-wielders."

Either my subconscious was even more messed up than I'd thought, or the girl did, in some way, really exist. In fact, now I looked around, our surroundings solidified into a hall-way. It looked like Central, with black glossy floors and towering elevators. My unconscious mind filled in the blanks and I had to focus my attention on the girl before my brain got carried away and conjured up images of actual people here.

"I like this place," said the girl. "Looks a bit like our satel-lite did before it left. Is there anything left of it now?"

I stared. "We're not there right now?"

"No, we're in the labs. They pulled us down a few at a

time, to prepare us for the transformation. Didn't you wake up for a minute during the transition?" She shook her head and smiled. "I haven't seen our planet in years. It's a mess. Might be worth waking up, just to see it for a moment."

"Listen—what's your name?"

"Angel." She laughed. "That was my screen name. Back in the day. We get new identities, right? Hold on." Her face turned serious, and settled on the image of a dark-haired girl, maybe sixteen or so. "They sent you. Didn't they?" She took a couple of steps back. "They sent you to tell me. It's my time, isn't it?" Her lower lip trembled. "I've lived in here all my life. I can't take the real world. Not the war. Not now."

I shook my head. "I've no idea what you're talking about, but I'm not working for the Stoneskins. I'm here to stop them."

"Not *them*," said the girl. "We *are* the Stoneskins—or, we will be."

Realisation sunk in. The original Stoneskins were from *here*. From Thairon. Trained in simulation for combat and awoken to be turned into soldiers for real. The bodies in the real world had been remade into those of invincible warriors. Their minds were programmed for battle. When they woke up, they'd be dragged into Enzar's war on the side of the magebloods.

This was the real reason Thairon had been cut off.

"How long?" I whispered. "How long has this been happening?"

The girl looked at me with sorrowful eyes. "Thirteen years."

The world tilted under my feet. That was the year contact had been cut off. Which meant Walker would have had free access to this place... he must have known. The Cethraxian goblin told me the Stoneskins wanted to kill Walker. The magebloods must have found out he planned to shut this place down.

So Walker had been telling the truth when he said he stopped the Stoneskin project. He wasn't in charge. Enzar was. But Walker had trapped me here, knowing that. He'd wanted to get rid of me *and* his enemies in one go. He never had stopped the project, and he'd never intended to set the prisoners free. He wanted to kill them, to stop Enzar gaining its army.

"Is there no other way out?" I asked desperately.

"You can't get out," she said. "You're hooked up to those wires, right? As long as the source keeps running, you're stuck here. Someone has to shut it down."

"There's a bomb. In the real world. This place is going to blow up."

Ada. Right now, she was the only person who could possibly stop it.

"Pity," said the girl. "They control the system. All of us. When we wake, we'll be theirs."

Mind control? "Are you real, or just another stream of digital data?"

"That's a rather personal question," she said petulantly. "As for you... I wonder if anyone will miss you when you wake and go to war for the Stoneskins. That girl? Or..."

Her appearance warped and changed into a woman of around thirty-five with thick, dark hair. The last time I'd seen her, she'd towered over me. Now we were the same height.

Elizabeth Walker.

"Stop," I whispered. "Stop that."

I closed my eyes.

A familiar voice spoke in my head. *"He'll be in London tonight, when I'm gone. Make sure you're careful, Kay. If you see anything, you know where to reach me."*

"Yeah. But you said you'd only be a day. Why can't I come with you? Why does it have to be you?"

"Because I'm the only person who can. Thairon needs me." Her voice sounded so close, I turned around, my eyes flying open. But there was no one there. The girl—whoever she really was —had vanished, and so had the illusion of my mother.

"I'll be back tomorrow..."

No. The echo of Elizabeth Walker's voice didn't even sound like her. I'd forgotten too much. Memory couldn't bring back the dead any more than magic could.

I never thought about before she died if I could help it. She was dead, there was no reversing it. But if not for Elizabeth, I'd never have been able to hang onto my humanity no matter what he made me do.

He'd tried to take the past from me. Tried to take my future. But in the end, he couldn't take away hope.

"Nice try," I said, aloud, "but you won't keep me here. I'm getting out."

Pain stabbed the back of my neck. I was suddenly flat on my back, looking at total darkness. No—grey smoke. The void, again. My hand twitched. My eyes flickered open. The cold metal table pressed into my back. I blinked repeatedly. None of it disappeared or reformed.

Was it... real?

Magic answered me, shivering under my skin. I gripped the table, never more relieved for the ever-present buzzing sensation. No simulator could create the exact sensation of magic.

I moved my hand to the back of my neck and found thin wires piercing behind my head. Swearing, I yanked them out. Magic sparked in response.

Magic.

The other Stoneskins remained in their glass capsules behind me. In front, half the room had collapsed. The floor was a mess of broken pieces of metal. Something had blasted open the ground. But there was a door behind me.

I shifted over the table, cursing as dizziness swept over me. At least the drugs, whatever they were, seemed to have worn off. I had to get to the bomb. If I was awake, the others would be, too...

But it also meant someone had switched off the simulator.

I grabbed the magic-gun from inside my coat sleeve. He hadn't even disarmed me. Not that a gun would do much good against Stoneskins, but if my father was still here, I'd show him no mercy. I walked as fast as possible to the opening at the back of the room. Whoever was in here must have gone through there—there was no way back to the front door now.

I froze, instinctively turning invisible, as a grating noise sounded behind me. Glass scraping against glass. The capsules were opening, which meant I wasn't the only one to wake up. The Stoneskins had, too. I moved quickly, knowing that if they saw me, they'd shoot me on sight.

Ada. Damn. I'd better not be too late.

Magic sparked higher, and it seemed to be coming from the direction I walked in. Strong magic, enough to press on me like a living consciousness. Angry. Livid, even.

The source is alive.

I rounded a corner, adrenaline flooding my veins as I heard voices. Another corner, and I almost ran into two people grappling on the ground. No—one was a Stoneskin. The other was human.

Ada.

I froze.

Ada, bleeding out in my arms.

Ada, alive, here, and struggling against the Stoneskin's grip, trying to break its hold on a gun.

"Kay," she gasped—I must have turned visible again in reaction to the magic sparking down the corridor. She moved suddenly, jerking out of the Stoneskin's arm, and hammered the side of her fist into its throat. The Stoneskin crumpled. At least the sciras was working… but the Stoneskins weren't in their right minds. They'd been brainwashed by whatever Enzar had put into the simulation.

Magic surged up, reminding me of the source. We needed to shut it down, fast. I ran to strike down the Stoneskin, sending him flying into the wall with one punch and grabbing the gun from its hands. No bullets left. I tossed it aside.

"The source," I said to Ada. "Walker said he planted the bomb *in* the source."

"I destroyed the bomb," she said. "Hey!" She kicked out at the Stoneskin as its hands grabbed at her leg. "Don't you come near me."

"They're brainwashed," I said. "They're all waking up now, thinking they're going to war. We have to shut down the source."

"Crap," said Ada. "The kimaros—it's around there. We have to stop it."

Yeah. We did. Not only was the army waking up, they most likely couldn't tell one enemy from another. They were pre-programmed killers—and Ada and I were the only targets in the building.

I followed her lead, activating the hover boots. Lifeless black ground stopped abruptly at the void. I couldn't see the world on the other side.

"Damn. We have to close it."

My skin buzzed all over, and the wounds on the back of my neck burned.

"Oh hell…" Ada pointed, wordlessly, at the haze of reddish-purple. It wasn't just residual magic. A pair of eyes gleamed from within. Living. Angry. A kimaros, bigger than any I'd seen before. Huge enough to blot out the void itself, and mask the grey haze spiralling up to the sky.

Oh, shit.

I went for my gun, for all the good it would do. How did you overcome something that strong? Even Ada wouldn't be able to channel so much power. She seemed transfixed, but the movement of her teeth over her lower lip told me she was thinking.

"Ada…" I raised the gun. If I amplified the charge, I might be able to do some damage to the thing. Or push it into the void. But Enzar was undoubtedly on the other side. Walker had thrown a bomb at the creature, but I had the sinking feeling even that wouldn't have been enough to sever the link between this place and Enzar… or Cethrax.

We had to close the doorway. I backed away, activating the tracker. Should have done that from the start. But the signal pulsing from the kimaros drowned out everything else.

"That creature… it's the source," said Ada faintly. "It's… it's Thairon's nexus, a living doorway. I don't know if I can…" She trailed off, staring. As did I.

The mist surrounding the void had gone transparent. I could see through it.

Right into Central's Headquarters.

It was so unreal, I almost thought I was still in the simulation. But through the glass doors was the familiar entrance hall—adamantine floors, glass elevators, high ceiling. Staff. Guards.

"Shit," said Ada. "Someone… Enzar found the way to Earth."

How? That was the only thought I had time for before the sight sunk in for real. The transparency revealed the other side of the void. There were two worlds, positioned alongside Thairon like a three-way portal. We stood at one corner.

Central at the other. And the third… was Cethrax. On the other side of the void. The doorway from here led there, not Enzar.

A line of hideous, monstrous shapes crossed from one world to another. Cethrax was invading Earth—directly into Central.

"It's my fault," Ada whispered. "If I hadn't destroyed the bomb… it'd have blown up the kimaros and the doorway would have closed."

"It wouldn't have worked. No bomb can destroy a living doorway." At least, I was fairly certain it couldn't. The kimaros appeared entirely unconscious of the three-way door that had opened over the place where the void had lay. The army marched on through Cethrax, without stopping.

The invasion had already begun. Offworlders and Earth people alike ran from marching chalder voxes, dreyverns, other nameless beasts.

Walker… what had he done?

"The lying bastard was working for them all along. Fuck." I grabbed Ada's hand, turning invisible. Even if they mowed us down, we had to stop them.

Still holding onto Ada, I activated the hover boots. The Cethraxians moved across the void from Cethrax through Thairon to Earth, in formation. Trained. Controlled by the kimaros.

I turned and impulsively fired the gun at the kimaros. It had no effect; the bullet dissipated in a shower of sparks.

Dammit. Most of Cethrax's creatures were magicproof, and the Stoneskins wouldn't be far behind. As for me, the magic vibrated underneath my skin, potent, agitated. If I got close to the kimaros, I'd get fried.

Ada tugged on my hand. Putting the gun away, I shifted over to the doorway, searching for a place to cross without walking into Cethrax's monsters. We couldn't fight the army here. We needed to defend Earth.

Ada and I flew through the void, landing in front of Central, as chaos erupted all around us.

A chalder vox bore down on a group of terrified-looking guards who'd clearly just left the building. I pulled out my dagger, jumping at the creature from behind. The onlookers stared, stupefied, as their enemy fell. Invisible, I could get the jump on any of these bastards, but that wouldn't help when the Stoneskins showed up. They were probably still waking up back in the lab, as the satellite descended with the rest of the army. Once they joined the fight… unless we shut the kimaros down, it was game over for Central. Walker didn't matter anymore. We needed to save Earth first.

Carl and two other guards ran at the enemy, placing themselves between another vox-kind and several novices. Most of the senior guards would still be in the Passages, because everyone had assumed the threat would come from in there. Not that Cethrax might have a direct link into Central. *God. I should have gone direct to the guard office before Walker got in the way.* But there'd been no time. Cethrax would have launched their attack no matter what.

Cursing the Multiverse, I cut down three dreyverns easily, drawing Carl's attention. "Who's there?" he demanded, staring as the dreyvern he'd been about to stab fell with its throat cut.

I switched off the invisibility, spearing another goblin with my dagger.

"Should have known." Carl kicked another aside. "How the *hell* is this happening?"

"A kimaros," I said. "It's controlling them, and the doorway, too. And the Stoneskins are right behind them. Thairon's linked to Cethrax, and they're both attacking on Enzar's orders. We need to evacuate."

"Evacuate the whole of London?" Carl swore as another vox materialised from shadow, swinging a fist at a young woman fleeing the chaos. We both ran at the creature, and I stabbed it while Carl shouted orders, waving his communicator. Central's alarm kicked up, siren-like, a strident tone. Everyone in the surrounding area would be able to hear it.

"Get anyone who can't fight into the building!" he shouted.

Central's adamantine surface would deflect any attack—I hoped—but one building couldn't hold back an army, not before they burned the rest of London to the ground. The void's smoky surface covered half the car park, and every minute brought a new enemy. Leaping dreyverns threw themselves into the fight with gleeful cries, while lumbering vox-kind reached out with huge hands to throw guards around. Fury rang through my whole body. Walker wasn't even here. Even though the goblin had *said* he was the target.

My dagger bit into the chalder vox's neck. I flipped over its head as it fell, trailing shadows, and saw Ada trading blows with two dreyverns. She fought alongside Amanda, who'd brought one of the guns with her and expertly fired shots at the Cethraxians' few weak points.

I ran to help Ada, but she had the situation in hand. Her dreyvern opponent fell under her dagger. I took out my own communicator, frantically hitting the warning buttons—for all the good it would do. A warning should be across the whole planet by now. Several messages had appeared, including one from Dr Helm on Valeria—but the signal faded in and out, probably distorted by the doorway.

"Shit," I said. "I can't get through."

We couldn't fight the whole of Cethrax. And if Cethrax or Enzar could connect the doorway here, it wasn't too big a leap to assume they'd figure out how to jump across the globe. Cethrax's monsters outnumbered Earth people capable of fighting against them by a mile—and that was *without* the Stoneskins.

The guards had collectively beaten back the first wave of monsters, their bodies heaped on the floor of the car park. But the link to Thairon remained, a mass of greyish smoke tinged red with the rising magic level. I reached desperately for the magic again, but I couldn't even see the kimaros. Just the void, and a new wave of monsters approaching like beasts clawing their way out of Hell.

"God*dammit*," said Carl. "I hoped it wouldn't come to this. Get back, all of you!"

No one needed any encouragement. We backed towards Central—guards, other Alliance employees, and all. No sign of Walker. I didn't want to run away from the army, but I needed to know if he had the faintest idea he was the intended target for the attack. I'd throw him to Cethrax without a second's thought if it'd stop them.

As we gathered on the inside of Central's doors, Amanda tapped her communicator, her expression grim.

"Danica and the tech team are trying to get through to Valeria and bring backup."

"Only a magic-wielder can fight the kimaros," said Ada, her eyes on the approaching monsters. "I have to go back. I can fly through the void, and I have a shield. I controlled that thing before."

"But the Stoneskins—" I started.

"We can't win here," said Ada. "I beat the Stoneskins last time. I need to get back to Thairon. I can't close the door from this side."

Damn. She was right. But going back put her in the firing line for two armies.

A grating noise sounded, and Central's doors slammed in front of us, abruptly. Wait—those weren't the same glass doors as usual. The doors were transparent, and humming with magic.

"Our shield." Carl tapped his communicator. "It's emergencies only. That doorway's already open so we can't do anything about ground level—but the rest of the building has an extra layer of protection."

"Good," I said. "But it doesn't help the people outside. In London."

"My family," said Ada. "Everyone. Those Stoneskins are pre-programmed soldiers. Even the guards out there won't be able to fight them all."

"I know." Carl nodded grimly. "I'll give you five minutes to come up with a plan. If I get a call from outside, I'll have to let the doors down. It'll only keep them occupied so long."

"Yeah," said Ada quickly. "I can explain later, but—look, I'm a walking magic lightning rod. I *need* to go after that creature."

"And I have to find my father." Damn it all to hell. The bastard had to know something about how to stop Cethrax. If nothing else, he had the other world-key.

And Ada… She'd beaten Veyak. She'd proven time and time again she could kick the hell out of a magic-creature.

"Where *is* Walker?" I asked Carl.

"He and the council barricaded themselves in that office." He pointed at one of the doors at the hall's side.

I swore. "Of course they did." I turned back to Ada. "I'll be back in a minute."

"You better."

I ran, half-expecting to have to break the door to the office down. Sciras activated, I shoved against the door with one shoulder. "I know you're in there, Walker."

Behind me, Ada spoke urgently to Carl and Amanda. I should go and check on Ms Weston, instead, or whatever the tech team was doing to set up more defences. Except if they'd come to assassinate Walker, I wouldn't let him get away with hiding while they trampled us all down.

The door opened, without warning. "So you survived after all. Pity."

Walker leaned against the back wall, where the doorway he'd opened to Thairon had been.

The other council members stood either side of him—except now they wore masks, Stoneskin-style armour covering them head to toe. *Dammit.* They had me beat by sheer numbers.

"Any reason you're hiding in a cupboard?" I enquired.

"You drove us into a corner," snarled Walker. He wasn't leaning on his stick, like I'd first thought—he was using it to draw on the floor. No, carve something. Symbols. World-key symbols.

"*That's* the world-key?" It explained how he'd got the damn thing into Central. He hadn't just been playing the sympathy card. "I knew you'd run like a coward."

The magic level surged, the floor quaked, and I threw a lightning bolt of magic at him. Walker snarled, bracing himself against the desk, but didn't let go of the world-key.

"How long have you been working for Cethrax?"

"You're mistaken," said Walker, his face greyish. "Someone else must have given them the means of getting to Earth."

"They used Thairon's doorway." To do that, they needed Earth's signal… "It *is* your fault. When you opened that doorway into Thairon's old headquarters, you left Earth's traces behind. Did you think they wouldn't notice?"

"If you had allowed my bomb to go off, Kay, that creature would be dead and the doorway closed. This is your doing."

"Yeah? Maybe if you hadn't tried to blow me up along with it, it might have worked. You don't know anything about magic," I told him. "Even those world-keys. I'll bet you never asked anyone how they worked."

Walker shook his head. "You arrogant little…"

"I'm not the person who used classified offworld substances without thinking of the consequences," I said quietly, rage pulsing through me. "Even if you hadn't tried to kill me, Walker, what you've done is good reason to lock you up forever, if we survive. And I'm not letting you escape Earth."

Magic sparked around me. If any of those Stoneskins got hold of me, I'd lose my advantage. But I had no intention of letting that happen.

In one movement, like I'd done countless times in simulation, I pulled the gun and fired one shot.

It would have hit Walker, had he not raised the stick. The bullet struck the magic coating and ricocheted off the room's wall, before striking the front of a Stoneskin's armour and dropping to the ground, useless. I activated the hover boots, moving out of range of the second Stoneskin's attack, and fired a bolt of pure magic.

I hadn't gone up to third level, but Walker collapsed as the magic struck him square in the chest. I ran to him and grabbed the stick from his limp hand, but the magic-shock forced me to let go. Ducking a blow from the fake council member, I grabbed the table for balance as another blast of magic shook the room. I backed out the door into the entrance hall again, thinking fast.

"Hey! Walker!"

I spun around in disbelief. What was Aric doing out of his cell?

"If you fight on their side, you'll lose, Aric," I said, with a glance over my shoulder. My father had collapsed from the magic-shock but remained conscious, and was shouting orders at the guards. *Crap.* Central really didn't need infighting right now. I needed to get my hands on that world-key. The stick lay on the ground where it had rolled out into the entrance hall. I crouched and grabbed it. This time, it didn't shock me through the gloves.

"I'm on the Alliance's side," snarled Aric. Those bastards aren't supposed to be here."

"Go ahead. Your funeral." I didn't have time to deal with Aric. One more fighter on our side might save our necks, if he didn't do anything stupid.

As Aric punched one of Walker's guards in the face, I ran to Ada. "I have a world-key, but I can't amplify it on Earth if I don't want to risk any more damage."

"I'll take it," she said. "I'll use it on Cethrax, they won't care about the damage. I have a plan—I think."

"There aren't enough of us." A crash behind me emphasised my point. I turned around to see the guard hit Aric hard enough to send him flying. He must be using sciras if he could hold his own against Walker's servants. "You let him out?" I asked Carl, but he was glued to his communicator.

"Yes, Kay," he said irritably. "He's a magic-wielder."

"They'll attack London again any second now." Ada turned the world-key over in her hands. "I have to go…"

Carl hung up the phone and ran to join Amanda in fighting the fake council members alongside Aric. Looked like everyone had access to sciras boosters now. But there weren't enough people here to take down an army of Stoneskins.

"Backup's on the way," said Carl. "Danica has it taken care of. Ada, are you *sure* you know what you're doing? We can only hold the fort here for so long."

"Yeah," said Ada. "It's risky, but it's the only thing I can think of. If I close the doorway to Thairon, I can send those Stoneskins somewhere they won't be able to escape."

"We'll create a diversion," said Carl.

"Hold on," I said. "*How* is the backup getting here?"

"I stole a world-key." Raj limped up from the stairs down

to the infirmary and the cells—the same place Aric must have come from. "I heard you lot shouting up here. I stole one of Walker's world-keys. He laid them out on the desk in the council room. 'Course, that's when he caught me."

I just stared at him a moment. "Damn."

"Hey, I deserved my shot at saving the world."

"Get back here!" Saki shouted from behind him. "You shouldn't be wandering around up there when you're injured."

As if to highlight her point, Aric chose that moment to land a punch on a council member, sending him flying into Central's front doors. Raj backed away.

"Ah, crap, I knew those guys were dodgy."

Ada checked her communicator. "Iriel's up in the tech room, she's working with Ms Weston. They're going to bring backup here. They're setting up a doorway port with the world-key you took from Walker, Raj. That was the plan."

"So where's everyone else?" Several guards had come up from downstairs, looking uncertainly at Aric's ongoing wrestling match with the former council members as if questioning who, exactly, they were supposed to be fighting.

"This is it." Carl shook his head. "A dozen of us guards, nothing more. We can't hold off the whole of Cethrax. I've asked the other guards from West Office and the Passages to come at the invaders from behind, but we're not equipped to deal with an attack on such a scale. And don't go near the void. It doesn't lead anywhere good."

"I'll go," said Ada. "Kay…"

She turned to me, and Carl looked away. I would have given anything in the Multiverse to walk with her into the void, but she stood a better chance of surviving than I did.

I folded her in my arms, sending one last amplified sciras boost into her hand.

"Give them hell, Adamantine."

17

ADA

I turned invisible as the entrance to Central began to slide open, inch by inch. Through the gap, I saw a transparent barrier over the doorway between Central and the worlds beyond. London, Thairon and Cethrax rotated before my eyes as the army marched from Cethrax through Thairon to Earth. They were a proper formation this time. Smaller figures in front—dreyverns—and hulking monsters behind. Alongside, still on Thairon, were two rows of people— humans covered in black armour. They moved slowly, as if they were just getting used to walking again. But in battle, they'd stop for no one.

And I was willing to bet the forcefield wouldn't keep them out of Central. The world-key shook in my hands, and the magic Kay had transferred over to me rattled in my bones. I drew in a breath. I needed to find the crux of the doorway… and that meant crossing over to Thairon again.

I stepped through the forcefield with no resistance.

The ground trembled. The whole of *London* trembled, buildings shaking, the sky boiling red-purple as the magic level surged. A doorway from a high magic world to Earth would mean major trouble if I didn't close it. It'd mean the world burning out, becoming a ruined husk of itself. *No pressure, Ada.*

The army turned around, as one, away from Central, breaking formation. On the other side of the doorway, a line of guards had attacked them from behind, and ran amongst the army, daggers and stunners in hand. West Office's guards had arrived—and offworlders were there, too, recognisable by the way magic reacted to them, lighting up the dark. Avians flew at the enemy, metal-armed Klathicans grabbed foot-soldiers and threw them into the air, and Valerians used hover-tech to attack from the sky. But it was too clear which army was bigger.

I ran. Ignoring the shaky ground, I turned in the direction of Thairon, following the rotating patch of air, grateful for the hover boots when the floor gave way to burned wasteland, pitted with craters.

And another army. The Stoneskins moved slowly, dragging their feet. I held my breath as two passed close by, shuffling into the formation. Behind me, the discordant sounds of the battle in front of Central broke apart as the doorway shifted like a rotating series of mirrors.

Magic pulsed all around me. The doorway shifted to the void again, clouded in smoke now dark reddish-purple with the climbing magic level. Magic buzzed so hard, it took all my effort to keep hold of the world-key. I still couldn't pinpoint the kimaros. It was too big, encompassing the whole doorway which fed on its power, growing wide enough to blot out the skies on all three worlds.

A whirring sound made my head snap upwards. A round disc-shaped metal object descended from the smog, and my mouth fell open. The satellite was coming into land, fast. The people aboard were the rest of the army. They were waking, thinking they were going to war. There hadn't been a pilot, so it must be pre-programmed to land. This had been years in the planning. Except I'd never in a million years have thought Earth would be the intended target.

Dammit. I activated the hover boots and zipped across the burned-out ground until the old lab was nowhere in sight. My heart beat fast in my ears. If this went wrong, I'd burn out the hover boots and wind up stranded here. Even the sky was blank, the smog obscuring the stars—if there were any. Blackened husks of buildings surrounded me, preserved in their decaying state as nothing in nature survived here to reclaim them. Aching sadness filled my bones. This world had been wrecked by magic. I couldn't let the same happen to Earth.

I reached for magic, letting it flow through the world-key and into my hand. The sky split open with a fork of lightning, my skin burned and buzzed, but I held on. There was only one place in this burnt-out world the magic could come from.

The kimaros would come to me.

But the magic-creature wasn't acting of its own free will, either. Whoever had been on this world originally had programmed it like a computer.

There it is. The kimaros appeared from the smog, visible even at a distance, like a shadow taking form. For a brief second I faltered, struck by an odd familiarity I hadn't consciously acknowledged until now. Then I reactivated the hover boots and moved closer, still tugging on the magic, visible in threads connecting the army. The simulator had spilled over into reality, and there were no wires this time.

"Let them go." My human voice sounded feeble, but I had to try. "There's no one controlling you anymore. Let them go."

The beast made an odd growling noise, shaking its smoky head. I gave another tug, pulling the magic into me. I was a conduit, a human lightning rod, and I'd control the kimaros. It *was* auros. Just like Veyak had been a living source, too. It was a nexus.

Realisation trickled through me as magic poured through my hands and the beast still didn't move. It was too strong, far too powerful for one person to contain. There was absolutely no way I could close the doorway alone.

The beast reached for me with a claw-like hand. Sparks sizzled from its smoky skin, leaving craters in the ground. Behind, the Stoneskins leaving the lab stopped. I'd distracted it. But not for long.

A hollow boom echoed and the ground vibrated again. The satellite had landed on the kimaros's other side. Another sound rang out, the grating slide of metal on metal. The second part of the army arriving to join the others.

I had only one idea left, and it relied on sheer luck. I could drain the life from a source. The kimaros might be a pure source, but at least some of its power was concentrated in the lab. Now the army was on the move, no Stoneskins remained inside the building anymore. Every one of them was in formation, heading to Earth through the point where Thairon and Cethrax met.

I used the hover boots, moved right up close to the towering form of the lab, and placed the gun to the wall. I didn't dare put my hands on it. It was possible my weapon would be destroyed right away, but before I could hesitate, I reached for the magic, and pulled.

Magic needed no encouragement. I was a lightning rod, and the storm had broken. Raging magic surged through me. Too strong. I dropped a few feet, my skin buzzing all over. Any higher and I'd have a serious case of magic burn... or die.

But underneath, I could still feel those threads. The individual strands of magic from the kimaros to the army it controlled. Being connected to Kay when he used the amplified tracker must have made me extra sensitive to magic signals, unless it was an effect of being in such a high magic world. Or maybe from controlling that Stoneskin through the link. I didn't know. But now, it was my only chance.

I tugged on those threads, and a Stoneskin stopped, turning to face me. The Stoneskin behind it kept on marching, pushing its fellow aside.

I grabbed another string. Then another. The Stoneskins were walking shields. I could control them.

Ten Stoneskins now formed a wall between me and the kimaros. I dropped to ground level, pulling them after me like puppets. A little creepily, they marched where I directed them: between me and the kimaros. Once again, I placed the gun against the side of the building, and dragged the magic into my hands.

This time, I let go the instant the buzz flooded my veins. The Stoneskins' line wavered as they lost their balance. I tugged again, and again, and on the fifth round, a Stoneskin fell.

Too long. It's taking too long. But it was working—the building began to lose its bright sheen as I drew the life out of it, through me to the Stoneskins. The building's shimmering surface went opaque as the bloodrock's effect disappeared, pulled through my body. Then the auros followed. The kimaros might be living, but at least part of it was tied to this building. Maybe that was what chained it to this world. I gritted my teeth and pulled harder, and the building trembled. It wasn't made of adamantine, and right now, I was a force to be reckoned with. If only I knew how to stop the kimaros. But I *could* delay its army.

I wildly grabbed for the threads controlling another swathe of Stoneskins. Inspired, I directed them to block one another's paths, or to move at a diagonal angle and disrupt

Cethrax's formation. Maybe I was just delaying their passage to Earth, but it bought me time to think. To build the charge from the building until its surface went flat black.

And to pull all the Stoneskins' power into me.

Finally, in a surge of crackling magic, the army stopped dead.

KAY

Cethrax's second army broke apart as Alliance guards and offworlders attacked it from behind. Earth's sky burned red and magic cast a haze over everything. It burned under my skin, demanding to be released. As tempting as ever.

I'd give magic free rein. I had nothing to lose.

I was first into the fight, my dagger slashing a dreyvern's throat. A smaller vox-kind wandered away from the pack, towards Central's doors, and it took only a second to slide the blade into its weak point. The bigger vox-kind appeared confused by the rampantly swirling magic and kept collapsing into their shadow-forms. They were used to fighting alone, using shadows to navigate the confined space of the Passages. Here, they were away from their usual terrain, forced to fight in a teamwork formation not natural to their kind.

Lumbering chalder voxes blocked each other's paths in an effort to get at their human prey, leaving room for guards to dodge their attacks and leap at them from behind. The smaller Cethraxians like dreyverns were more dangerous because they were used to teaming up, but the magic level seemed to be driving them crazy. They ran about, screeching loudly, as the guards attacked with guns and daggers alike. But our own army numbered fifty at most. Not enough to take on Cethrax, let alone the second army rapidly approaching.

The humans under mind-control, thanks to the simulator.

I let the charge build in my hands, second level, and fired magic at the ground, knocking the nearest batch of dreyverns back. Every step took me closer to the void. I hoped Ada knew what she was doing.

A gap in the fighting appeared. Magic swirled in from Thairon, forming two snarling, lion-sized shapes. Kimaros. I ducked as sparks rained down on us, deflecting the worst with the side of my dagger. Hell. Like the Stoneskins weren't bad enough on their own.

"Use your stunners!" Carl shouted.

Or guns. I drew mine, sending a wave of magic through it. The first kimaros was thrown back. I let the charge climb higher, putting myself between the beasts and Central. *We won't let you take us down.*

The first kimaros broke apart, and magic swirled across my vision again. The doorway was rotating between worlds, making it impossible to see where I was going. As the floor tilted under my feet, I activated the hover boots, zipping over through to the other side of the car park to chase the other kimaros. The creature must have figured I was a magic-wielder, because it'd turned its back on me and flew towards a bunch of Alliance guards in a hail of sparks.

I caught up before it could strike. Magic shot from my palms, striking the kimaros in the back of the head. It whirled, hissing, and I hit the hover boot's heel, moving too fast for it to knock me down. Sparks flew, leaving sizzling black marks on the tarmac of the car park. The creature might be pure magic, but the open doorway fuelled my own power. My skin hummed all over, heedless of the magicproof uniform. Purple-red light arced from my hands and struck down the kimaros in a blaze far brighter than any stunner I'd ever fired. My bones hummed in resonance as the charge built in my blood, an amplifier standing at the heart of a source.

This time, my attack swallowed the creature whole. Reddish purple exploded from my fingertips, dashing the kimaros against the tarmac. It burst into pieces in a shrieking howl, burning into my irises, until all that remained was a blackened outline on the surface of the car park.

I activated the hover boots again and flew to help the guards fighting a new pack of Cethrax's monsters. Magic-wielders fought too, and—so did Nell, Ada's guardian, her eyes blazing, dagger slashing. They'd joined the fight from the car park's other side, where the doorway cut a jagged slash through the world. Offworlders and guards fought side by side, driving Cethrax's forces back.

I cut down two dreyverns, dodging a flash of magic as a cyber-enhanced Klathican grappled with another. Magic-shots flew wildly, but it struck me none of these people had been trained in magic-based combat before, let alone against Cethrax. The army had a clear advantage even when they didn't work as a team.

The second kimaros rose from the fog, spitting sparks. Those unlucky enough to get hit collapsed, yelling. I cursed, firing a magic-shot of my own. The creature dodged, blurring into reddish-purple, its fur-like protrusions standing on end.

"You can only hit it with magic!" I yelled at those behind me. I pushed against the monster, aware the magic I drew on was likely part of the other kimaros, the one holding the doorway open. The smaller creature shrank away from the magic crackling from my fingertips, recognising a superior enemy. Rather than wasting bullets, I fired a bolt of pure magic, amplified, and it collapsed into smoke.

The ground trembled, and Central itself appeared to shake, deep cracks appearing in the car park's concrete floor. I cursed and sped over to intercept a chalder vox that had knocked two guards to the ground. Before it could land the fatal blow, I'd speared it in the back of the neck.

Sparks flew out from behind, and as I turned that way, the view shifted to Thairon, and a new flood of enemies. More people under the kimaros's control, accompanied by Stoneskins. The real army was here.

I used the hover boots to re-join the guards fighting directly in front of Central's doors, firing magic at the ground to knock the approaching foot-soldiers off balance. Apparently undeterred by the magic, a group of goblins leaped at Carl from behind. I intercepted one of them, my dagger plunging into its throat. Even the adamantine knife handle vibrated in my hand from the magic pulsing through the air. The doorway had knocked out the Balance in London—maybe across the whole of Earth.

Another tremor shook the ground, and magic exploded overhead. I threw myself flat to avoid the sparks, twisting to see where they came from. Maybe a kimaros, maybe a reaction. *This* was why using world-keys directly into another world wasn't allowed. Three worlds were literally being torn to pieces, and Earth was one of them. If Ada didn't close that doorway, and soon, Earth would become Thairon—with no satellite as backup. Everything would turn to ashes.

Rolling to my feet, I stabbed another dreyvern, blinking to clear magic's glare from my eyes. All I could do was fight, and keep fighting until the threat was gone. This was what I'd been made to do.

Blood dripped down my dagger. I should be tiring by now, and my movements had begun to slow, but the hover boots made it easy to dodge attacks which would have knocked me down otherwise. More than that—the constant buzz of magic in my veins made me feel like I was plugged into an electric charger. Hell, maybe *I* was amplifying the magic and making it all worse. But I could no more stop the magic affecting me than I could cut off my own arm. Even chalder voxes bowed under its power. I stabbed one in the back of the neck, using my hover boots to propel myself out of the way as its huge body fell. Cethrax's army had fallen under the guards who'd arrived to boost our ranks… the real problem was the Stoneskins.

They moved slowly—the only reason they hadn't overrun Central. Carl and two others had cornered one of them, while Aric grappled with one of the false council members.

"Stop that!" I shouted, as Aric shot magic at him again. "It has no effect!"

But Aric's eyes had blanked out, a red haze surrounded him, and lightning crackled from his hands.

"Aric, snap the hell out of it!" I yelled. I couldn't see my father behind him in the entrance hall, nor the other two council members. The bastard had probably made a run for it. No time to worry about him now.

Aric aimed another magic-shot, and I ran at him, shoving into him. The second level jolt went right through my bones, knocking me to the ground. Every nerve flared, my skin burned, my eyes flew wide open. My head snapped back as Aric's fist connected with my face. The pain was enough to snap me back to reality.

"I'm trying to help you," I gasped. I could feel blood streaming from my nose, but I didn't have time to check on the damage. "If you're gonna throw magic around, don't do it here!"

I rolled to my feet, dodging a kick from the fake council member. Aric had actually made a dent in his adamantine-enforced helmet, but it wasn't enough to break the armour. My head throbbed and the magical aftershock shook my limbs. Then magic flooded my body again, and I knocked Aric flying.

A deafening noise behind me drew my attention. I spun around, heart plummeting, as a flood of people appeared inside Central. Running downstairs, through the entrance hall. Ms Weston led the way, followed by guards, by Valerian officers, Klathican cyber-guards, and too many others to count.

She'd opened a doorway, and brought in the Alliance.

I didn't dare let myself feel relief, but ran to intercept Cethrax's next attack. They must have sent a new wave to Earth.

This time, however, we had a proper army of our own.

Armoured guards, Klathicans and Valerians ran from Central, joining Central's forces beside the void. Cethrax fell under the assault. I joined them, fighting with magic and blade, and my own hands.

When the adrenaline died down, I found myself alone, surrounded by severed swamp-creatures' limbs. I'd lost track of Aric, but now I looked, he rolled past the doors to Central, grappling with a Stoneskin. Cethrax's army had blocked some of them reaching Earth, but they'd slowly begun to join in the fight. What they lacked in speed, they made up for in sheer brutality.

I kicked the hover boots into action and zoomed over to where one stood over the lifeless body of a guard. Abandoning my dagger, I activated the sciras and slammed my elbow into the back of its head. Recalling how Ada had beaten the StoneKing, I spun the bastard around and shot magic into its eyes.

The Stoneskin collapsed, howling. I ducked a blow from another, the one Aric was fighting. He looked half-crazed, his buzzed hair standing on end, sparks flaring out every time he moved. The veins in his hands stood out, glowing red. Had the rising magic level made the magic-booster go out of control?

A bolt soared over my head, confirming my guess. Dammit.

"Get out of here, Aric." He didn't seem to hear me. He'd pinned the Stoneskin down, but a second struck him from behind before either of us could react. Aric fell head over heels, blood streaming from the back of his head. On his feet, he staggered, firing a bolt of magic into the air seemingly at random.

Cursing, I hit the first Stoneskin as hard as I could, knocking him into a group of dreyverns crossing the void. I hadn't realised how close I was to the edge.

"Hit them in the eyes!" I yelled at the other guards, but the clamour of the battle snatched away my voice.

Aric yelled, stumbling into view. The glow around him had pulsed black, like a clinging shadow. I took a step towards his attacker, but was thrown back by the blast. Only instinct, and the hover boots, stopped me falling over the edge. I swore, seeing the Stoneskin must have caught Aric in the face, which was a flayed mess of blood.

I cursed again when a kick sent him through the doorway, into Cethrax, and a chalder vox's concrete foot came down. Fighting the magical backlash pouring from where Aric had stood, I knocked the Stoneskin flying with one punch and crossed to Cethrax, plunging my blade into the back of the vox's neck.

But it was too late. Aric lay dead, magic still spilling from his hands.

Cethrax shook with another blast of magic, and the backlash knocked a group of goblins right into the void. The link between the three worlds wasn't anywhere near as stable as it looked. Whether because of the kimaros, or the backlash of linking worlds with drastically different magic levels, I didn't know. Numbness filled me at the sight of Aric lying there on the void's edge. I hesitated, then dragged him back from the swirling current of magic visible in the gap between Earth and Thairon. I left him outside Central, amongst the other dead.

Turning away from Aric, I aimed to re-join the army... and stopped as the void went transparent, revealing the other side. Cethrax fought on, but now I knew why there were so few Stoneskins. They'd paused, dead still, some halfway on the brink between Thairon and Cethrax. In fact, there looked to be total confusion over the other side of the door. Some of the army had formed a wall, blocking others from getting through. One Stoneskin rampaged through the centre, knocking its fellows flying. Others ran amongst the Cethraxian formation, causing confusion. Nobody seemed to know who they were meant to be attacking. Had Cethrax— or Enzar—lost control of their army?

I stared, and only reflex stopped me being jumped by a dreyvern. I kicked it hard enough to send it flying over the barrier to heaven-knew-what-world—my eyes were on Thairon, and the army which had stopped in its tracks.

Ada.

Icy fingers dug into the back of my neck. The buzzing magic had masked the assailant's approach, and I knew before I turned around my father had come after me.

His grip tightened. I gritted my teeth against the pain. The number of times when I was a kid I hoped he'd finally snap and finish me off rather than leaving the simulator to do all the work... but that was before. And when you lived your own death a thousand times, a strange thing happened. You got addicted to living.

I drew the magic still sparking in the air, and he yelled,

letting go. Lucky for him I'd not hit third level, but it was close.

"You ungrateful bastard," he spat. "I would have shown you mercy."

"You don't have a fucking clue what mercy is." Magic swirled around me, masking everything, shaking the gun in my hand. "Come to join the army? Whose side are you really on?"

I spun to intercept another attacker. Two of the fake council members had got away. Mrs Grey's face was hidden behind a mask, and so was Mr Shean's. Not that it mattered. I couldn't take them down with magic.

I activated the sciras instead. Mr Shean got out a dagger, but my hover boots carried me out of the way of his attack. The doorway shifted, reflecting magic in planes that dazzled my vision, but I forced myself to focus. Forced myself to ignore the presence of the kimaros pressing at me like a creature beating the walls of a cage.

My rage was my own, and I would control it.

One kick sent the fake Mrs Grey sprawling. The battle had started again on the doorway's other side. Cethrax's monsters' cries mingled with screams, but all was obliterated by a familiar roaring in my ears. I kicked the fake Mr Shean down, knocked the knife from his hands with the heel of my palm, and pressed his own weapon to his throat. "I wonder if you're really unbreakable?"

The ground shook with another magic-shock, sending the fake council member's lifeless body tumbling towards the void. The other staggered to her feet, and I grabbed her arm, knocking her weapon to the ground. Her wrist broke under my hand.

With the magic level this high, I can break them.

The fake Mr Shean cringed away from me. Behind him,

Lawrence Walker stared, the blazing magic reflected in his dark eyes.

"What the devil are you?"

The magic level surged high, the sky burned red, and bolts of lightning rained down on London.

"I'm what you made me, Walker."

18

ADA

I hit the heel of the hover boot and glided above the ruined ground as the magic roared over me. My whole body shook, uncontrollably. I had to do something. Get the creature under control.

On the other side of the doorway, magic rained over London and Cethrax alike. Red bolts lit up the sky above the armies.

I did that.

"No!" I screamed, aloud, wrenching on the magic.

The army stood frozen as one, the kimaros's power thrumming through me instead. I didn't know if I could control all the Stoneskins at once. I wasn't sure I *wanted* to. But I wouldn't let them kill people on Earth. Never.

Magic sparked from my hands, hitting the floor, leaving craters where it struck. The ground trembled even more intensely. I pulled on the kimaros's magic again, and cracks appeared across the burned out wasteland.

Stop, whispered a voice in my ear. It sounded like Nell. *The Balance.*

The Balance had shifted towards Earth, and it was too late to turn it back.

Close the doorway.

The army had stopped here, but on Earth, war raged on. Cethrax's forces continued to move across from the swampland to London, lumbering beasts and crawling goblins alike. Gripping the world-key in one hand, I used the other to fire my gun at the monsters, sending a wave of magic over them. Those with little armour fell, creating a gap, and I zipped across to the swampland. Heart racing, I knelt, carved three symbols into the ground, only stopping to kick away a goblin that had grabbed for my legs.

I floated back over the void, raised the world-key, and called all the magic to me.

Red light flared over Cethrax. Lightning speared downwards, breaking the ground under the army's feet. It opened, and the Stoneskins and monsters were dragged through.

Higher. Climb higher. My teeth rattled, my bones shook, and somehow I stayed upright, bolstered by the hover boots, as the enemy fell into the void. I'd disconnected the worlds. The void wavered, obscuring Cethrax first, and a wrenching sensation ripped the air in two as their world was smothered in fog. The void's smoke cleared enough for me to see Earth remained on the other side. Cethrax, and their army, had gone.

Trembling, I activated the hover boots and flew the rest of the way to Earth.

My eyes fell on a single figure, highlighted against the burning red sky. Kay.

The crumpled forms of the fake council members lay at his feet. At least one was dead, lying where the void had been. The shifting smoke had moved a few feet back now I'd broken the link with Cethrax, but the Stoneskin army remained, and I wasn't sure I could hold them forever.

Lawrence Walker shifted. He was alive, but barely. I turned to Kay, and my heart dropped. Blood streaked his face, bruises marked his neck. His eyes reflected the lightning searing the sky, and didn't seem to see me.

"Kay." *No. It can't be.* The kimaros couldn't have got him. Not this time.

I hit the heel of the boot again and zipped over to join his side. My feet touched down on Earth, which trembled under the magic thrumming from the ever-present void. The link with Thairon was still here, and the kimaros along with it.

I held out the world-key, and pressed it into Kay's hand. He didn't respond, but magic flooded me again, like my shock at what I'd done had momentarily blanked it out. The amplifier bolstered the world-key, and I let magic flow through it.

The kimaros filled my vision. Now the fog had cleared, I saw the links between each of the Stoneskins, pale wire-like threads of magic linking them to the living doorway floating above them all.

I pointed at the kimaros with one hand and grabbed Kay's hand with the other. A dark, quiet part of me screamed in horror, screamed for him to come back. But I needed an amplifier. I needed the power, and I sent it all at the kimaros.

The chasm again, wreathing everything before us in fog. The pulsing threads of magic flashed through my head and for a brief, dizzying moment, I floated above the void, my power linking the Stoneskins together. A second later, I was Ada again, pushing at the magic, driving the kimaros further into the void.

At the same time, I *was* the kimaros, snarling in fury as my tenuous grip on the Stoneskins broke, one thread at a time.

As Ada, I watched its power drain away, and then I floated again.

I was the army, frozen in its tracks.

I was the doorway, each world's voice like a song. Two were almost lifeless, and as the void closed, became one, linked with another whose song was familiar... so familiar...

I jolted back into my own body as Kay's hand shifted in mine, then squeezed.

The flood of magic drained back into Thairon, and I *pushed.* No, we all did. All the magic-wielders had assembled on the edge of Earth. We pushed at the kimaros, and the more of us who drew on its power, the weaker it became. The smoky monster hissed, driven back into the void, and the smoke faded away, leaving London. Leaving us. Our army. The Alliance.

19

KAY

"Kay." Someone said my name. Over and over. I shook my head. The buzz of magic in my head blocked out everything else.

Now it all came flooding back. I'd seen it all—seen the army stop, seen the void open and swallow the Stoneskins and Cethraxians left behind after the doorway to Cethrax abruptly vanished. I'd seen the doorways merge and the Thaironic army, controlled by the simulation, stop in their tracks. And finally, the kimaros had broken its control over the Stoneskins and was thrown back into the void.

My feet hit the ground. The hover boots had stopped working, worn out. In fact… I could hardly feel magic at all, aside from the aftershock. Ada gripped my hand, and I couldn't feel that, either.

Am I dreaming?

Am I back in the simulation?

"Kay, say something. Please. You're bleeding."

I willed the world to come back into focus. "Ada." It felt like I hadn't spoken for days. "You…"

"Kay. I thought you were…"

Sensation began to return. The world looked odd, until it clicked that the red haze had faded, and London was once again grey, even the sky. There was no doorway. In fact… the world-key was between our clasped hands. The buzzing sensation was raw, but more the absence of magic than the real thing. Aftershocks. My body shook with it.

"I'm sorry," Ada said. "I needed an amplifier…"

My thoughts moved slowly. Like magic had knocked all sense out of me. Maybe it had. The battle had been a blur, but now I focused on the details…

"Hell," I said. "Walker. Where is he?"

Ada shook her head. "I don't know… oh, crap. Thairon. I think… I think I killed some of them."

She leaned against my side, her body trembling.

"Hang on. What exactly happened? You—you were on Thairon." I'd seen her floating above the void, hands outstretched, eyes unseeing. But half of me thought I'd imagined it.

"I closed the doorway. But the army—some of them were stuck on Cethrax. I couldn't… couldn't save everyone."

"It wasn't your fault."

"It wasn't *their* fault they were brainwashed." She clutched at my arm, which I wrapped around her, pulling her closer to me. Blood stained my hands, and my gloves were shredded. Guess that was why I'd managed to channel magic through my hands.

"What happened to the kimaros?" I asked.

"Either it fell into the void or it ended up back on Thairon with its power gone. I felt it—I felt most of its power disappear into the void."

"Damn," I said. "We'll have to check on Thairon later." I stepped forward, unsteady on my feet. "Come on. We need to go back."

Now the doorway was closed, the way back to Central

was just ahead—and littered with bodies. The ones that hadn't fallen into the void. I was conscious of the blood dripping from my hands, and as sensation returned, I could feel the sting of cuts that had broken through the uniform's protection. The magic level had climbed high enough that even the Stoneskins had broken under my touch. And Aric's.

It looked like half the Alliance were here. Everyone from West Office had come, and Ms Weston's doorway must have brought dozens from Valeria, Klathica, Alvienne, and every other world within reach. None of Cethrax's army had survived here. The void had closed, meaning Thairon wasn't linked with them anymore, but we needed to do something. They'd been speaking to Enzar, somehow…

"Oh, good," said Markos, walking over covered in ashes and what looked like dreyvern blood. "You're alive."

"Same to you," I muttered, absently wiping blood from my face. Aric had hit me.

Aric was dead.

I didn't even know what to think about that. I turned to Ada instead, who looked about as dazed as I felt. Pulling myself together, I said, "I'm gonna check if anyone needs help."

"*You* need help," said Markos. "You're bleeding everywhere."

"I'll live." Most of it wasn't my blood. I didn't know how many I killed. Didn't want to think about it, either. Just like those war-scenarios in the simulator…

"Hell," I said, suddenly. "Where's Walker? Did he get away?"

I about-turned and headed for the doors again. Behind me, I heard Ada say, "Amanda!"

Ms Weston's younger sister lay on the ground, near the doors. Ms Weston herself crouched beside her, her face stark white. "She's alive," she said to Ada. "But we need a doctor over here now."

Ada rushed through the doors, yelling for help. The medical staff were on the way up from the infirmary's stairs, probably called the second the fight had ended.

As for me, I found Walker to the east of Central's entrance. He lay on the ground, stirring feebly. He wasn't dead. We might have bigger problems, but I wouldn't let him walk away. I grabbed him roughly, hauled his arm over my shoulder and dragged him behind me, back to Central.

Carl intercepted me in the entryway. "He's dead?" He didn't sound particularly displeased.

"Alive," I said. "But I want him locked up. He tried to kill me."

"He *what?*"

Exactly the answer I'd expected. A small crowd had gathered, mostly guards, some offworlders. Despite the dead lying all around, everyone looked at me.

A roaring in my ears, like waves crashing against a cliff. I closed my eyes. "Lawrence Walker is a liar and a murderer," I told them. "He locked the council up on Thairon, trapped them in a simulator, and brought his own false council members to replace them. They were Stoneskins." In the battle, I suspected most people would have been too busy fighting for their lives to notice the council transform. They'd never in a million years have thought Walker didn't intend to fight on their side.

I let the gasps of surprise and questions roll over me, until silence fell again.

"He claims to be against Enzar. But not a word he says can be trusted. When he realised I could challenge him, he locked me up on Thairon, too. Then he tried to kill me during the battle. I used magic against him, but the shock will wear off soon. He should be locked up with the other prisoners until we can question him."

Silence. I opened my eyes. Horror-stricken faces leaped out of the blurred world. Like nothing existed but the man at my feet who'd wrecked so many lives. My hands itched to break his neck like the false council member's.

I'm not him.

"It's true," said Ada.

"Agreed," said a voice, and I started.

Mr Shean, the council member, approached me. I stared in astonishment—he'd clearly escaped Thairon in the fighting before Ada had closed the doorway. A single marble line stretched down the length of his face and one hand was now grey, but he must have avoided the worst of the Stone-skin transformation.

"It seems I have you to thank, Danica, for keeping Central safe in our absence."

I hadn't even realised Ms Weston had come out of the building, behind me. Like everyone else, her gaze went straight to Walker.

A measure of dread crept over me. I said to Mr Shean, "Walker's the one who left you on Thairon."

"I am aware," said Mr Shean, darkly, "and we will deliver the punishment as we see fit, once we've determined our course of action in the light of this latest threat to Earth."

"What about the other council members?"

Mr Shean shook his head. "They were on Thairon… the transformation took them." He turned to the remaining guards. "Bring Walker into the cells."

I declined all offers of help, but five guards tailed me down to the cells. Maybe they thought I intended to let Walker escape. As it was, I wouldn't leave until I was certain the door was locked and bolted. Even then, I had the constant sense of eyes on my back.

The dead numbered nearly thirty in total, including Aric. Including some of the controlled people who couldn't be saved. A fair few hadn't made it over the threshold of the doorway before it closed. Some would be stuck on Cethrax, some back on Thairon.

That was just one point we needed to bring up at the meeting. There *was* a meeting, eventually—an informal one. Though Ms Weston closed the doorway port she'd opened, a large number of the Alliance members from other worlds elected to stay behind. And those from the other Alliance branches on Earth, too. Considering Central had only one remaining council member, it was probably for the best.

While the meeting between council members assembled in another ground-floor room, I found Ada. She'd been with Amanda, who was lucky and expected to recover from the wounds she'd sustained in the fight. Ms Weston stormed about, barking orders at everyone. Even the offworld council didn't dare argue with her.

"Guess we really are the Inter-World Alliance now," said Ada. "I can't believe she got so many people in here."

"Apparently Central's had the parts for a doorway port under lock and key for a while," I said. "That's our emergency backup. Actually, I think they might even have used it the first time Central was attacked. I didn't really pay attention at the time."

Even now, so many details escaped me. Battles weren't simple. Knowing who was on which side, who'd been controlled, was nigh on impossible in the chaos—let alone what remained on Thairon. Central itself was a shambles. No one seemed fazed to see all of us, guards and council members alike, were battered, bandaged, and covered in the enemy's blood and our own.

Ada rested her head against my shoulder. "How are we

going to explain all this? Like, controlling the kimaros? I don't even know how I did it."

"Wait," I said. "You *controlled* the kimaros?"

"Yeah. It's how I destroyed the bomb. I sort of piloted one of the Stoneskins. I did the same in the battle."

"You did *what?*"

Ada looked at the ground. "It wasn't fun, not at all, but I had to do it. Like... like when I used your amplifier. I'm sorry. I didn't know if you were alive, but I—I had to do it." She shifted her gaze back to me, eyes brimming over. She knew what confessing it would cost me. But I was too numb, too tired to feel the creeping terror the idea of someone else using my power would usually conjure. It was what I'd always feared—I'd wake up from the simulator to find it had seeped into the waking world, controlling me. In the end, it had never needed to. All the decisions I'd made, I'd made on my own.

"I know," I said, simply.

Her hand closed around mine, and it was almost enough to push the darkness back. If only for a second we could step out of the world and forget this.

There was no turning back. Cethrax's army had been acting on the magebloods' orders, and we hadn't killed all of them. They'd want retribution for this. Making a deal with the Vox was even less likely than before, let alone searching the swamp to make sure no more links with worlds like Thairon were left.

The council seemed to have forgotten entirely that Ada had been the one who closed the doorway. Their plans left the pair of us on the outskirts, descending into arguments about the future of cross-world security and Passage use. Klathica liked the idea of ambushing the next monster we found in the Passages and torturing them for information. Valeria and several other worlds found that notion appalling.

Nobody asked for my opinion. Probably a good idea in the end, because all I wanted was to be in charge of Walker's interrogation. The rest could wait.

Nobody here personally knew Walker, and securing the Passages was paramount in case Cethrax planned a double attack. As the meeting broke up, Ms Weston approached me.

"Your father—"

"Let me speak to him first." I didn't *want* to talk to the bastard, but I trusted no one else to get answers out of him.

"If you're certain, Kay," Ms Weston said. "I'll consult with Carl and the other guards first, but we'll have to move him to a more secure cell no matter what."

I nodded. "Yeah. Good." Let him experience some small part of the horror he'd inflicted on me.

Walker, who'd come to his senses by now, was wide awake when I entered the cell. He sat on the bed, watching me in silence.

I closed the door behind me. He was cuffed. He couldn't reach me. I wouldn't let him see my fear. A camera clipped to my jacket would record our entire conversation. Every confession I managed to pry from him.

"Well, now," he said. "I suppose you have a lot of questions for me."

I really wasn't in the mood to play any more games. "Did you kill Thairon's council?"

"Yes."

I blinked, surprised at the directness. He must know the council could hear every word he said. Should have expected he'd do exactly what I didn't anticipate.

"You'll stand trial for attempted murder. Attempted genocide," I said. "The rest of Earth's council will be more than happy to see you locked up forever. The entire Alliance, even. Some are in favour of using the death penalty, but unfortunately, we don't do that here." My voice shook with fury. "I don't care if you really did think you were working in the Alliance's favour. You've got a lot of people killed."

Walker shook his head. "I admit, I never guessed you'd turn out a ruthless killer. You were always a weak, scared little boy."

"You were always a bastard," I said. "And I want to know if it's true—if the Walker family really did finance the Stoneskin project."

"It's true," said Walker. "I claim full responsibility for the Stoneskins' existence. It was to be my project, inherited from my father. But when I realised the magebloods were ignorant of the consequences, even of magic sources, I stopped the project. I should have stopped the simulation, but it was too late. The people within it were beyond reach. The fiasco cost my wife her life, and when I finally got hold of a world-key and found my way back to that place, it was to fall into my own trap. There never were any negotiations. I was a prisoner there, and would have remained, were it not for the void opening and the magebloods demanding more Stoneskins. When I was moved back down to the planet's surface, I temporarily awoke from stasis long enough to escape."

"And you decided to trap the council there?"

"Something had to be done," said Walker. "I needed Earth to be on the defensive. The current leadership is weak, and it wouldn't do to have people asking unwanted questions. No —best to quietly assume leadership."

"Well, that failed." My voice rose in anger. "Seeing as you almost got Earth wiped out and started a cross-world war."

"I saved this world, twice, since I returned," said Walker. "As the son of the founder of the KimaroTech Institute, it was my duty to stop the monsters my family created from overrunning the Multiverse."

"And what about your human experiments? Were they an accident, too?"

"You're the only survivor," Walker studied me in a shrewd way I didn't like. "I spoke with a representative of Klathica, and he tells me *you* killed the others."

"Was this the group of scientists you got to inject me with magic?" I asked.

"Times were desperate. Thirteen years ago, I discovered that Thairon's entire population was under an influence ready to wage war on Earth. It was clear, too clear, we were lacking in defence against an invasion. Earth has the least magic of any of the allied worlds, and during a meeting with my trusted advisors at the KimaroTech Institute on Klathica, someone postulated the idea of injecting magic into non-magic-wielders. Almost everyone on Klathica is born with magic, so they'd never tried it."

"From what I gather, they didn't have a clue what they were doing. Earth's magic levels are too low even for a magic-wielder to use magic, unless the Balance is knocked off—which it is now, thanks to you."

"So that's the missing connection," said Walker, musing.

My hands clenched. "That's it? A child on a high-magic world could have told you as much. Do you really know *nothing* about magic levels, about the goddamn Balance?"

"Don't you dare mock me, Kay," said Walker. "If I had known, you'd be dead. You were supposed to be the beginning of a new army for Earth. Our defence against offworld. Magic-wielders."

"Some defence, if you don't even know…"

Did he not even know I was an amplifier? If not, I wasn't about to give him that advantage. I glared instead. "Klathica. KimaroTech. Were they the ones you got to throw the bomb at us?"

"Does it matter? The assassins are dead."

"And that kimaros at the market had people building a bomb, too. I'm guessing that has your name on it as well.

Which seems to contradict your claim to know nothing about magic."

Walker's eyes flashed. "I claim absolutely no responsibility for the existence of those *monstrosities*, but when one escaped onto Earth, my servants saw fit to put an old strategy of mine into action. We needed to see if a bomb could survive being near a source."

"So you'd be able to do the same on Thairon. You knew the doors would open again."

"It was a controlled setting," said Walker. "No harm came, in any case."

"*You'd* say that," I said. "What about that kimaros on Thairon? I'll bet that one's a bit beyond your control. No wonder you're such a coward, stuck for five years on a planet ruled by a magic-god."

"You think of them as gods?" Walker shook his head. "That Enzarian girl's influence is clearly warping your perspective."

I stared. "You what?"

"She hasn't told you? Or could it be that she's ignorant of the twisted practises of her people."

"You've a nerve calling anything 'twisted'," I said savagely. "So, Enzar are the ones who created the kimaros?" *Like the Vey-Xanethans.* I didn't know why it came as a shock. Nobody had known where the kimaros had come from, after all, even on Vey-Xanetha. Apparently they weren't the only ones who'd had the idea. Enzar was behind it all.

Walker shifted position on the bed, leaning forward. "Imagine having so much magic at your fingertips, you could contain it not only in an object, but in a living creature. I believe it started as a specialty of the Royals."

Damn. I was right.

"You seem to know a lot about it."

"It helps to know our enemies," said Walker. "Of course,

that knowledge is irrelevant now Enzar is cut off from this side of Cethrax, but I imagine those magic-creatures are giving the guards a lot of trouble."

"You'd know," I said. "So, they somehow locked magic into living creatures, which went berserk. How the hell'd you get them to give people instructions, then? Sounds awfully like that simulator."

"The principle is the same," said Walker, apparently unconcerned. "Magic feeds on life itself. The one thing that can combat a magic force… you know the name."

Antimagic. Adamantine. His Stoneskin minions were *made* of the stuff.

"So you asked your Stoneskin servants to dominate the kimaros… right?"

"One of them volunteered for the job. It seems the abominations had past experience with controlling magic-creatures."

Hell. It must have been one of the group who'd kidnapped Ada, and enslaved Veyak. "You call them abominations, even though they served you?"

Walker's eyes narrowed. "You're just like Elizabeth. Too concerned with terminology to care that the offworlders will be your undoing."

"So were you controlling *all* the Stoneskins?" I asked. "I'm seeing a massive hole in your story. You claim to have had nothing to do with the magebloods, but it looks like they were operating on Thairon all along. You can't expect me to believe you weren't the one who controlled the Stoneskins, too. They escaped the same year my mother died."

"Thairon and Enzar remained linked even after they were both cut off from the Passages," said Walker. "I tried to break that contact thirteen years ago, but with the result that a number of specimens escaped from the labs into the Passages."

No. He did it?

"You set the Stoneskins free?" I stared at him. "They kidnapped Ada."

"I was imprisoned in simulation for five years," said Walker. "Forgive me if I do not pity you."

"I don't give a crap about your miserable existence, but like hell do I believe for a second you didn't do it on purpose. Look, when you open a doorway, you leave a trace. Tell me: does that mean Enzar has *our* trace now? Earth's? Because it sure looks like that to me."

"If the doorway on Thairon is closed, you don't have to worry about that," said Walker. "They don't have world-keys on Enzar. Even you ought to have guessed. If they did, they would have invaded Earth along with all the allied worlds and reduced them to rubble."

"How dramatic," I said coldly, though some of the tension eased out of me. Enzar wouldn't make an immediate attack. They'd enslaved that kimaros, the living auros, but the way to Thairon was cut off even from Cethrax. If Enzar had once had access to advanced technology, the Alliance still had the Passages, and all the auros. Though I made a mental note to tell the other Alliance branches to be careful with those doorway ports.

"As it is," said Walker, "I was unpleasantly surprised to find Enzar still using Thairon as their laboratory. I have taken care of the problem."

A chill crept up my spine. "What do you mean by that? The population will wake up naturally."

"Oh, they won't," said Walker.

"What do you mean by that?" *Hell.* "The world-keys. Where are they?"

"These?" Walker got out a familiar black-glass stick. "You don't want to open a door there. The air's still probably full of magic-based shrapnel."

My heart dropped. "No. You can't be serious."

I stood still, heart now thudding in my ears, magic sparking to the surface.

"Don't, Kay, it's pointless. The magical bomb will already have detonated by now."

For an instant, I stared at him, unable to believe what I was hearing.

"We destroyed the bomb," I said. "Ada destroyed it."

"That was a decoy. The real bomb was coated in blood-rock, the last of it, as a precaution. I believe it was underneath the place where the satellite landed."

No.

"You *what?* Is that some kind of sick joke?" *Someone will know. It has to be a trick.*

"Fortunately for you, you got back before the second device detonated."

A roaring kicked up in my ears. Magic swirled around me in a dark red cloud. Earth still had enough left to get to third level.

"It's too late, Kay." Lawrence Walker's face twisted into an expression I'd never seen him wear before—something like defiance, self-mockery and resignation all in one. "They're dead. Killing me won't bring them back. Thairon is no more."

"Who said anything about killing you?"

Walker's stick swung at me. The goddamned thing was charged like a stunner. Every nerve in my body blazed. I couldn't even lift my head to see my father move to stand over me. He didn't strike me again, simply shaking his head before moving for the doors.

He was getting away—with the world-key. He'd used bloodrock to disguise it.

"No!" I shouted. I drew my gun, which vibrated in my hands. The first three shots bounced off the walls, and the split second it took to duck was enough to give my father the chance to shove the door open. I took off after him, cursing the magic-shock in my nerves, gripping the gun hard. Guards shouted and scattered as Walker hit them with the stick. I shoved my way through them, chasing after him. The bastard was quicker than I'd given him credit for.

Lawrence Walker reached the top of the stairs and pressed the world-key to the wall, drawing something. He was going to escape, without a care for how much damage using a world-key would do in here.

Before I reached him, Ada tackled him from the side, blasting him with magic that sent even me flying back again. I braced myself against the wall, scrambling to get a hold on the trigger. The world shook. Ada was thrown back as Walker surged to his feet.

I raised the gun. Squeezed the trigger, and fired my own magic into the bullet.

The air shimmered, then lit up, pulsing red and black as the bullet sliced through the air, past Walker. A fresh wave of tremors shook my body, but my father was caught in the blast, too. The bullet didn't strike him, but the aftershock threw him aside. He hit the wall and fell to the ground, unmoving.

The tremors stopped. Ada rushed towards me, eyes wide. She must have waited outside in case Walker tried to make a break for it. The haze of magic cleared from my vision. Walker remained still.

"Ada, are you hurt?"

A shake of the head. She looked at my father.

"You killed him?"

"I don't know. The level might not have been high enough." If there was any justice in the goddamned Multiverse… but there wasn't. A world had just been obliterated. If I'd trusted my instincts—if I'd just killed the bastard when I'd had the chance…

No. I had to keep it together. For Ada's sake. For Central, now Walker had pulled the final trigger against Enzar.

People ran out of the meeting room at the top of the stairs. I stood, fists clenched at my side, knowing what to expect. The scene looked like Walker's son had cracked at last and shot down his own father.

Ms Weston was the first to reach Lawrence Walker, wearing a marked expression of distaste. "He's alive," she said. "And this—" She picked up the world-key—"is highly illegal to use on Earth."

"He disguised it with bloodrock," I said. That wasn't the important part. Words blurred together in my head, meaningless. "That man," I said, into the silence, "just admitted he killed everyone on Thairon."

The silence became a shocked one, then broke into mutters. Whispered questions. Accusations. I spoke louder. "He activated a bomb near the satellite." I turned back to Ms Weston. "I'll take him back to the cell."

As our eyes met, everything froze in a heart-stopping instant as if she was going to refuse, to turn the words on me, imprison the son along with the father…

"Do it," she said to the nearest guards. "Now. Kay, you are to report to me first."

Dizzy, numb, still shaking with the magical backlash, I watched the guards lock Walker back into his cell, then turned back to the entrance hall. If word didn't get out, fast, if we didn't prepare for the consequences… Enzar would find another way to attack us. They'd got at Cethrax already. We'd be next.

I walked upstairs with Ms Weston, speaking, my voice as numb as I felt. "He left a bomb there. On Thairon. He planned to stop Enzar's magebloods turning the rest of the population into Stoneskins. He wanted to kill them first. We thought we'd destroyed the bomb. With the magic level so high, we'd never have found another. He disguised it."

Ms Weston drew in a breath, her eyes unreadable. "Enzar and Thairon are cut off from one another, you say?"

"Did you know his plan?" *No. Please not her, too.*

"I never guessed he'd go that far." Ms Weston closed her eyes, her face pinched. "But I knew we had a madman in our midst. We need to assemble all the magic-wielders here at Central—those in London, that is. The shelters are no longer safe."

I stared, uncomprehending. "Here? Why?"

"Because they'll be targets," said Ms Weston. "Now that Earth is at war."

My heart missed a beat. "The doorway closed…"

"And Enzar will point the blame at the Alliance for cutting Thairon off and destroying their army, both on Thairon and Cethrax. They've lost twenty thousand potential Stoneskin soldiers."

Twenty thousand dead. The stark fact seemed unreal as the simulation. I gripped the wall on my left with one hand. *Hold it together. Someone has to.* Small fucking consolation that everyone knew what Walker really was now.

"Walker may have, in his own twisted way, tried to defend us," said Ms Weston. "But anyone can put the pieces together and know that the bomb was planted by someone from our world. It'll start soon."

Our communicators buzzed in unison.

ADA

I stared out at the sea of faces, my whole body trembling. Walker—he'd really done it. He'd really killed off a whole world, supposedly in some twisted way to keep the Alliance safe.

But nowhere was safe. Not now. He'd aggravated Enzar, drawn attention to Central, and we all had targets on our heads. Me, most of all. The crowd of council members and guards felt confining, stifling, like their accusing eyes were levelled against me. No. Not only the council. Everyone who'd fought in the battle had assembled, including magic-wielders I knew from the shelters. Who could have brought them…?

"Ada!"

I spun around, finding the familiar face in the crowd. Nell, with Alber just behind. And Jeth was there, too. My family. I ran to them, heart lifting despite myself—*they're safe, they're here.*

"Ada." Nell's expression stopped me in my tracks. Fear was etched on her every feature.

"Enzar declared war on the Alliance."

The world tilted, relief giving away to horror. *It's happening. It's really happening.*

They'd been watching, somehow, maybe from the moment I'd arrived on Thairon. Maybe through the kimaros, since they'd been the ones to link Enzar with Thairon and make the Stoneskin army. They'd know only someone with a powerful magic source could have closed the doorway like I had. Which meant they knew I was fighting on the Alliance's side. Against them.

My communicator buzzed in my pocket and I jumped. *Oh god. What now?*

I took out the device with trembling hands. Symbols appeared on the screen, along with the icon that indicated the Alliance's translators were working. Cold sweat dampened my palms. I watched, mesmerised, as the letters revealed themselves on the screen.

We are coming, Adamantine. You are ours.

"Enzar," I said, my throat dry.

"What's that?" Nell said sharply. With trembling hands, I turned my communicator screen around to show her.

"My name," I whispered. "They know my name."

"I will *not* let them threaten you." Nell's jaw clenched, but her eyes were as horrified as my own.

"It's not a threat," I said. "It's a promise. My homeworld's coming back for me."

We are coming, Adamantine. You are ours.

ABOUT THE AUTHOR

Emma is the New York Times and USA Today Bestselling author of the Changeling Chronicles urban fantasy series.

Emma spent her childhood creating imaginary worlds to compensate for a disappointingly average reality, so it was probably inevitable that she ended up writing fantasy novels. When she's not immersed in her own fictional universes, Emma can be found with her head in a book or wandering around the world in search of adventure.

Find out more about Emma's books at
www.emmaladams.com.

www.ingramcontent.com/pod-product-compliance
Lightning Source LLC
Chambersburg PA
CBHW050809190726
48285CB00005B/1851